KATIE COX

GOES

COX

VIRAL

Marianne Levy

sourcebooks
jabberwocky

Published by Sourcebooks Jabberwocky, an imprint of Sourcebooks, Inc.
P.O. Box 4410, Naperville, Illinois 60567-4410
(630) 961-3900
Fax: (630) 961-2168
www.sourcebooks.com

Originally published as *Accidental Superstar* in 2016 in the United Kingdom by Macmillan Children's Books, an imprint of Pan Macmillan.

Library of Congress Cataloging-in-Publication data is on file with the publisher.

Source of Production: Versa Press, East Peoria, Illinois, United States
Date of Production: November 2016
Run Number: 5008001

Printed and bound in the United States of America.
VP 10 9 8 7 6 5 4 3 2 1

The picture quality's not the best. But even so, it's clear I'm having a good time. I'm smiling so much you can see all my teeth, and I'm shutting my eyes on the high notes and everything. And my voice sounds all right, I think. Not perfect, but not terrible either.

It's too bad you can also see a pack of extra-strong acne lotion on my desk. And piles of clothes on my bedroom floor. And something round and fuzzy sticking out from under the bed that I think was once a pepperoni pizza.

If I'd known that two million people were going to be watching, I'd probably have done some cleaning up.

AMANDA, WILL YOU PLEASE TURN it down? Some of us are trying to work."

Basically, my sister got her first paycheck and bought a new stereo that she has on pretty much 24/7. Even at night. Especially at night.

Meanwhile, my friend Lacey cut her own bangs, and because it didn't look completely terrible, she's putting serious pressure on me to join her. Honestly. You get whole, entire lectures on how to deal with people offering you cigarettes and drugs, but no one prepares you for your best friend clicking a pair of scissors in your face and saying, "It'll really show off your eyes."

Oh, and Mom and Dad's divorce was finalized. So there was that.

Otherwise, it was a normal sort of Saturday morning, and I was lying on my bed supposedly doing my English but actually doodling lyrics because that's how I like to warm up before doing homework. Of course, sometimes I spend so long on the warm-up that I run out of time before I reach the main event.

The problem is that writing songs is just so much more interesting than homework. Writing songs is more interesting than anything. Except listening to songs that other people have written, which is the *other* way I warm up before doing homework.

It is possible that I don't spend as much time on my homework as I should.

But this song wouldn't leave me alone. The hook had been following me around all morning, something about "breakup makeup" with a little pause, then a defiant *flick-flick*, like the notes were turning around and walking away.

For a second I had the whole thing there in my head.

> "Gonna break out my makeup
> For this stupid breakup"

And then the pause, and then—
Thump thump thump-thump thump.
"Amanda, will you turn it down, just for a second? I am in the middle of studying."

For just a second, the bass boom did stop. Then it started again.

I was beginning to realize that I'd been wasting my life. All those years of Amanda not having a new stereo. Glorious, peaceful years, when I could take a nap on my bed or talk on the phone with Lacey or think of a tune—

The noise started up again.

"*Manda!* My walls are *vibrating.*"

"You said just for a second!"

I opened my lyric book and wrote everything down before it got away from me again, then pulled my guitar across the bed to get the tune into my fingers.

At that moment, the door opened.

"Katie, I thought you were doing homework?"

My big sister stood in the doorway and gave me one of her looks.

Amanda is tall, with a long face and a long nose and long fingers. But even though all the sticking-out parts of her are thin, the middle parts are pretty solid. By which I mean, she's got broad shoulders and biggish boobs, and they make her look heavier than she is. I'm allowed to say that because I have them too. (Thanks, Mom.) Then there's the Cox hair, which is insane, half-curly, half-straight, and the Cox skin, which is pale with an oily T-zone.

"Actually, I am about to start a very important essay on *Julius Caesar.*"

Her eyebrows shot up. "And you're writing it on the guitar?"

"If only."

Which Amanda took as a signal to sit down on my bed, giving Shakespeare a close-up view of her butt. Which seemed as good a moment as any to call it a day.

It's like I always say with homework—you can push it too far. It's really important to know when to stop.

"I liked what you were playing just now," said Amanda.

I played it again.

"Does it have words?"

I made an attempt at singing it. Only it didn't come out fun and defiant like I'd intended it to. It just came out sort of sad.

"Do you think," said Amanda, "that maybe you've written enough songs about the divorce?"

"What do you mean?"

"It's over, and we're okay. So stop dwelling."

For the record, there hadn't been *that* many. Which I told her.

"'Four-Fingered Twix' wasn't about the divorce! And 'Home Sweet Home' wasn't either. Well, maybe a little bit."

"*Good-bye, bedroom,*" sang Amanda.

"*Good-bye, past. Homes like ours aren't made to last.*"

"Er, how is that not about the divorce?" she asked.

She had a point. But saying good-bye to the literal home of my entire childhood—how could I *not* write about it? All the good memories—the guinea pig babies and Easter egg–hunting and the neighbors' cat falling in the wading pool—were in that house, and when Dad left, we had to sell it. He used his half of the money he made to rent a place in California, where you can sometimes see dolphins from the kitchen window. We used our half to rent an apartment in Harltree, a nowheresville just outside of London, where all you can see from the kitchen window are foxes going through the garbage cans.

In the end, divorce affects everything. Even the wildlife.

"You're bringing us all down," said my sister.

"Oh, blame it all on me. The big bad apple on the family tree."

She laughed. "You should put that in a song. Anyway, things change. People move on."

"Dad certainly seems to have."

"*This is what I'm talking about.*"

"I'm supposed to be miserable! I'm a teenager. That's just me!"

"Doesn't sound like the Katie I know," said Amanda, which was kind of her, given that it did sound like the Katie *I* knew, for the last few months at least.

"You know what? You're right," I said. "From now on, I

will be *upbeat*." I waved at the window—and any potential trash foxes—and plucked out a bit of a tune.

"*So* much better," said Amanda. "And anyway, it's not all doom and gloom. Mom's got a boyfriend."

My fingers froze. "What? No she doesn't."

"She does."

"Amanda, Mom isn't seeing anyone. She knows it's way too soon for that. I've told her."

"Which is why she hasn't told you."

"And she told *you*?"

Amanda looked away. "Not specifically. But there are signs."

The thing about Amanda is that she's read too many fairy tales about happily-ever-afters and handsome princes and things like that. What she doesn't realize is that we had the perfect family. We were the perfect family. And then we weren't. And we never would be ever again.

No biggie.

"What signs?" I said.

"Okay." She ticked them off on her fingers. "She's been singing in the shower."

"Practicing for karaoke."

"She bought a new jacket."

"It's been cold!"

"She's got…"—Amanda paused for effect—"the glow."

"She went to a tanning salon!"

"And why do you think that is?" said Amanda.

"I told you," I said. "It's been really cold. Can you please get your behind off my books?"

"Okay, but listen—"

"No," I said. "*You* listen. Mom was really messed up by all the Dad stuff. It took her forever to get even slightly straightened out, and she's only just gotten herself into anything like an okay place. I don't think she'd go and mess that up with someone new right now."

Amanda stood up. "Not with you telling her she can't—*ugh*! What's that?"

I looked where she was pointing. "Pizza."

"Katie, we had pizza three nights ago. You are revolting."

"Then you are free to amuse yourself elsewhere."

So she got up and left.

♪ ♫ ♪

After that, I did *try* to do my homework. I tried to write a new song too because that tune I'd come up with was truly catchy. I played it over and over and over again, only instead of lyrics, all I could think about was Mom.

It was slightly disturbing to think that I'd been holding her back because all I care about is her happiness. And mine, I guess, but mine is kind of dependent on hers, so it's all the same, really.

So I was determined to talk to her about it at the earliest opportunity.

That wouldn't be for a while though because Mom was taking loads of extra shifts at the hospital. Still, if I had to wait a day or two or even a couple of weeks for the chance to have what would probably be a pretty awkward conversation, then that was just how it would have to be. Too bad.

Suddenly, I heard her key in the door.

"Katie? Are you home? I feel like you and I haven't talked in ages!"

Sometimes I think that maybe the universe is using me to have a bit of a laugh.

"I'm in my room," I said.

"Coming!"

There was no way she was glowing, although it was true that Mom did look a little happier than she had been. Probably just the result of her new jacket. And the haircut. And was that an actual manicure?

"So," I said. "How're things? It's all been pretty tough lately, hasn't it?"

"I suppose so," said Mom.

"Because of the move," I said. "And this place being so cramped."

"It's growing on me," said Mom.

"Like mold," I said.

I guess I should describe our apartment, but there's not much point. It had somebody else's curtains on the windows and someone else's hairy, old carpet on the floor. So it wasn't really ours at all.

Mom was still going. "I know things have been... well...but I feel like we're really turning a corner."

"We as in—"

"Me, you, Amanda. Us."

Which made me feel a little better. "Maybe."

"Definitely," said Mom. "It's like there's been a dark cloud over us, but you know what? Summer's on its way. We're settled here now. We've made it, Katie."

"Are you sure?" I said.

"I really do think we're going to be all right," said Mom. "So cheer up. Promise?"

I wasn't going to promise, but I did say, "I'll try," which was pretty much the same thing. Because maybe we would be all right now. Amanda was pretty annoying, and I wasn't at all sure about Mom's taste in jackets. But all things considered—and there were a lot of things to consider— we'd made it through fairly well.

"Are you all right to do dinner without me tonight?"

"Sure," I said, doing a little dance inside. The things

Mom does to food would be considered torture if it wasn't already dead. "What's the occasion?"

"It's karaoke at the Dog and Duck, and for once I'm not at work."

Mom is a complete karaoke fiend. I think her version of "My Way" is better than the original. And the Elvis version. It's maybe even as good as the Nina Simone one.

"Is that why you're in such a good mood?" I said.

She flushed. "They're a nice bunch of people. They don't ask about your father. And they like my singing."

Of course they liked Mom's singing. How could they not?

"So *that's* why you're so happy," I said. "It's funny because Amanda thought you had a new boyfriend!"

There was this pause.

And then Mom said, "Clever Amanda."

"What? Why? Amanda isn't clever. Amanda doesn't know anything. You don't have a boyfriend."

"His name is Adrian," said Mom. "I'm sure you'll like him a lot."

I wanted to say, *Adrian? How long has this been going on? And didn't you think to maybe ask me first?*

"Adrian? How long has this been going on? And excuse me, but didn't you think to maybe ask me first?"

"Only a couple of months," said Mom. "And I don't need your permission, Katie."

"But I thought…" And then I ran out of words and just stared at her.

"He saw me singing a few times and said I had a nice voice, and then one thing led to another and…" I had to tune out for a while. I came back in on, "I'd never have started seeing him if I hadn't thought you could deal with it. He's nice, Katie. I promise."

"If he ever hurts you, I'll kill him with my bare hands. And my hair straighteners, which are pretty lethal when they're heated up."

She laughed, which was annoying, because I meant it.

"I'll have him over for lunch on Sunday. I'm sure you'll get on like a house on fire."

She went back downstairs. And I *did* feel like a house on fire.

But I don't think Mom meant it like that at all.

Chapter Two

I'M A BAD PERSON," I said.

Lacey and I were walking along the canal to school, which sounds all pretty and lovely and like it's full of boats and ducklings but, in fact, is quite a risky way of getting somewhere because of all the sixth-grade boys and the incredibly dirty water.

Which isn't to say that there aren't nice parts. There's a really friendly cat that likes to hang out on top of the barges, and once a year the geese have chicks or geeselings or whatever baby geese are called.

Mostly, though, it's graffiti and seagulls picking things out of the trash. And people sitting on benches chatting, which seems fine until you notice that (a) they are all drinking beer and (b) it is eight thirty in the morning.

"What do you mean you're a bad person?" said Lacey.

"You're supposed to say, 'No, you're not,'" I told her.

"Okay, no, you're not. Why?"

"Because Mom's found a new boyfriend and she's really happy, and I know I should be happy too, but I'm not."

"That's not so bad," said Lacey.

"But you think it's a little bad?"

"A little," said Lacey, and I decided I wouldn't be asking her for any more advice for the time being.

We stopped for a second to watch one of the boys trying to climb into a Dumpster.

"Did you know that Savannah's having a party?" said Lacey.

"Nope," I said, still watching the boys in the Dumpster.

"It's not for a while, but she's already got this exclusive guest list," Lacey went on.

"You're making Savannah sound like some Hollywood A-lister," I said.

"She probably *is* a Harltree A-lister," said Lacey. "Which makes us Harltree D-listers, I guess."

"Stop it, Lacey. You're overwhelming me with joy."

"Maybe we're C-listers?" said Lacey, hopeful.

"Nah, we're definitely D-list. If that."

"Well, she can't just have A-listers at the party, or there'll only be three of them there."

That sounded like my last party. Me, Lacey, and Amanda, dancing to my collection of vintage NOW albums. "That's okay," I said. "As long as it's the right three people."

"Yes, but her dad's spending a load of money on it. There's going to be a tent in her garden. A really enormous one, with caterers and a light-up dance floor and everything."

"Just how big is this tent?" I asked.

"It's so big," said Lacey, "that it even has its own toilets. That's what Paige told me."

"Savannah won't allow her guests to put their butts on her proper toilet?"

"No," said Lacey, snickering. "Only Savannah's beautiful behind gets to sit on that."

This was especially funny because last week a picture had gone around of Savannah's bare butt. At least it was supposed to be Savannah's. Savannah herself denied all knowledge, and it *was* a suspiciously perfect butt, even for perfect Savannah.

Still, we all shared it. Because, you know… Butts.

"Do you really think she'll invite people like us?" I said, thinking that maybe if she did, I might get a shot at standing somewhere in the vicinity of Dominic Preston, who is gorgeous.

Lacey looked a little offended. "She's invited me. Maybe it's my bangs. I think my hair is B-list, even if I'm not. You really need to consider cutting yours, Katie. It would completely open up your face."

"I am considering it," I said.

"I could do it tonight," said Lacey. "If you've got some sharp scissors."

I made a mental note to text Amanda and get her to hide the scissors.

"I think Adrian's going to be there tonight," I said. "Maybe we could go to yours."

"Is he that bad?"

"I did try to like him," I said sadly. "For Mom's sake. I did try."

♪ ♫ ♫

I'd opened the door to him the day before.

"All right? I'm Ade."

He was wearing a tight black T-shirt, which was not even slightly appropriate for a man of forty or fifty or whatever he was, and jeans and a huge, cracked leather jacket.

"Hello, Ade…rian."

"You Amanda or Katie?"

"Katie."

"Mind if I come on in, Katie? I'm dying to pee."

He came on in, his jacket making a creaky noise, and an invisible battle started up between the lunch smell of roast chicken and his very strong aftershave. The chicken was just making a retreat back to the oven as Adrian emerged from the bathroom.

"Is that him?" Amanda was at my elbow.

"Shh," I said. "Just watch for a second."

We stood in the doorway as he went through to the kitchen, kissed Mom, then poured himself a glass of water. He headed straight to the right cabinet and even knew to do the funny twist thing to make the water come out of our touchy faucet.

"What?" hissed Amanda. "What's the matter?"

"*He's been here before.*"

"So?"

Was it while I was at school? I reran two months' worth of breakfasts, me jabbering away over the Nutella, thinking I had Mom's full attention while all the time she must have been counting the minutes until she could get rid of me and see lover boy.

Or had he come around at night? Did Mom wait until Amanda and I were in bed and then sneak out to let him in?

All those times she'd given me McDonald's money to go and meet Lacey in town, had she really been trying to get rid of me?

Judging by the evidence—whose hand was now caressing my mother's back—the answer was yes.

Now there are a lot of ways you can spoil a Sunday lunch. You can burn the chicken. You can drop your headphones in the gravy. Or you can sit down across the table from a man with two hairs sprouting out of his nose. By which I mean, the skin on top of his nose. Not his nostrils, which would have been disgusting but at least normal.

"Good chicken, Mom," I said.

"Yes," said Amanda.

"It's not too burned, is it?" said Mom.

"Not at all."

"It's terrific."

"Your best ever."

"It really tastes…like…chicken."

There was a pause, which might have lasted a moment or maybe a hundred years.

"It's delicious," said Adrian, and then he leaned over and kissed Mom on the mouth. While she was still chewing. With tongue.

After five of the most awkward seconds of my life, he finished eating my mother and went back to his plate. "So Amanda, Zoe tells me you play bass?"

"I guess so," she said, looking at her lap. "Sometimes."

"I used to be in a band once. A while back. Split up. Creative differences. You know."

"Oh, right," said Amanda.

"Still got a lot of industry connections. You should meet my pal Tony. Tony Topper. The stories he could tell—"

"I bet."

"So are you any good?"

"I'm…okay."

"Just okay?" Adrian leaned forward, and I noticed he had a piece of squashed carrot stuck to his elbow. "Who are your influences?"

And that was it. For the next ten minutes, Amanda was off in Amanda Land, talking about the music she loves and the bands she's going to see and the people she'd like to see but can't because they're not touring at the moment or they've split up or they're dead and *blah blah* infinite *blah*.

And Adrian was doing it too! For every band she wanted to talk about, he had an actual opinion, which is not what you do when Amanda starts up on one of her music rants. You keep quiet until it's over. Nose Hairs, on the other hand, was encouraging her. And all the while, Mom was nodding and smiling and stuffing her face with chicken.

"You know," said Adrian, "I could use someone like you in the store. Vox Vinyl, you know it?"

Amanda nodded like it was Christmas and her birthday and she'd won the lottery. Twice.

"We're a little short-staffed right now, and it's so hard

to find someone who knows their stuff. You free to do a few hours next week?"

"I can be," said Amanda. Seriously, I thought she might faint. I mean, I know she'd always said she dreamed of working in a record store, but I hadn't realized it was her life's great ambition. Until now.

"Great," said Adrian.

"I just have to tell the café I'm leaving, but that's fine. I'm a lousy waitress anyway."

"I don't know that we're busy enough to justify you coming on board full-time."

"That's all right," said Amanda. "I'll just—I'll be really useful. It's fine."

"Is it?" I said.

He turned his attention to me. "I've heard you and your sister like jamming together?" Then he did a little burp. "'Scuse me."

Mom giggled.

"I've got some instruments kicking around that I've been meaning to sell. Some Gibsons, a couple of Fenders— you'd be welcome to come and mess around with them."

"That would be amazing!" said Amanda.

I said something that can only be written as, "Mblm."

"Katie writes songs," said Amanda. "About her life and stuff. She's like Lily Allen used to be, sort of. Kooky."

I'd planned on keeping quiet, but this was too much. "Don't call me kooky! Kooky is for girls who wear plastic flowers in their hair and have names for their toes."

"Feisty?"

"No. Feisty says, 'She's so out there, which is really surprising because she's a girl.'"

"Quirky?"

I mimed being sick.

"All right then," said Amanda. "How about *different*?"

I thought for a second. "I will accept different. Thank you."

There was a very long silence.

"So Katie, how's school?" said Mom.

"Fine," I said.

"Tell Adrian what you're studying at the moment."

"Nothing much."

"It's okay, Zo. When I was her age, school was the last thing I wanted to think about. Especially on the weekend. Bet you're too busy chasing the boys, right, Katie?" Then he winked.

"We're doing a play called *Julius Caesar*," I said, "which is where this annoying guy who thinks he's the best ends up getting stabbed."

And then I did my most evil stare. And then I choked on a roasted potato.

♪ ♫ ♫

"It was all pretty grim," I said to Lacey, as we slumped into our homeroom. "So grim that I only managed to eat half my dessert. Which is saying something."

"But you went back for the rest later, right?"

"Of course I did," I said. "Things are bad enough. I can't risk malnutrition too."

"And Amanda's going to be working for him?"

"She's giving her notice at the café today. I tried talking her out of it, but all she's interested in is whether he'll give her an employee discount. As far as she's concerned, getting 20 percent off the latest Alabama Shakes album is more important than the fact that there is this man in our flat, groping our mother."

"Mad Jaz alert," said Lacey, which is our code for when Mad Jaz is in the vicinity. Okay, it's not much of a code.

"What's she doing here? I thought Jaz was finished with school?"

"Look! Nicole's filming her. This should be good."

We watched as Jaz opened a can of Fanta and poured it into Ms. McAllister's top drawer. Then, like she'd finished her work for the day, she turned around and left.

"She is so crazy," said Lacey. "And that is such a waste of Fanta."

"What is?"

"Katie? Earth to Katie?"

"Adrian drinks Fanta," I said.

"You need to forget about him," said Lacey. "Focus on Savannah's party. Or writing a song. Or your new bangs."

But I couldn't. He was all I could think about. How, when we went for a walk in the park, Mom and Adrian had held hands. And how, when Adrian took Amanda into his shop to show her how to work the cash register, she was so excited that she'd given him a hug.

And last night, when it got later and later and later and Adrian didn't leave and didn't leave and didn't leave, and at midnight, when I knew he was next door in Mom's room in her bed, all I could think about were those two nose hairs lurking—just a yard away—in the dark.

Autocorrect

You ask if I've finished, and I say can
you wait
But before I can stop you, you're
clearing my plate
You ask, "Am I happy?" and I say "I'm
trying"
Your voice says that's great, but your
eyes know I'm lying

I guess if you want to earn my respect
Can you maybe turn off the autocorrect?

When you talk to your folks, I couldn't
be better
The undisputed star of your epic
Christmas letter
My behavior's amazing, my grades are
great too
It's kind of a pity that none of it's true

I get that there's stuff that you have to
protect
But please can we turn off the autocorrect?

It's late and I'm lonely, and though you're
next door,
There's nothing to link us but walls
and a floor
I don't want to lose you, but I know I
might
No way will we talk when he's here for
the night

Mom, if there's any chance we'll ever
connect
You'll have to turn off the autocorrect.

Chapter Three

AFTER THAT, ADRIAN WAS JUST always *there*. Leaving his stupid jacket on top of the laundry basket or coming out the bathroom with his chest all hairy or using the kitchen table as an imaginary drum kit.

"You do like him, don't you?" said Mom on one of the very few occasions where he wasn't standing next to her.

"Um, yeah," I said, which was about as positive as I could manage.

"Because—"

"It's just—"

We'd both started at the same time.

"You go," I said.

"What were you going to say?"

I was going to say that I thought it was all going kind of fast, but Mom had a funny look on her face, so I decided I'd let her finish.

"It's just…we were thinking we might move in together. He's here most of the time anyway!"

I did a few fish gulps before I managed, "But…there's not enough room. Doesn't he have ten million records or something?"

"Ten thousand. But there's plenty of space for them. And us. You girls would each have a room. And there's a decent-sized kitchen and a garden. With a shed. And a pond, sort of. Either a pond or a drainage problem, it depends how you want to look at it."

"Hold on. We're all moving somewhere new? Together? As in us and him? Sharing a house? And…a bathroom?" I don't know why this was the most horrifying thing to me, but it really was.

"Actually," said Mom, "our bedroom has its very own bathroom. I don't think even your father's place has that. Not that you're going to tell him. Well, maybe you can."

"I did. Last night," said Amanda.

"Is everyone in on this except me? Because it's starting to feel like some kind of conspiracy."

"Of course it isn't," said Mom.

"Then how come Amanda already knows?"

"I guess I might have mentioned it to her. But look, it's not definite yet—"

"Mom showed me pictures," said Amanda, "and it's nice. Well, it could be."

"The lady who had it died, and it's really cheap," said Mom, digging into her purse, probably so she wouldn't have to look at me. "Adrian thinks—"

I was about to launch into a long speech about taking things slowly and thinking of others. And was she absolutely sure? And even if she was, maybe she should at least check that everyone else in the household was on board. But, before I could, the man himself came barging in.

"What?" I said. "What is it that *Adrian thinks*?"

"About what?" he said, looking from me to Mom. She waved a crumpled scrap of paper at him, and I spotted an upside-down photo of a house.

He grinned. "Ah! The place is a bargain, Katie. A real gem. If we move fast, we can get it before anyone else even knows about it."

"Isn't it exciting?" said Mom.

Going to live with Nose Hairs in the house of a dead lady. "Yaaaay."

They put in an offer, and it got accepted right away, so I had to drink sparkling wine and plaster on a fake smile while Mom and Amanda decided what we would take with us and which of my childhood memories they would throw away. (Spoiler alert: all of them.)

And every night as we built up to the move, I was asked to help wrap stuff and pack it away when I could have been sitting in my room with my guitar. Instead I was forced to be a part of Team New Home, stacking box after box in teetering piles up against the walls, which was incredibly dangerous, and when I stopped looking where I was going even for a second, they came crashing down on my head, which meant that everyone got mad at me for breaking their stuff at the exact moment I might have given myself permanent brain damage.

Fun times.

♪♫♪

"Bye-bye, geese," I said to the geese paddling along the canal. "Bye-bye, footbridge. Bye-bye, old mattress."

"I can't believe you'll have to ride the bus with those guys," said Lacey. "They're messed up."

"Thanks for being so supportive."

"What can I say?" said Lacey, who clearly knew exactly what it was she was going to say and was about to continue saying it. "You've got Finlay from seventh grade, who has the mental age of a six-year-old. Then there're the sixth-graders. Like, about a billion of them. And Nicole, who's a sophomore."

"At least she's interesting," I said.

"Apparently, she got her ear pierced last week right at the top with this really tiny stud. Only it swelled up in the night, and the stud part disappeared into her ear like her skin had eaten it. She had to go to the emergency room and get it taken out. Mad Jaz filmed the whole thing and put it online."

"That is so disgusting," I said. "Have you seen it?"

We slowed down so Lacey could show me. The camera zoomed in close, and there was even a little blood. It finished with Jaz giving the nurse a high five.

"Eighty-seven views," said Lacey. "Seriously, who watches this stuff?"

"I know."

"In fact, I think Jaz gets the bus too."

"No, she doesn't," I said. A dose of Mad Jaz was the last thing I needed. Mad Jaz with her gothy clothes and pale skin, like she's some dead lady from a hundred years ago who just crawled out of the grave in order to hang around, looking spooky and making snarky comments.

"She does," said Lacey. "She lives down near those yellow fields by the rotary. Poor you."

Which was much more like it.

"Exactly," I said. "It's like, the divorce was the worst thing in the world, and we'd just managed to get through that, and then Nose Hairs comes along, and now I'm bussing it with Jaz. Poor, poor me."

"Poor you," said Lacey. "Hey, so Paige and Sofie had a fight over who got to buy these navy sling backs at Topshop, and they're not speaking. So Savannah's uninvited them both to her party until they figure it out."

Sometimes I think that Lacey isn't quite as interested by my problems as she should be.

"Honestly. Who even cares about shoes?"

"Not you, apparently," said Lacey, staring at my scuffed Doc Martens.

"Lace, can't you just be nice for five more minutes? We are never going to do this walk again, and I don't want my last memory of our time together to be of you trolling my footwear."

She blew her bangs out of her eyes. "I'm just grumpy because I'm going to miss you. Okay?"

Oh. "Don't say that! We'll still see each other all day. And we can talk to each other on the phone the entire way in, so it'll basically be like we're walking together."

"I guess."

She stopped under the tree with the picnic bench, where we'd sometimes share a Dove Bar.

"What?" I said.

"Nothing," said Lacey. "Just…"

She looked kind of worried, standing there, her white-blond hair blowing in the cold breeze that always came off the water, and I wondered whether she'd planned for something unpleasant to happen as a going-away present.

That's the problem with Lacey. She's not the best judge of that kind of thing. She could just as easily have gotten me a special Dove Bar as she could have arranged for the boys to toss me into the canal.

I readied myself, and then—

"Surprise," she said awkwardly and pulled a little box out of her bag.

"What?" I said.

"Open it."

So I did, carefully, and—

"Lace!"

My best friend had lined the box in violet tissue paper, my favorite color.

"It's mementoes of our best walks. There's the noise-maker from your birthday. I saved it. And the song we made up about the geese babies. I know you've forgotten it, so I wrote it down—"

"And a pair of Dove Bar sticks!"

My insides got as gooey as chocolate pudding. In fact, I was starting to think of a new song, maybe called something like "Walking with You," about friendship and memories and how beautiful it all was when Lacey said, "Other surprise!"

Suddenly, the rest of the canal crowd jumped out from behind trees and dumped me in the water.

I walked home and dried off and sat down on my bed, surrounded by boxes, some of which I hadn't even unpacked from the last move, and thank goodness I had my stereo because otherwise I think I might have exploded or crumbled or something.

That's what I love about music. There's always a song that knows how you're feeling.

I played *Back to Black* over and over, Tom Waits, some Leonard Cohen, lots of Patty Griffin, and Joni Mitchell. It was when I was listening to *Blue* for the third time that there was a gentle knock on my door.

"What?"

"I bring word from the rest of us," said Amanda.

"Which is?"

"Message received, okay? We know you don't want

to move, but can this soundtrack of extreme misery please stop?"

She was kind of smiling as she said it, and even though I really did not want to, I found myself smiling too. "All right. But only as a favor to you."

"Play me that tune again," said Amanda. "The happy one you were doing a few weeks ago. Dah-dah-dahdah-daaaaah?"

I played it, and it sounded…hopeful. So I played it again.

"Does it have words?" said Amanda.

It didn't. Now, though, with Amanda next to me, I tried:

I got mad skin,

I got mad hair,

I borrowed your stuff, and I don't even care."

"What did you borrow?" said Amanda.

"Your yellow sweater. Deal with it, sister," I said, leaning over to scribble in my lyric book. "Go grab your guitar? I want to hear it with a bass line."

Amanda got her guitar and sat down to pick it out carefully and precisely.

"Like that but faster," I said. "Speed it up a little."

Which she did, and I sang:

I got mad skin,

I got mad hair,

I borrowed your stuff, and I don't even care.

I'm the big bad apple on the family tree.
Deal with it, sister. That's just me."

"I like that," said Amanda. "And I would also like my sweater back."

We played it a few more times.

"Is there any more?" said Amanda.

"It's a work in progress," I said. "I've just been finding it…hard."

"I do get it, you know," said Amanda.

"You nearly do," I said. "There's just that funny part toward the end. It needs a pause after 'Deal with it, sister.' You're rushing."

"I meant about the move. I'm nervous too. And so's Mom. It's *not* just you, Katie. It isn't easy for any of us."

I leaned over to get another line into my book before it evaporated.

"We're all finding it hard."

"Then why are we doing it?" I asked. "Can't we just wait a few months?"

Amanda thrummed some more on her guitar. "Maybe Mom wants to get going with the rest of her life. The divorce went on long enough."

"Yeah," I said. It had gone on long enough.

"We'll move," said Amanda. "And we'll unpack, and then everything will get back to normal."

"I guess," I said. "Want to see something funny?" And I showed her the video of Nicole's ear.

"Eeeurgh! How have eight and a half thousand people watched that?"

"Have they?" I looked at the view counter, and they had. "Wow. It's gone totally viral."

We were silent for a second, thinking of all the people out there watching a close-up of Nicole's ear and sending it to their friends. Or maybe their enemies because it really was disgusting. If one person sent it to two people, then they each sent it to two people, then each of *them* sent it to two people…

"But why?" said Amanda. "Will you forward me the link? Adrian will love it."

Chapter Four

S O WHAT'S IT LIKE?" ASKED Lacey the day we moved into the new house.

I was about to tell her that the phone reception was terrible, but then my phone went and hung up on her, so I guess that said it for me.

Our new house was great. In a sort of really dark, horrible kind of way, where the floors creaked and everything smelled a little moldy and the windows didn't open right and when you did get them unstuck, you couldn't shut them again.

"It's got so much character," said Amanda, who'd dropped her keys between the floorboards and couldn't get them back out.

And when I went out to explore, all the neighbors were about eighty and said things like "Good morning" and "Nice day to wash the car" and "Watch where you're going,

young lady" just because I happened to be walking and tex-
ting at the same time, which is completely normal everywhere else, and it's hardly my fault that mobility scooters
can't get out of the way.

"There's such a sense of peace," said Amanda, who was
listening to Black Sabbath.

And we were in the middle of actual nowhere. There
was just a pub, a load of smelly pigs, and a field of oilseed
rape, which really needs to get itself a new name.

And Adrian had stuck his drum set right under my
bedroom window, so even after I'd unpacked my boxes and
put all my things away, the room still didn't feel like mine.
All I could see were mountains of flattened cardboard and
cymbals and walls the color of pee.

I thought I'd write a song about it, but the pee thing
made it sound like the whole situation was funny, and it
wasn't. At all.

Then I tried finishing "Just Me." I had two verses but
no ending. And after half an hour, I still had no ending,
just a whole pile of things that didn't rhyme with other
things and a sore brain.

So instead I tried moving the wardrobe over a little in
case that helped things.

At which point the wardrobe door fell off onto my
actual face.

"Mom? Mooom!"

It wasn't Mom who appeared outside my bedroom door but Adrian.

"You mother can't come upstairs right now. She's lying down."

"Why?"

"She's had a small electrical shock."

"From what?"

"The oven."

"Do ovens usually give people electrical shocks?"

Adrian looked a little uncomfortable. "Not usually, no."

Our thoughtful moment was interrupted by Amanda, who was looking flushed and upset and distinctly non-Amandaish.

"It's fine, but I was looking under my bed for my hairbrush. I can't find it anywhere… And I saw a mouse. Well, mice, I guess. Three mice. At least three mice."

"What do you mean *at least*?"

"They move really fast," said Amanda. "And I didn't want to look at them closely because they were mice."

"Probably pets left behind by the last people who were here."

"The dead lady?" I said. "Maybe they came out of her *corpse*."

"Katie!"

So we all sat down and had our first ever family gathering to list all the things that were wrong with the house. It went like this:

- strange smell (even after opening the windows)
- windows that open but don't close again
- a really big hole in the floor of the pantry
- oven electrocutes you
- mice
- the toilet flushes with hot water (two words: poop soup)

"It's not so bad," said Amanda in a way that made it clear that even Miss Optimism thought it was bad.

"I'll talk to the real estate agent," said Adrian, tapping out the world's slowest text message with one of his massive thumbs. He stared at his phone. "It's not sending. Why won't it send?"

"There's reception if you lean out of the window, so it feels like you might be about to fall out," I said helpfully. "Or at the end of the driveway." And off he went.

The rest of us stared at one another.

"Did you not notice any of this when you came to look around?" I asked Mom, trying to make it come out light and nonaccusing.

"We only looked quickly," she said. "It was such a bargain…"

She looked all small and hopeless, and I wanted to yell at the universe for being so mean.

"We'll figure it out," said Amanda cheerfully. "Really, it'll be fine. Better than fine. We're all in this together."

"I'm going for a walk," I said.

"Now?" Mom asked.

"To see the bus stop. Since I'm going to have to be there tomorrow morning anyway."

I left her in her room and went off down the driveway, past Adrian on his phone, past Amanda's hairbrush, which I went back and retrieved from the recycling heap, and off into the sunshine.

Now I want to be clear that what I am about to say does not in any way mean that I was happy or that I liked the new place or that I wanted to be there. No way.

It was just…there was something really nice about walking down the driveway and along the sidewalk with the grass smelling green and fresh, all beaded with drops of rain and glimmering in the light. Hardly any cars came past, and the sky felt high and open, empty and waiting to be filled.

I let loose a few bars of "Just Me," and it sounded even better outside. Especially after I adjusted the melody just a little and sent the last verse spiraling up toward the watery sun.

"I got mad love,
I got mad hate,
I've got my whole life to come, and I just can't wait.
And here's the thing, I think you'll agree,
We're all in this together. It's not just me."

The words fell into place like they'd been there all along.

I did a twirl and then another. There's nothing quite like using a hairbrush as a microphone.

"Are you all right, dear?"

There was the bus stop. Complete with two old ladies.

My face was hotter than the sun. Hotter than the sun on fire. Which I think it is anyway, but still.

"You have a lovely voice," said the nearest one. Then, to her friend, "Doesn't she have a lovely voice?"

"She's the one who ran into my scooter," said the other lady.

"Oh, *is* she?" said old lady number one, eyeing me closely. It was then that I decided to turn around and go home.

♪ ♫ ♪

When I got to the end of the driveway, my phone started ringing in my pocket. When I saw who it was, my heartbeat went syncopated, which is fun when it's music, but biologi-cally speaking, probably not the best.

"Dad!"

"We're just taking five, so I thought I'd check in on my special girl."

It's the miracle of phones that even though he was in the United States, his voice sounded so clear that if I shut my eyes, I could pretend that he was standing just behind me, his hands on my shoulders, holding me close.

"I'm all right," I said. "We've just moved into the new house."

"And?"

"It's fine," I said. I didn't want to spend my precious Dad minutes on anything even slightly Adrian. "How's California?"

"All good."

"Hot?"

"Oh, yes. You really must visit."

"You know Mom won't let me come while school's in session."

"Honestly, your mother. You can't be doing anything important."

"Only schoolwork."

"Exactly," he said.

"Or," I said, trying to keep the hope out of my voice

and failing, "you could always come here? We have lots of space now."

"Soon," he said. "Work's pretty busy at the moment, but soon."

Dad's a session musician, which is the coolest of the cool. He's an amazing guitarist. Plus he also plays bass and the keyboard and the clarinet, although I have no proof of the last one, and he does have a tendency to exaggerate.

Even so, he's basically the best guitarist in the world, and I'm not just saying that because we share chromosomes. You can hear him on zillions of tracks, from cereal commercials to stuff by very major rock stars who I'm not allowed to name because it's supposed to be them playing, not him.

The only difficult thing about Dad being so awesome is that his work is not very regular, so when he does get offered a job, he kind of needs to take it.

"I'm still planning on coming over just before Christmas," he said.

"Of course. And Christmas isn't that far away."

"Only a few months."

For all the magic of cell phones, I could feel the whole distance between us. Every last millimeter.

"Written anything good lately?"

"I'm working on a couple of things," I told him. "Hey, what did you think of the last batch?"

"Oh, fantastic. All of it."

"Really?" My heart did another flip. "I wasn't sure about 'Wet Weather.' But if you like it—"

"I love it," said Dad. "The lyrics are phenomenal. Your best yet."

"'Wet Weather' was the instrumental number. The one with a ripply part at the beginning that was supposed to sound like rain?"

"Of course it was. And I thought it was amazing."

Now it was a good thing we were on the phone, or he'd have seen me crying. "Thank you, Dad."

"I've got to go back into the studio now, sweetheart. Sorry this is such a quick one. You take care, won't you?"

"I will. And Dad—"

And at that point, the stupid, stupid, stupid reception cut out, and he was gone.

So I stomped back up the driveway, and then I stepped on a snail and felt bad and tried to walk a little more delicately and then stepped on another snail anyway, which just goes to show that sometimes there really is no point to anything.

And then I thought about having to ride the bus with Finlay and Nicole, who were sophomores, and Mad Jaz, and my mood got even worse, if that's possible, which it was.

We'd started calling her Mad Jaz as a sort of joke, although it isn't that much of a joke because Jaz has a tendency to go crazy.

Like, once there was this stretch of muggings downtown, and we had a policeman come in to show us self-defense. He needed a volunteer to demonstrate his techniques and picked Jaz, and to cut a long (and violent) story short, Jaz ended up being arrested.

I'd been keeping away from our resident psychogoth, which luckily had been pretty easy to do because Jaz seemed to have made the decision to stop coming to school. Of course, now that I thought about it, that meant she almost certainly wouldn't be riding the bus anymore. After all, why would you go all the way to school if you weren't planning to be in any classes?

I walked through the front door to find that everyone had mysteriously vanished.

"Hello? Hello?"

Nothing. Just some distant guitar noise.

"Manda?"

I went upstairs and across the landing.

The door to Mom's bedroom—no, not Mom's bedroom; Mom *and Adrian's* bedroom—was open, but there wasn't anyone in there. Just the faint scent of Mom's eau de toilette and the not-so-faint stench of Adrian's deodorant.

I must have inhaled it ten times a day, but even so, every single time was a shock. I hadn't even known my old life had had a smell until he'd come along and swapped my home and bought Mom a different perfume and sneaked cigarettes at the back of the garden. Now I knew things were messed up without even having to go to the trouble of opening my eyes.

I knocked on Amanda's door. "Manda?"

He was there. Sitting on a chair by her bed, guitar under one arm. "Hey, Katie."

"Oh. Hello."

Amanda was propped against her desk, head bent over her own frets. She didn't meet my eye. "Katie."

"What are you two doing?" It came out more confrontational than I'd meant. But surely Amanda couldn't have been playing guitar with…him.

I mean, there was making the guy feel at home and then there was out-and-out sisterly betrayal.

Playing together was *ours*. We'd done it with Dad since we were little—Amanda banging a drum while I sat on his knee and he held my fingers in place on the strings. We got older and better, and there were nights after a really big fight when the music was just about the only thing keeping us together.

And now here she was, strumming away as if it was just normal.

"We're not doing anything," said Amanda as Adrian said, "You'll like this—"

"She won't," said Amanda, actually holding her fingers across his strings to stop him from playing. Absolutely right too.

While Amanda had at least noticed that she was in trouble, Adrian was still grinning. "Go on, Katie. Grab your guitar. We could use your expertise here."

"My fingers are tired," I said, which made no sense whatsoever, but there you go.

"So are mine," said Amanda quickly. "Should we call it a night?"

Adrian's head swiveled between us. He picked up his guitar and started to leave, pausing to say, "I'll put on a pepperoni pizza, okay?"

"Katie—" Amanda began.

"No, it's fine," I said, heading for the door. "You play with him if it makes you happy."

"Really?" said Amanda.

"*No.*"

Mobility Scooting
on the Pavement

Got a head full of blame
And a knee full of hurt
Got a heart full of shame
And a face full of dirt

Lady,
You'd think you'd have a bell
Or perhaps a kinda hooter
Somewhere on your mobility scooter

You're a Triple-A holder,
And I was in your way
One day I'll get older
But first I need to say

Lady, please,
Get yourself a bell
And a really giant hooter
And put them onto your mobility scooter

And if you won't do that
Then lighten my load
And ride the stupid thing
Along the stupid road.

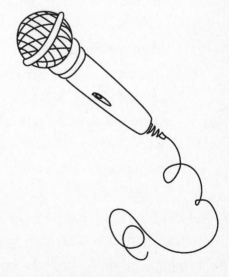

Chapter Five

S HOWING UP AT A BUS stop on a school morning is a little like jumping into a den of tigers—or something just as deadly but not so endangered. Like jumping into a bowl of cashews if you've got a nut allergy.

To avoid making it completely obvious to the bus crowd that I was Katie-no-friends, I made sure I got there nice and early. Which didn't work at all, as, in fact, I was the first one to arrive. I ended up standing around completely on my own, fiddling with my phone.

Okay, not fiddling. Trying to call Lacey so we'd at least be able to talk to each other on our way in like we'd planned. But her phone just rang and rang and rang.

She probably had it on silent or something.

Which left me with a dilemma. How many times should you try calling a person before you start to seem like you're kind of mental? I stopped after fifteen attempts and went back to staring out at the road instead. I couldn't even try to look cool. It was guitar lesson day. So I had to stand there with this huge thing strapped to my back like a kind of deformed tortoise.

My mood wasn't helped by the fact that the bus stop closest to our house would not have made it onto a list of Harltree's best bus stops. Not even a top one hundred. The bushes around it were filled with candy wrappers and pieces of Styrofoam. The shelter's seats had been ripped out, and on the piece of plastic protecting the time schedule, someone had taken a permanent marker and scrawled a picture of something Gran would call obscene.

Suddenly, just a few minutes before the bus was supposed to turn up, it was the Harltree version of Piccadilly Circus.

A bunch of sixth-graders were doing something complicated with playing cards, and Finlay was poking his fingers into an egg salad sandwich. Then Nicole announced she could make her eyeball pop out by pinching her nose and blowing it at the same time. She couldn't—she just got snot on herself.

That was really funny, and I did a big laugh to show how much I was in on the joke, only no one seemed to notice.

And I thought of Lacey and was about to try calling her again when—

"All right, Katie?"

Oh no.

"Jaz!"

"What are you doing here?"

Out on the street, she looked scarier than ever, the pimples on her chin oozing yellow stuff and piercings all the way up both ears. She'd even managed to put a stud through that little triangle part in the middle. The part that, strictly speaking, is not ear but head.

"I'm taking the bus now," I said.

"Why?" Jaz was wearing a school uniform skirt, but instead of the required navy-blue sweatshirt on top, she had a black bodice thing with sleeves that billowed out at the top and narrowed from her elbows to her wrists and finished up with rows of tiny buttons. This, combined with her piercings and a fairly extreme level of makeup, made her look like a twisted Victorian doll.

"Because Mom has just bought the world's worst house with the world's worst man and…"

I trailed off because it was possible that Jaz wasn't truly listening. I could tell because she had turned her back on me and because she had started talking to Nicole.

I'm aware that there are more unfortunate people in the world than me and that being lonely at a bus stop isn't the same as being in a famine or getting shot or catching a deadly disease. But somehow, knowing that didn't really seem to help.

Just then, my deep and interesting thoughts were interrupted by the sight of Nicole walking backward off the sidewalk and into the traffic.

"Aaaargh, careful!" I lunged forward to pull her to safety.

But, instead of thanking me for saving her life, Nicole shook me off, and Jaz said, "You've ruined it now."

"Ruined what?"

"We're videoing." She turned to Nicole, "Okay, start again."

Jaz held up her phone while Nicole started wobbling off toward the road again.

And part of me wanted to stop them because obviously it was incredibly dangerous. But another part of me was really interested to see what would happen. Nicole was just veering off the pavement when, thank goodness, the bus drove up, stopping just before it squashed her.

My plan had been to stay safely in the front near the driver, but just as we were getting on, Jaz put her face right in mine and said, "You can sit in the backseat with us."

And suddenly, I was pining for the good old days when it had just been me, the bus stop, and my guitar.

So we all piled on, shoving past a bunch of people who had left their bags and legs sticking out. One of them, this thin, veiny man, said, "*Excuse* me," in a really pointed way, and Jaz just laughed.

The veiny man caught my eye, and I made a face that said, *Sorry about her. She's not my friend or anything. I'm new to this bus actually, and I'm finding it kind of difficult.*

I'm not certain I managed to get all that across because the veiny man scowled and said, "The nerve. In my day you'd have been whipped."

So anyway, the bus took off really slowly, like it had to visit every last street it could before getting us to school, and we were all sitting at the back—Finlay and the sixth-graders shoving themselves between the seats, Nicole in the middle, plucking her eyebrows with what looked like a pair of pliers, and Jaz in the back corner like some kind of public transportation queen.

"Katie?"

"Um, yes?"

"Finlay is trying to open your guitar case."

I turned around, and he was.

"Oh. Thanks, Jaz."

Mad Jaz was being nice. Weird.

"I don't think I've ever seen you without Lacey. It's like you're joined at the hip or something."

"Nah," I said, thinking of the zillion missed calls Lace would be finding the very second she looked at her phone. "We're not actually even that friendly anymore. You know. People move on. Apparently."

"Do you want me to get Finlay to egg her?" said Jaz.

"Um, no, that's fine. Thanks, Jaz."

"'Cuz he will."

And in fact, I was so upset at Lacey for not phoning me back that I almost thought about saying yes, only at that exact second, my phone rang, and it was her.

"Lace! Where've you been all my life?"

"Oh, you know." She sounded distant. In all the ways you can be distant. "We were walking along."

"You and who?"

"Just…people."

I considered bringing up our pact to talk to each other on the phone and then decided it would just sound needy and that I wouldn't say anything about it.

"It's just…I thought we were going to talk on the way in. Like we'd said."

"Sorry. Something came up."

"Well…" *Just leave it, Katie. She clearly isn't interested. Let her go.* "Want to spend the night tonight and see the house of horrors? We've got mice and everything."

"Maybe."

"Oh, come on. I'll make Mom give us money for fish and chips."

"Fish and chips?" The reply was immediate and very enthusiastic. Unfortunately, it hadn't come from Lacey. It had come from Mad Jaz. "I like fish and chips. And Nicole likes them too."

And suddenly, I was hosting the world's scariest sleepover. And that wasn't even including our exciting new pets.

"Um, Lace, ring me back in a sec, okay?"

I put the phone down and was about to explain that it hadn't been a general invitation, only I discovered that Jaz was going through the contents of my bag like that was a completely normal thing to do.

"Ha-ha, look. It's Katie's secret diary."

Of course, she'd found my lyric book. People like Jaz can smell that kind of thing a mile off.

"No, it's not."

She flicked it open. "'Just Me.' What is this, please?"

Only Jaz could make the word *please* sound like a threat.

"I write songs."

"Seriously?"

"Yes."

"Since when?"

I thought back and realized, quite interestingly, that I couldn't ever remember *not* having written them—the song for Amanda's fifteenth birthday, which had made her cry, even though she pretended it was an allergic reaction to her new mascara. The divorce songs, which made *me* cry. And the ones about silly stuff like types of breakfast cereal and the weather and never being able to find shoes that look nice that I can also walk in. Actually, that last one isn't silly at all. It's very important.

"Since forever."

I genuinely couldn't tell whether Jaz thought this was good or bad. Her face was pretty hard to read, what with it being covered in eyeliner and cakey foundation that was supposed to hide her acne but in fact just made it look like acne under a layer of foundation. And because Jaz pretty much always scowls, even when she's happy. Especially when she's happy. It's one of the ways you can tell.

"Sing one."

She said it in this laid-back, not-bothered kind of a way, so quietly that I'd almost have ignored it, only when I looked up, her eyes were staring right into mine. Like it was a test.

"Really? It's not like they're any good, Jaz. You won't be that interested. It's just stuff I do when I'm—"

"*Sing one.*"

So there I was, new on the bus, surrounded by sixth-graders, Finlay, Nicole, and a bunch of people who were going to work or wherever it is that adults go on a bus at eight in the morning, which I guess must be work because otherwise, you'd obviously stay in bed.

We were just going around the Old Ewe beltway, where Amanda had failed her driving test. There were drops of water running down the insides of the windows, and the air smelled like gasoline and bad breath. Most of the nonschool people had headphones on, so there was this *tick-tick-tick* sound of leaked-out bloblets of music, all mixed in with the noise of the engine and a siren from outside the window.

Not exactly an ideal environment for my very first public performance.

And I was about to point this out, only then I realized I was actually more scared of what Jaz would say if I *didn't* sing than if I did.

So I took a deep breath and then another one, as though I were standing at the top of the high diving board at the rec center—except that's a poor example because I've never managed to jump.

But I did sing.

"I've got mad skin,
I've got mad hair,
I borrowed your stuff, and I don't even care.
I'm the big bad apple on the family tree.
Deal with it, sister. That's just me."

And…it was okay. Better than okay.

"I've got mad beats,

I've got mad moves,
I know your mom really disapproves.
If you're up for a laugh, then you're my cup of tea.
Friends forever, that's just me."

I could feel without even having to look, that everyone was listening, leaning in, as if my words were a sort of a net drawing them all together, and for maybe a minute or two, the whole bus faded away.

"I've got mad love,
I've got mad hate,
I've got my whole life to come, and I just can't wait.
And here's the thing, I think you'll agree,
We're all in this together. It's not just me."

I finished, and in the pause just after, I saw a new light in Jaz's eyes. Because I'd done it. I'd opened myself up and earned her respect.

She opened her mouth slowly, her surprisingly pink tongue running across her bottom lip. "Katie?"

"Yes?"

"Finlay just dropped your phone out the window."

Chapter Six

I'M GOING TO TRY TO be very calm about this and not go over the top or anything, so all I will say is that it was like the world had ended, and leave it at that.

Just getting my phone back into my hand was hard enough on an alien bus in the middle of who knows where. And when I did, the screen was cracked, the back was smashed, and it wouldn't turn on.

I cradled it in my arms, hoping it knew how much I'd loved it.

"Finlay, you are a jerk," said Jaz.

So it wasn't shaping up to be the best of days.

There was a small moment when I arrived at school with the bus group, and Lacey was there with the canal crowd. I was going to talk to her, but somehow a pack of boys got in between us, and by the time I'd squished past, we were all on our way into morning assembly. You can't talk there, or McAllister murders you and strings up your guts on the information board.

Then we were in the hall but not next to each other, which had never happened in the whole history of Katie and Lacey. Not that I minded or anything. I mean, I knew we'd have to sit apart eventually. I guess. I just hadn't thought it would happen quite so soon.

We'd met on the first day of school, when we were the teeniest, tiniest kids walking along the canal, and we'd teamed up right away in a friendship that, at least to begin with, was based on not wanting to get thrown in the water.

No, there was more to it than that. Lots more. We both loved long baths—not together, whatever Devi Lester would have you believe—and going for walks around the athletic fields right after it had rained.

We could drink whole rivers of Diet Coke and stay up until four, talking about what exact dog each of us would have, who we'd most like to go out with, and the truly vital things you should get from a Chinese takeout food restaurant. (For the record, it's a Labradoodle, Robert Pattinson when he was Cedric in the Harry Potter films, and shrimp crackers and Peking duck.)

We even had the same hairstyle, or at least we did until one of us got trigger-happy with the scissors.

"So for my birthday," Savannah was saying as we shuffled back out after twenty minutes of some woman talking about saving the bats, "I'm thinking I'd like a MacBook, a pair of diamond studs, and as much Clarins stuff as they'll give me. Plus tickets to the Glastonbury Festival. Because of my creative spirit."

The idea of Savannah at Glastonbury with its eccentric music, theater, and performance lineups was so spectacularly hilarious that I almost didn't say anything just so she'd go and I could hear about it afterward. But that would have meant denying someone else the chance to go. Someone like Amanda. Or me.

"Savannah, do you know what Glastonbury *is*?"

She ran her fingers through her perfectly highlighted blond hair. "Katie, how can you not know? It's this amazing party where Cara Delevingne and Alexa Chung go to drink champagne and wear Hunter boots." Her head flicked over to Paige. "I should ask for Hunter boots too."

"So you're okay with sleeping in a tent?" I said.

"I'd stay in a hotel, babes."

"I don't think there is one. I think you have to sleep in a tent and use a portable toilet. And honestly, it's mainly about listening to music. You know, bands. While standing outside. Even when it's raining. And it usually does."

"Ew. How do Cara's brows cope? Okay, not Glastonbury.

Maybe I'll get a Miss Sixty handbag instead. Would that honor my creative spirit, do we think? The new season is pretty out there…"

All the way through this, I'd been trying to catch Lacey's eye, but she was deep in conversation with Paige, and then it was time for my guitar lesson.

The story goes that when I was four, I found Dad's guitar and started playing it. Mom discovered me plucking out a reasonably decent version of a TV show theme, and together, they decided that I was some kind of prodigy and that I ought to have lessons.

The funny (not in a *ha-ha* way) thing about this is that I'm not a prodigy or anything like one. I'm actually terrible. In my head, there's Jimmy Page making it sound like his fingers are taking an actual stairway to heaven, and then there's the reality that is Katie Cox mashing up cords in a portable classroom.

The lessons have been going on so long that I've run out of things to learn, which sounds more impressive than it really is because there's no exam in being Eric Clapton. You either are, or you aren't.

I am not.

I was running out of guitar teachers too. There'd been a nerdy guy in his sixties who declared me "unteachable" and took to reading books while I played and a geeky man in his twenties who, to be frank, could have used a few more lessons himself.

My latest victim was this tall, nervous woman named Jill, who had enormous buggy eyes and a mane of long, red, perfectly straight hair. It was a little like being taught by a small deer.

"I've got something I'd like to finish off this week," I said to her as I unzipped my case, half expecting to find an egg salad sandwich nestling into the strings.

She was fine with that as she always was, and so I sat down and played "Just Me," stopping every time it sounded less than perfect, which was a lot.

"If you're up for a laugh, then you're my cup of tea.

Friends forever, that's just me."

"No. That's not right," I said, stopping myself. "It needs something else."

"Maybe just hold the E for a moment longer?" offered Jill.

I tried it, and it was better.

"I've got mad beats,

I've got mad moves,

I know that your mom really disapproves.

If you're up for a laugh, then you're my cup of tea.

Friends forever, that's just me."

I faltered, and, as usual, my hands wouldn't do quite

what I needed them to. "*…that's just me. J-just me. Just me.*" The notes fell away from my fingers. "Sorry."

"Katie, it's really good."

"Well…" I was so embarrassed that I thought my cheeks were going to melt and start dripping onto the carpet. "Thank you. Can I have one more try?"

"Um," said Jill, "you've been here nearly an hour, and in theory, it's only a twenty-minute lesson, so—"

"*What*? Why didn't you say anything?"

Jill mumbled some stuff about talent that was just her covering up the fact that she was too sweet to kick me out.

So I cut her off and raced to the hallway to meet up with Lacey.

"Good lesson?"

"It was fine." I didn't really want to get into my extended one-woman show. "Anyway," I said casually, "what did I miss this morning? I bet lots of stuff happened."

"When?"

"When you were walking along the canal. While I was getting the bus from our new house for the first time ever. A bus I was on with Mad Jaz… I'm sure there're lots of things you need to be telling me, so I'll shut up about everything going on in my life and let you talk."

"Devi Lester has these new sneakers. He kept going on

and on about how expensive they were, so Kai pulled one off and kicked it onto a barge."

"Wow. That sounds a little like something that happened to me on the bus this morning—"

"And when Devi went to get it back, this woman came out and screamed at him—"

"Because Jaz started going through my bag—"

"And so he waited until she'd gone back inside and tried to hook it out with a branch, but he couldn't reach. So he's going back later with a hockey stick."

"It was really intimidating. I just didn't know how to stop her."

Lacey looked up from dissecting her sandwich. "Jaz was upsetting you?"

"Yeah."

"Then how come you came in together? Why stay with her if she's so intimidating?"

"I wasn't 'with her,'" I said. "We just happened to be standing next to each other."

She shrugged. "So am I coming back to your place later?"

"If you'd like," I said.

"Do you want me to?"

"Yeah, but no pressure."

"'Cause I don't have to come."

"*Lacey*," I said, possibly a little more loudly than was really necessary because a lot of other people turned around and stared at us. "Please will you come and stay the night at my house?"

"All right," said Lacey. "No need to be weird about it."

Everything was going to be better again. I could feel it.

School ended, and Lacey and I walked to the bus stop, where Finlay didn't seem to notice us at all, and when the bus came, we sat at the back, which was the worst seat, what with all the darkness and gasoline fumes and being jolted every time we went over a bump. But with Lacey next to me, sharing a Kit Kat, it was like we were in our own little nest. No one knew we were there.

"So you didn't answer my calls because you were afraid they'd throw your phone in the water," I said. All things considered, it did sound reasonable.

"And you didn't answer when I rang you back because your phone got broken."

I lifted its poor, sad body out of my bag and onto my lap. "It's no good. I can't look."

"Maybe we should bury it in your garden."

"Not the best final resting place," I said, thinking of the

weeds and the pool of gray sludge. "It was a good phone. It deserves more."

"So the house isn't as nice as Adrian claimed?" said Lacey with her usual understatement.

"It's grimmer than grim." I filled her in on the latest horrors, including Mom putting her hand through the side of the bathtub and how we'd all heard something moving around in the loft. "And the worst of it is that we can't say how hideous it all is because then it sounds like we're going after him."

"And it's not his fault?"

"It's totally and completely his fault. But if I say so, then I'm basically saying I don't like him."

"And you can't say that because…?"

"Because it would be the equivalent of saying that I don't want Mom to be happy. When really I do want her to be happy, just…differently happy. With someone else. Anyone else. Or no one. Who needs men anyway? What is this complete obsession society has with everyone coupling up?"

Lacey's expression told me that she was starting to have second thoughts about coming over.

"We don't need to talk about him anymore," I promised her. "You can do my hair—*not* my bangs—and we'll watch *Mean Girls*."

"What about the mice?" Lacey wanted to know. Through the window, I saw that we'd pulled away from all the nice roads full of houses and shops and sidewalks and other useful things, and we were heading out toward the fields. "Because if you've got mice running around everywhere and I'm sleeping on the floor, then—"

"My room's fine. Honest. Other than that somehow I've ended up providing a home for Adrian's drum set. But I'm vermin free." The bus went over a bump. "Maybe don't leave any food lying around though. Just in case. Hey, this is our stop."

And so we came tumbling off the bus, me and Lacey and a broken phone and a guitar, ready for some full-on friendship.

To find Nicole and Jaz waiting for us.

Chapter Seven

I TOLD MYSELF NOT TO PANIC.

"We've got big plans for tonight," said Jaz. "Nicole wants to pierce her thumbnail. So we borrowed a staple gun from the art room. Well, not borrowed, exactly—"

"I didn't know you were invited," said Lacey, and she didn't seem very pleased.

I was desperate to tell her that, in fact, the person who'd invited Jaz was Jaz.

Only I couldn't because the person standing next to me was Jaz.

"So where's your new place?" Jaz said, and all I could do was start walking there and hope that she and Nicole would get a better offer somewhere along the way. Meaning within the next four minutes.

We ambled alongside the fluorescent-yellow field at the end of our road, then past the house of the lady who'd been giving me evil looks all weekend. She was watching me out of the front window, so I tried to give her my best "we're friends now" smile. It might have worked if Nicole hadn't tossed a half-drunk can of Sprite into her front garden.

Lacey wasn't saying anything at all. And Jaz had her headphones on, nodding away to music so loud that it was drowning out the traffic. Part of me wanted her to switch it off so I could make another excuse and get her to go away, but most of me wanted her to keep listening because then I wouldn't have to speak to her.

We got to my front door.

"Are you sure you want to come in?" I said. "It's going to be pretty awful if I'm being honest."

"I might just head home," said Lacey.

"Not you. I meant—" Only I didn't get to finish the sentence because at that point the front door opened.

"Ladies!"

Apparently, in the moment before you die, your whole life flashes before your eyes. Thinking about it, I guess it can't be your *whole* life. Partly because it would have to go so fast that you wouldn't be able to notice any of it and also because a lot of the flash would be taken up with things like being asleep and looking very closely at the skin on the back of your hand and leaving voice mails.

"Adrian," I whispered. "What are you doing here? You're not due back for another two hours. Minimum."

"Business was a little slow, so I thought we'd call it a day." Adrian grinned. "Having a party, are you?"

"No!"

"Too bad. I was going to open a beer."

"Yes, please," said Jaz.

Stay calm, stay calm, stay calm.

"Well?" Amanda was hovering in the hall. "Are you coming in or what?"

♪ ♫ ♫ ♪

Let's just recap.

Mad Jaz.

Nicole from tenth grade.

Adrian.

Amanda.

Lacey.

And me.

We were all sitting down eating fish and chips *like everything was normal and fine.* Amanda was telling us the fascinating story of how many sales they'd made that day (it was three), and Adrian was telling Mad Jaz all about his days in a band.

"Me and Tony, we were signed and everything. Tony Topper—you know him?"

"Of course she doesn't," I said.

"Still got my drum set. Couldn't bring myself to part with it."

"Then why is it in *my* bedroom?" I asked.

Adrian launched into a whole thing about how the leak in his and Mom's room wasn't good for musical instruments, but before he could finish, Jaz's eyes went all glinty and crazy.

"Can I try it?"

There was a miniscule pause as Adrian clearly thought about how much he didn't want anyone messing around with his precious drums but also how much he was enjoying having an audience.

"You know what? Katie's been using them as clothes hangers. We should set them up, have a jamming session!"

"In my bedroom?" I squeaked. "There's really no need to go up there. It's incredibly messy, disgusting actually. Why don't we bring the drums downstairs? Or we could just leave it—"

"Maybe you should have thought about cleaning up a little before you invited so many people over," said Amanda, and right then and there, I decided that her yellow sweater wouldn't be making its way back into her wardrobe, however much she asked for it.

Despite my many, many objections, we all ended up

cramming into my room. Amanda started picking out odd notes on her bass in the way she does, while Jaz sat down on the edge of my bed and didn't play the drums so much as physically attack them. Seriously, if I'd been on the receiving end of what she was giving out, I'd have dialed 911.

"Reminds me of the glory days," said Adrian, who was sitting cross-legged on the floor next to my dirty jeans pile, balancing a keyboard across his lap. "Great technique you've got there, Amanda. And Jaz, that's some real…energy."

This pleased Jaz so much that she whacked the biggest drum hard enough to knock it onto the floor.

"You two going to join in?" said Adrian, looking at me and Lacey.

"I can only play the recorder," said Lacey in a way that made it clear she didn't even want to do that. Nose Hairs didn't seem to notice her moodiness though and offered her a tambourine.

"But I don't…" Lacey began. "I thought we were going to watch *Mean Girls*, Katie. I'm going home."

This could not be allowed to happen.

"Lacey, please. Let's just do this. Then we'll absolutely watch *Mean Girls*. Promise."

Very slowly and in a way that made it clear she found the whole thing incredibly stupid, Lacey took the tambourine from Adrian, who gave it a little shake as he handed it over. "Wicked. Nicole?"

In answer, Nicole held up Jaz's phone.

"She's videoing it," said Jaz. "For posterity."

"Yup, yup," said Adrian. "Katie?"

This was awful. But on the plus side, if we were playing, then Lacey couldn't fight with me, and Adrian couldn't be too embarrassing. And Jaz couldn't...do whatever the terrible thing it was that Jaz was surely about to do.

I unzipped my guitar from its case and tuned up.

"Let's go," said Adrian. "One, two, three, four—"

There was a minute, maybe two, where the air in my bedroom turned into this music casserole, guitar twangs, drumbeats, and the tinny notes from the keyboard all floating around together and taking turns to come to the surface. It was a complete mess.

Then Adrian began playing.

"That's your song," said Jaz. "The one you sang on the bus this morning."

Exactly how did Adrian know the tune to "Just Me"?

Then I saw Amanda's guilty face, and I knew.

And she knew that I knew.

"I just went through it with him a couple of times the other night. That's all. It sounded nice with two guitars, and I thought—"

"You played *my* song?" I said. "You sat down with him, and you played something that is mine? With him?"

"Yeah! And we got it pretty good," said Adrian, who clearly hadn't quite grasped the epic treachery going on right beneath his hairy nose. "I've worked out a keyboard backing. You do the guitar and vocals, okay?"

No.

No.

There was no way I was singing *my* song with the Cox Family Destruction Collective, featuring drums from Mad Jaz. No way.

They were all looking at me.

"I really don't want to," I said.

They kept looking.

"Seriously."

More stares.

"I guess…" I said hopelessly. "But does it have to be 'Just Me'? We could do 'Bohemian Rhapsody' or 'Yellow Submarine.' Or 'The Wheels on the Bus.'"

"I like *your* song," said Jaz, and I honestly couldn't tell whether she genuinely did like it or just wanted to see me squirm.

"It's just quite personal," I said.

And Lacey said, "Not that personal, is it? If you sang it to everyone on the bus."

There was nothing—and I really mean nothing—I could do. Except maybe get up and walk out, but I didn't think of that until afterward.

So I hummed the tune—just a little—and then, in that way that sometimes happens, the music sort of took over, and I hummed it louder.

"Cool, cool," said Adrian, nodding his head to the beat.

Then Jaz started playing at the exact speed of the song, *boom tish boom boom tish*, like she'd been a drummer all her life. Which, come to think of it, was perfectly possible.

"Nice," said Adrian, and together, we sort of mashed through the song, stopping every now and then for Amanda to twiddle or for Jaz to get a little overenthusiastic, which was often.

"Again?" said Adrian, and we did it again, and this time it almost sounded really good.

"Well, this has been fun," I said. "Should we call it a night?"

"Once more," said Adrian. "And this time you should sing."

"Nah."

"If you don't," said Adrian, "then I will. *I'm the some-thing apple in the fa-mi-ly…*"

Hearing him singing my words, or at least a version of them, was deeply cringe-inducing. As if I'd come home to find him trying on my clothes.

"It's *I'm the big bad apple on the family tree*," I said.

"Sing it," said Adrian, and Amanda said, "Oh, go on, Katie."

Years and years ago, I remember we did this poem in English, something about choosing between two paths. And how once you go down one path, your life changes forever, and you can never go back and see what was down the other path. I think there was a hard part about leaves and undergrowth in there too that I never quite understood.

Anyway, the point is that sometimes you have these major moments that decide lots of stuff, not just for a while but forever.

Now given how things turned out, I'd like to say that I knew I was having one of those moments as Lacey, Amanda, Mad Jaz, Nicole, and Adrian all paused and looked at me. I'd love to be able to state that I looked out into my future down those two paths and knowingly chose the one that I took.

Honestly, though, it wasn't like that at all. Jaz and Adrian came in on the intro, Amanda picked up the bass line, Nicole held up the phone, and I just opened my mouth and sang.

Because singing is what I do.

"I've got mad skin,
I've got mad hair,
I borrowed your stuff, and I don't even care."

It started out fairly quiet, and I could feel everyone settling into their instruments while my voice kind of floated around somewhere up above. Like a feather or a kite or the time Paige made Lacey's math homework into a paper airplane and sailed it off the top of the science lab.

"I'm the big bad apple on the family tree.
Deal with it, sister. That's just me."

And while Lacey's math homework had drifted down into the school pond, my voice stayed up. And got louder and better as underneath me the instruments went from being separate into one unified sound—into, I guess, music.

"I've got mad beats,
I've got mad moves,
I know your mom really disapproves."

By the time I got to the second verse, I'd stopped feeling embarrassed. In fact, I was hardly thinking at all.

"If you're up for a laugh, then you're my cup of tea.
Friends forever, that's just me."

Saying this is incredibly embarrassing, so I'll do it quickly and just get it over with, but as I was singing, I really did feel as though I was growing stronger. I guess it was a sense of togetherness with everyone, which is deeply bizarre, as we were the least-together group that had ever existed on the face of the earth.

The end was pretty intense.

"I've got mad love,

I've got mad hate."

Much bigger than it had been on the bus too.

"I've got my whole life to come, and I just can't wait."

Not just me, but everyone: Adrian thumping out his chords, Jaz whacking her drums, Lace giving it some on her tambourine, and Amanda doing a cool sort of flourish.

"And here's the thing, I think you'll agree,

We're all in this together. It's not just me."

Chapter Eight

AND THEN WE WERE ALL laughing our heads off, and Adrian was giving everyone high fives.

"That was excellent!"

"So cool!"

"I never knew you had such a good voice!"

It was exclamation-mark central.

"Oh, you know…" I said, trying to make the jump from worried hostess to lead singer.

"Did you get it all, Nicole?"

"I love that riff you did right at the end."

"Is anyone eating these chips, or can I have them?"

The chips were stone cold and slimy and stuck together and soaking in fish grease. Even so, they were the most delicious things anyone had ever eaten in the whole history of eating things.

"It sounded like a real song," Lacey said. "You know,

like the songs that you hear on the radio. It sounded like one of those."

"I can't believe we made that noise."

"I know."

"I know!"

I swear to you there was a glow in the room. Not the scary, radioactive one there'd been to start with either. This glow was like the ones you see in makeup ads. Everyone and everything right down to my dirty jeans pile just seemed to shine.

In that moment, in fact, I could almost believe we *were* all in this together. That we were all on the same team, that the house wasn't so bad. That Adrian and Jaz weren't so bad either, because how else could we have made that music?

Nicole and Lacey were doing this *boom boom shake shake* thing between them, Amanda was laughing, and Adrian was saying, "I wish Zoe had been home for this. She'd have been so proud of you both."

At which point I thought of just how much I'd have given for it to have been Dad with the keyboard on his lap rather than Adrian—and the happy bubble exploded. Or rather imploded.

Anyway, it was gone.

"Mom's always proud of me," I said. As I spoke, it was like the room snapped back into focus again. It was just me and a load of people who didn't really like one another, surrounded by a tube of skin cream, mountains of clothes, and something that might once have been a pizza.

"Yeah, but if she'd just heard that—"

"Whatever," I said, shooting the word full of ice. "And Nicole, can you please stop filming everything? You're creeping me out."

"Katie," Amanda said in her big-sister voice.

"I'm just saying," I said.

"What?"

"Nothing."

"Sorry," said Adrian. "I didn't mean to—I don't understand—"

"No," I said. "Clearly, you don't."

"Sorry to interrupt," said Lacey, "but you should know that Jaz is in your underwear drawer."

She wasn't literally in there. She was just digging through mounds of underwear and twisted up ropes of tights, and stuff was falling out onto the floor, which, let's be clear, was already pretty busy.

"Jaz, why are you looking through my underwear?"

Jaz turned around and grinned as though it were socially acceptable to meet people on the bus and then come back to their house and play music with them and dig through their underwear drawers.

"Because if you've got anything hidden, it'll be in here."

"Like what?"

"Whiskey," said Jaz, "or handcuffs. Or maybe a secret diary." She reached right to the back of the drawer, putting her arm all the way in a little like a vet I'd once seen on television who'd been helping a cow give birth.

"Jaz," I began as Adrian got to his feet, which took a while.

"You know, I think I'll leave you ladies to it."

Thank the Lord he left. But then Amanda jumped up too, and I really didn't want her to go. The atmosphere was already toxic, and that wasn't even including Nicole's body spray.

"You can stay if you want, Mands," I said with a hopeless smile.

But I'd said it too late.

"Ade and I are going to talk about restocking the shop."

"Great. Okay. Fine," I said. "You two go and do that."

"Okay," said Amanda, heading out the door. "Have fun."

"We will," I said as Nicole grabbed Lacey's bag and Frisbeed it out of the window.

"Ha-ha-ha," said Jaz. She didn't actually laugh—she just said the words while looking Lacey straight in the eye. Clearly, my underwear wasn't as amusing as trying to irritate my best friend.

"Yes, very funny," said Lacey, also not laughing in the slightest. "Are you going to go and get it then?"

That's when Nicole started climbing out of the window.

"No!" I said, rushing forward and pulling Nicole down off the sill before she could actually kill herself. "We're really high up. You'll fall for miles."

"If anyone's going to fall out the window," said Jaz, "it should be Lacey."

"What?!" Lacey's head snapped back around. "Why?"

"Put you out of your misery."

This was not looking good. I had to get Jaz to leave before something truly terrible happened. But how, seeing as how I hadn't actually invited her in the first place? Even with vampires, you have to ask them inside.

So while Jaz tossed Nicole chips and Nicole tried and failed to catch them in her mouth and Lacey pretended she was deeply interested in my Amy Winehouse memorabilia (which from past experience, I knew she wasn't), I made a mental list of ways I might get Jaz to go away so I could talk to Lacey in peace.

1. Say the evening is over and go to bed. (No. Jaz would climb in with me.)
2. Fake a serious disease. (No. Nicole would probably catch it.)

3. Have a huge fight and make Jaz storm out. (No. Jaz would win, and I'd storm out, and then I would be homeless, and although the new house was not much fun, it was better than a park bench.)

4. Use reverse psychology and tell Jaz that I want her to stay. (This could actually work. Nice one, me.)

I grinned and lay back against the wall, very casual, trying not to notice that Nicole was pulling the shade off my bedside lamp. "So, this has been a really fun evening."

"Huh," said Lacey.

"I'm so glad I'm riding the bus with you now," I said to Jaz. "It's brilliant."

"It's all right," said Jaz, but I could tell she was pleased.

"What's great about it, Jaz, is that we get to hang out some more," I said. "I feel like I've hardly seen you at school because of all the...all the..."

"Skipping school?" said Lacey.

"And now we can do stuff. Which is why you should definitely stay a lot longer if you want. Stay the night even!"

I threw a quick glance at Lacey with an expression that made it clear I was doing some very clever mind trickery that was going to get rid of Jaz pronto, so we could enjoy some one-on-one friend time.

"If she's staying, then I think I'm going to head off."

"What?! No, Lace, you don't understand. I don't...I mean, I want you *all* to stay. *Especially* you. Nicole, maybe don't put that in your mouth. I don't think it's a good idea."

"I gave up seeing Grandma's kitten to come over here. Because I thought we were going to watch *Mean Girls* together." Lacey's skin was normally this soft, milky color, but now she'd flushed a bright and—I have to say, quite unattractive—shade of tomato.

"We can watch *Mean Girls*," said Jaz. "I've got this great game. Any time Lindsay Lohan sits down, you have to drink—"

"I thought *we* were going to watch *Mean Girls*," said Lacey, blinking fast. "To make up for not walking to school together."

"And we will—"

"So how come you invited Mad Jaz—oh, dear."

"*Mad* Jaz?" said Mad Jaz.

"That's Katie's secret nickname for you," said Lacey. "It just slipped out. Whoops."

"Why do you think I'm mad?" said Jaz as I inwardly curled up into a tiny ball and rolled under the bed while outwardly I tried to look unbothered and respectful of Jaz.

"Just, you know."

"No, I don't."

"Oh, dear, this is embarrassing," said Lacey, looking the happiest she'd looked all evening.

"It's j-just," I stuttered, "that you sometimes do things that are a little…unexpected."

"I love it. Mad Jaz! Best nickname ever. Thanks, Katie. Are you drinking that beer?"

"Maybe everyone should go home," I said, "Lace, it's not late. You could probably still see the kitten. And Jaz, you can…go and do…Jaz stuff."

Amazingly, it worked. Everyone got up and started moving toward the door.

"Bye," I said, shepherding them all down the stairs, which made ominous creaking noises as they went. "Great seeing you. So much fun. Bye. Bye-bye!"

Then they were picking their way through the weeds in the front yard, and thank goodness it was almost over. I was just deciding to pretend that none of it had happened when I had this sudden thought.

"Er, Jaz?" I called down the path. "You won't post any of this online, will you?"

Jaz turned and smiled, her teeth shining white through the dusk. "I already have."

Chapter Nine

A T BREAKFAST THE NEXT MORNING, there was kind of a tense atmosphere. I know this because I was the one creating it.

"I see you had a party last night," said Mom, looking meaningfully at the pile of fish and chip wrappers next to the trash can. "I hope you had a good time."

"Not really," I said.

"I had fun," said Adrian, giving his hair (head, not nose) a quick fluff. "And your friend Jaz? She's quite something."

"I hate Jaz," I said. Amanda raised her eyebrows. "Okay, not hate, but…she's not my friend, all right? She's just someone I know who came over for the evening. That's all. And from now on, can everyone please mind their own business?"

"What's upset her so much?" said Mom.

"You know Katie," said Amanda as though I wasn't standing right there next to them. "Drama queen. We're running out of Cocoa Krispies. It's the world's greatest ever disaster."

It was pretty disastrous, actually. But it wasn't why I was so upset. Although I have to say, it didn't help.

What's the first thing you do when someone tells you they've put a video of you online?

You go and watch it.

Only I couldn't because my phone was dead. And the Wi-Fi, which had been the one thing that had been okay about the new house, suddenly ceased to exist.

I'd given it an hour and tried turning the box off and on and then off and then on. And smacking it against the wall just in case. It was working because the lights were on, but however much I refreshed the connection, our Wi-Fi wouldn't come on.

I'd gone to bed with this itchy, crawly feeling that there was all this stuff out there and I couldn't see it. Not to mention all the other stuff I was missing. Devi Lester's latest conspiracy theory, whatever disgusting thing Nicole was up to, the pictures of Lacey's grandma's kitten. It was like not being invited to a party. And as I literally hadn't been invited to Savannah's party, I wasn't feeling too great.

"Can someone *please* tell me why the Wi-Fi has stopped working?" I said.

"Oh. Yeah. That's switched off for the time being,"

said Adrian, who was wearing his leather jacket at the breakfast table, the weirdo.

"What's the time being? Because I'm going to need it tonight."

He creaked. Or his jacket did. "The foreseeable future."

"What?" My breathing became shallow. "I cannot foresee a future without Wi-Fi."

"Money's kind of tight right now. Business is a little down. There are a few things wrong with the house that need to be fixed—"

"Like having no Wi-Fi."

"It was either that or turn off the water!" he laughed.

I wasn't laughing. "Then I'll go without water."

"Adrian, why don't you go and unpack…something?" said Mom.

He shot out of the kitchen, and, simultaneously, Mom and Amanda leaned in.

"How can you be so rude?"

"It's not his fault."

Which was pushing it. "He told us to buy the house, didn't he?"

"You should be nicer to him," said Amanda.

"You're right," I replied. "I should *jam* with him and maybe play all my private songs that I thought were just between the two of us."

She flinched. "I'm going to help Adrian unpack… some…thing."

Now it was me and Mom and a table's worth of breakfast dishes.

I wouldn't say anything else, I decided. Not while I was so worked up. I'd only talk my way into trouble.

Unfortunately, Mom has this killer technique for getting me to open up. I think she learned it at nursing school. It involves kneeling down and brushing the hair out of my eyes and saying, "Katie, love, what is it? Are you okay? Because I'm worried about you."

I lasted all of nine seconds.

"It's just the house."

Wrong answer. She stood back up again.

"We're all upset about the house," said Mom.

"And I guess, Adrian."

"What about Adrian?" asked Mom, swinging around to the sink.

"Um."

"Do you have a problem with Adrian?" Now she was doing some really intense washing up. The sort of washing up that made it clear she didn't want to hear the answer.

"No," I said.

More big long gap.

Don't say it, I thought. It won't help.

Scrub scrub, splish splish.

"It's just…I thought you weren't going to go out with another musician. Because of Dad and everything. You kept saying it all through the breakup. And now—"

"Adrian is *not* a musician," said Mom, and she said it very fast and very sharp. "He's in retail."

"He was in a band though."

"That was then."

"And he's always noodling around on the guitar, isn't he? Him and Amanda—"

"I think Amanda's been terrific recently," said Mom. "Very calm, very supportive." I was clearly being invited to consider another member of the family who hadn't been quite so angelic.

"Yeah," I said. It was becoming obvious that Mom didn't want to know *why* I'd been such a grump. She just wanted the grumping to stop.

"And what's the big deal about the Wi-Fi? Why can't you use your phone?"

"Ah," I said. "About that. It's sort of…broken."

Mom did that thing she does when she is being Ms. Calm-in-the-Face-of-Adversity. The current adversity being me. "You broke your birthday present?"

"I didn't break it, okay? This boy on the bus threw it out the window."

"I guess I thought you'd take better care of it. That phone was incredibly expensive."

She wasn't hearing anything I said.

"If I hadn't had to catch the bus in the first place, this wouldn't have happened," I said. "It's not *my* fault we had to move."

"Katie, I have a headache coming on, and you're not helping."

"Well, I'm sorry I'm such a pain," I said. "And I guarantee that from now on, you will hardly notice my existence. It'll be like I've disappeared."

"Katie—"

"You won't even notice I'm around. Then, one day, you'll find the Cocoa Krispies box is empty, and you'll be all, like, 'Oh, yes, my other daughter,' and—"

Mom took off her rubber gloves and stood back in a way that told me this conversation was over. "Katie, knock it off."

Which made me completely furious because she'd started out like she cared when really she'd just wanted to take a shot at me.

That's the problem with parents. You think you're talking about one thing, and you're not. You're talking about something else entirely.

Since I wasn't really up for hanging around at home anymore, the next day I got to the bus stop even earlier than I had the day before.

No one should ever have to wait for a bus without a phone. It's unnatural. I mean, what are your hands supposed to even do? Why do humans have thumbs if not for messaging?

I was forced to look at the world around me, and it was not pleasant. Traffic whizzed past. A couple of pigeons fought over something brown. And the plastic wrappers that had been shoved through the wire fence had piled up on the ground to provide an interesting record of the snack choices of the number 53 bus. (If you're interested, Mars Bars were the most popular, followed by Kit Kat, and then it was a tie between Snickers, Twix, and M&M's.)

I spent a second thinking about what archaeologists in five hundred years would think of our litter and whether any of them would understand the gloriousness that is a Snickers, and then I got distracted from my scientific considerations because Finlay had arrived, and he was staring at me.

I tried a small smile on him to show that I'd forgiven

him for destroying my beloved phone. I hadn't, but I just couldn't face him destroying anything else.

He said, "You're really messy."

"I am messy, yes," I said because I guess I am. My hair was, as usual, a little all over the place, and my eyeliner wasn't at its best.

Then he smirked. So I decided he was an idiot, and I decided to ignore him while I dealt with the sixth-graders, who all arrived at the same time, singing the chorus of "Just Me."

They had the words and tune down perfectly, which was pretty impressive, given that they'd only heard it that one time on the bus. And they sang it over and over and over and over and over again.

"That's great. Thanks," I said, thinking it would shut them up. Instead it seemed to put them into overdrive.

"All right, maybe you can stop now," I tried, which, of course, made it infinitely worse.

Then Nicole turned up. I wanted to ask her about the video and whether I could watch it, only before I could, she started telling me a long story about her tuberculosis vaccine scab, which ended with her picking it off and eating it.

"Maybe we could talk about something else?"

"Maybe you could wash your clothes," said one of the sixth-graders, and then they all snickered.

Honestly. In my day, we showed our elders a little more respect.

I smoothed out my sweatshirt, which, come to think of it, *could* probably have used a spin in the machine. Then the bus showed up, and we were all thundering on and taking our seats, sixth-graders in the middle, Nicole and Finlay on the backseat, and me floating around somewhere in between.

No sign of Jaz.

I spent the entire bus ride trying to keep Finlay from shoving tuna salad down the back of my neck, while Nicole seared her name into the seats with a compass and her lighter. What with having to make a quick trip to the bathroom to de-fish myself, I only just made it to general assembly, and as I sat down, everyone giggled.

"What?" I said just as McAllister came in and said, "Assembly. All of you. Now."

Assembly that day was a lecture on plants, how we are all like plants and should grow toward the light and something about chlorophyll.

I'm a little hazy on that last part because I'd only been listening vaguely, probably scratching my nose or drooling or feeling around in one of my back teeth for trapped Cocoa Krispies or something similarly embarrassing when I started to notice that things were slightly…off.

Like how you don't realize for a little while that you're running a temperature and instead find the world has gotten a little funny? Well, I could feel the weight of a thing happening. As though I was heating up, only I wasn't, or like I'd accidentally sat down under a hand dryer, which I hadn't.

My eyes slid from the stage, down to my lap, and across to the next row. A bunch of jumbled-up arms and legs, frayed pieces of school uniforms, a few things that definitely weren't uniforms, a smell of feet and farts and—

Eyes. Eyes everywhere—all of them looking at me.

The heat that I'd been feeling was the collective gaze of 950 people. There were 1900 individual eyes looking at me, although really I should say 1899 because there's a poor kid in seventh grade who has to wear a patch.

The principal finished her speech, and we all stood up. We're not allowed to talk in assembly, and on the way in, people are pretty good about it. On the way out though, everyone's in a hurry, the teachers are distracted, and everything's a little more chatty.

Which is when I heard snatches of "Just Me."

Not just from my bus crew.

Not even just from my classmates.

But from every corner of the hall.

And it just didn't make sense. No one knew about that

song except for me and Lace and Amanda and Adrian. And Nicole and Jaz and Jaz's phone…

Oh, God.

Oh, *God*.

The sixth-graders singing on the bus.

Finlay calling me messy.

The whole entire assembly hall.

OHGODOHGODOHGOD.

It was Savannah's butt all over again.

Only this time, the butt was me.

According to the clock, I had eight minutes until the start of math. So I tore through the crowds and up the stairs into the tech lab. I logged in with shaking fingers and hammered my name into Google. And there was the video. Jaz had tagged it "Katie Cox sings 'Just Me' Quirky Kooky Feisty SO REAL," and there'd been 757 views, and it was—

Blocked.

Stupid school computer!

I tried again, and it came up and just as quickly went away again.

But it was there. It was definitely there…like an escaped animal from the zoo.

And everyone had seen it.

I raced back down the stairs, and there was Dominic

Preston by the lockers, watching me with his gorgeous eyes—eyes that must have seen the video because then he actually smiled at me.

Aaaaaargh!

I raced all the way into homeroom. I was panting now, and I didn't even care because there was Savannah with her gold-plated phone.

"Can I please borrow that?" I said, making a grab for it.

She gave me a Savannah look, one of the particularly withering ones, and said, "Er, you do not touch my phone. Thanks, babes."

"But the video…" I said.

"It's my phone," said Savannah. "Get off."

I went in for another swipe. "Please?!"

"*Do not touch my phone*," said Savannah, with Paige and Sofie sliding in on either side of her as backup.

The bell was ringing for math. I couldn't go back out into the hallway—not with the whole school laughing at me. Maybe I should go to the office and tell them I was feeling sick. Or I could skip that step, do a Mad Jaz, and just walk out.

Even I could see, though, that trying to skip out after the entire school had spent assembly staring at me probably wasn't my finest idea.

So instead, I took a few deep breaths.

"Savannah, I don't want to touch your phone. I promise. I just want to watch the video because I haven't seen it. Apparently, I'm the only one."

She rolled her eyes, and then amazingly, she unlocked it and let me lean in.

There I was, singing away, everyone else playing in the background, while in real life, Savannah hovered beside me in her nonuniform heels, smelling of Gucci *eau de toilette*.

I looked at the screen, trying to make sense of it. Something odd was going on. Perhaps my eyes had gone funny. Or maybe the shock of it all had given me brain damage.

Because just a few minutes ago, there'd definitely been 757 views.

But now, there were ten and a half thousand.

Chapter Ten

THOUGHT I MIGHT PASS OUT. Everything went hot and cold and then hot and then kind of swirly.

"Ten and a half thousand," I said. "Ten and a half thousand. Ten and a half thousand."

Voices, faraway.

"Why does she keep saying ten and a half thousand?"

"Maybe she's sick."

"She looks sick."

"No, that's just her face."

"Katie? Katie!"

"Put your head between your knees…"

"Er, can I have my phone back first? OMG. Paige. She has eleven thousand hits."

"Maybe that's why she's passing out. Katie!"

It was the most intense moment of my existence. I'd never felt so… Well, I couldn't put a name to the feeling. Should have worked harder in English, I guess.

First, there was embarrassment—huge and monstrous like I was being stomped on by the Godzilla of cringe.

Then there was shame. On so many levels. The shame of my hideous room, which wasn't even unpacked and also wasn't even in the right house and was a complete and revolting disgrace. And that's before we even got anywhere near my clothes, my hairstyle (or lack of), and my face…

Yes, that was the worst. That I was just singing away into the camera as though it was totally normal. As though no one was watching me.

And I'd have probably died of the cringe right there on the spot only here's the thing: we—I—sounded all right.

But still though. But still.

I opened my eyes to see Savannah's face entirely filling my vision. Interestingly, her cheeks had this microscopic coating of white, fuzzy down on them like a peach. I examined the fuzz for a while until I noticed that her mouth was moving.

"Babes. Babes! You need to focus. You have eleven"—she glanced down at her phone—"*fourteen* thousand hits. Also, you need to go to math."

My legs somehow began working again and lifted me up and into an approximation of a normal-type person.

"Fourteen thousand?"

"It's going up again," said Sofie.

And Savannah said, "Can people *please* stop touching my phone?"

I made my way over to math, and the world seemed to be crackling with electricity. Walking through the hallway and up the stairs, all I could think was, *Who are all these people?*

And why are they listening to me?

I plunked down into my seat next to Lacey. Whatever craziness was going on in my life right then, she would rescue me. I wouldn't be facing it alone.

"I cannot believe this is happening," said Lacey.

"I know," I said.

"Everyone in the school has seen it. Like, everyone."

"And—"

"*Everyone*," said Lacey.

"I know. I just saw. Fourteen thousand people! Probably more by now. I don't think I can even imagine what that looks like!" I thought about it for a moment. "Nope. I can't."

"Fourteen *thousand*?" said Lacey. "This is crazy, Katie. This is bananas."

"Isn't it?" I laughed semihysterically.

"Why are you laughing?"

"I don't know!"

"When you've made me look so stupid!"

Hold on. What?

I thought back to my bedroom floor and my blackhead cream and my school uniform and the boxes and the way my eyes closed when I sang the hard parts and the fish and chip wrappers, and I said, "*I've* made *you* look stupid?"

"People keep telling me to cheer up. And asking me what I've done with my tambourine."

"It's Adrian's tambourine."

"*Katie!*"

"What? I'm just saying."

In films, you have major dramas on the tops of buildings or cliffs or jumping between spaceships. Not in math class, third row back.

"You have to take it down."

"I didn't put it up! Jaz did! Lace, I'm as embarrassed about it as you are!"

"Are you?"

"Of course I am! It wasn't like I planned for this to happen."

"I never gave you my permission. I know you sound nice, and it's catchy and everything, but I'm not going to be a part of this."

"I'm sure it'll fizzle out pretty soon," I said. "I mean,

that's what happens with these things, right? They come, they go, they—"

"Good morning, everyone." Miss Allen swept in, all big jewelry and scarves. "Katie, stop talking. Now."

"I'll ask Jaz," I whispered after the teacher scolded me. "I'll get her to take it down."

"Promise?"

"Promise."

♪ ♫ ♫

But it wasn't that simple tracking Jaz down, what with her not behaving like any kind of normal person. For example, if I'd wanted to find Lacey, I'd have tried the vending machine. Or the top hallway radiators, because Lace is one of those people who is always cold, even in the middle of summer. I called her Elsa for a while, but it didn't go over well, so I stopped.

To find Jaz, I'd have to think outside the box. I'd have to use all my cleverness and cunning. I'd have to investigate places I'd never been to before, really get into the underbelly of the school, all the dark corners I'd never normally visit.

Or I could get Nicole to text her, which is what I did.

And it turned out she wasn't in school anyway. She was spending the day in town.

That worked for me since my need for a new phone had gone from dire to extra-super extremely desperate. All those zillions of people watching me, and I couldn't even get online.

They could use it as a form of torture. I figure it would break anyone. Even James Bond.

After the slowest, strangest day in the history of time, where every classroom echoed with verses of "Just Me" and even the teachers were looking at me funny, I finally got myself to town.

According to the tourist information leaflets, Harltree's downtown is one of the two main attractions of Harltree. The second one is the train station, and I'm not completely sure that counts as a Harltree attraction because if you're going there, it's because you're trying to leave.

I looked all around, my Mad Jaz radar on full alert. The usual suspects were out in full force—mothers and their tank-sized strollers, some kid screaming over a dropped ice cream cone, a group of scary-looking men and their scary-looking dog. And—

"Katie!"

She was standing right next to me.

"Hey, Jaz. I was just looking for you!"

"Want some body lotion?" Jaz opened her bag and showed me about ten bottles. "I've just been to Superdrug."

"Why did you buy so much body lotion? Oh, you didn't buy it. I see. No, thanks. I mean, it's kind of you to offer, but I'm okay for lotion just now." I walked her around the corner in case a security guard was about to come running out and throw us into prison for the next hundred years. "Um, about the video."

"I know. Have you seen?"

"Not recently," I said. "Because of Finlay breaking my phone. I was just on my way to get another one."

"Great," said Jaz, striding off toward the phone store. "I need some new headphones."

Trying not to think about whether Jaz was planning on paying for the headphones, I followed her inside. The salesclerks were all busy, mostly talking to each other, so I went and stood as far from the headphones as possible.

"Here's the thing about the video," I began. "You need to take it down."

"Why?"

"It's really embarrassing."

"Is it?"

"Yes!" I said. "I know you put it up for a joke and everything but—"

Jaz was contemplating an iPad, which, thankfully, was bolted to the wall. "I thought you liked writing songs."

"I do."

"And you sang for everyone on the bus."

"But this is different."

"Is it?" said Jaz. "Or is it the same but better?"

"The whole thing has been humiliating," I said.

"I thought you sounded fine," said Jaz, which was the sweetest thing she'd ever said to me, period.

I decided to try something different. "Look, Jaz, everyone's seen it now."

"If everyone's seen it," said Jaz, "then why take it down?"

I didn't have a good answer, which was a shame.

"And anyway," said Jaz, "not *everyone* has seen it. Two hundred thousand, seven hundred twenty-one people have seen it. That still leaves the rest of the world that hasn't."

"Two hundred thousand?"

"You're smiling," said Jaz.

"I'm in shock."

"You're pleased," said Jaz.

She was looking at me, hard, and I thought all over again how strange it is that someone can be making a complete mess of her life and yet still be incredibly clever. Jaz could see exactly what I was thinking even before I'd quite realized it myself, and yet she hadn't noticed that she was a disaster area who terrified everyone around her and was probably about to get expelled.

"For the record, I am not pleased. I am horrified. And

humiliated." I picked at the loose skin around my thumb. "Sorry, did you really say *two hundred thousand*?"

"Last time I checked. It's probably gone up since then."

"When did you check?"

"I don't know. Maybe half an hour ago?"

"So it probably has gone up…"

"Can I help you?"

A bored-looking guy came ambling across the shop. He didn't look like he wanted to help me. He didn't look like he wanted to help anyone.

"Er, yes. My phone's broken. I need a replacement." I gave him my name and address.

He scrolled up and down on his computer until he found it. "Got you. Replacement phone, yes?"

"Yes, please." From the corner of my eye, I could see Jaz doing something awful to a rack of leaflets.

"That'll cost 180." He said it in this bored way, clearly not noticing that his words meant misery and doom.

"It's 180?"

"Yeah."

Cold sweat came trickling out from wherever cold sweat comes from. "I don't have 180. I've got fifteen." I mentally added on my emergency ten and a few days' worth of lunch money. Lacey would share her sandwiches. "Maybe forty. At most."

"Then you can have this," said the man, and he pulled out the worst, most useless, brick-iest phone anyone has ever seen.

"Does it have Internet?"

"Nope."

"Apps?"

"You can use it to make calls," said Mr. I Really Don't Care. "And text. Oh, and we're giving away Karamel's new single as a free download with every purchase. But you won't be able to play it on that."

"Okay," I said, cursing inside that I wasn't old enough to have a job and earn money and instead had to depend on Christmas and birthday presents to meet my technology requirements. "Thank you." And I went to the register and handed over my cash.

Jaz was waiting by the door. "Got it?"

"Yeah, but it's pretty much useless." I showed her the box. "Did you check? How many?"

"Three hundred forty thousand, two hundred and thirty-three. This could change your life. You could…" Jaz stopped walking for a second, clearly trying to think of some things that could happen. "You could get a decent phone. One made of gold like Savannah's."

I wouldn't normally go to Jaz to predict the future— also, silver looks better with my skin tone—but I did begin to think that maybe she might just have a point. Maybe somehow this *could* change my life. I wasn't quite sure how, but—

"If you want me to take it down, I will," said Jaz. She had her phone out, her thumb hovering over the screen. "I can do it right now."

For a moment I hesitated.

Because I had promised Lacey.

Because having the whole entire world look into my bedroom was spooky. No, scratch that. The bedroom thing wasn't nearly as weird as the fact that I'd sort of shown the whole entire world the contents of my head.

But on the other hand, wasn't it sort of great that they'd seen it? That they were watching because they liked it?

And then all at once, I knew I just couldn't ask Jaz to take it down—not when it was by a million miles the most exciting thing that had ever happened to me. I'd have had to be insane to have put the brakes on at that moment.

"Maybe leave it," I said, trying to sound casual. "For now. Might as well see how far it goes."

"All right," said Jaz, swinging off toward the bus station, her bag hanging heavy and low with body lotion and goodness knows what else.

I'd just tell Lacey that Jaz had refused. It was believable enough.

And it wouldn't be a lie, exactly—or at least, it would be only a very small one.

It was, I told my stomach, definitely the right decision.

Song for a Broken Phone

I loved your camera
I loved your apps
I loved your GPS and your maps

I loved your screen
I loved your charger
I loved the way you made pictures larger

But your screen is smashed
And your case is broken
Messages gone
Voice mail unspoken

He threw it as a joke
But it wasn't very funny
And I can't upgrade you
'Cuz I haven't got the money

Chapter Eleven

ADRIAN CAME HOME THAT NIGHT as happy as anything with a great big bag of ham and pineapple frozen pizzas.

"On sale! Love some pineapple on my pizza."

And then he started asking Mom about her day while simultaneously nibbling at her earlobe.

"Mainly," said Mom, who for once seemed to be finding Adrian's attentions as annoying as I did, "I spent the day talking to people who'd come to tell me they'd seen you all on the Internet. Perhaps next time you could tell me *before* you decide to become famous?"

I sat up a little straighter. "You saw it! What did you think?"

"Whoa there, horsey," said Adrian before Mom could tell me how proud she was and how terrific I'd sounded and stuff like that. "We're online?"

"Jaz put it up," I told him. "I didn't ask her to, but she did. And it's doing really well."

"Nice one," said Adrian.

"Well…"

As I spoke, I found that I hadn't thought how I'd tell them all. And half of me wanted to pretend that it wasn't a particularly big deal, that stuff like this happened to me all the time, that Adrian's stupid jam session hadn't been an event or anything, and that I was basically totally chill about it.

That half of me was almost immediately overwhelmed by the other half, which was hugely excited and couldn't keep its mouth shut.

"Actually, it's better than that," I said. "I've… We've… It's gone really big. Thousands of people have watched it. Hundreds of thousands."

"What the—"

Mom stood up just as Amanda spilled her juice all over the table, which Adrian was drumming with his hands. "Katie, this is huge."

And Amanda said, "Why didn't you tell me?"

"Because you were at work," I said. "And anyway, it doesn't mean anything."

"*Of course* it means something," said Amanda. "Of course it does!"

"It's just one of those things that goes around. Like

Savannah's butt. Which I don't think was even Savannah's, honestly, because it was so incredibly perfect and—"

"Can I see it?" said Adrian.

"What? No! Oh, you mean the video." I set my face to the full *I told you so*. "If we just had broadband like I'd said—"

Amanda held her phone out so we could see she'd pulled it up.

"There," I said. "More than four hundred thousand views!"

"That's nearly half a million people," said Mom, and I saw that she was shaking. "Good grief, Katie."

"Sorry," I said.

"Don't be. It's not… This is…" She rubbed her eyes. "I can't get my mind around it."

"Me neither."

We all huddled around the screen, and for a second, I thought about how, in the olden days, everyone used to huddle around the fireplace and whether modern times were a good thing or a bad thing, but then I gave up on my historical musings because there I was on the video, singing, and that was much more interesting.

Without a bunch of people talking and clattering up and down the hallway, I could hear the sound clearly and all the words. And yeah, it was sort of amateurish, and there were parts where we weren't quite together. But in a way, that made it better. It gave it credibility.

"That girl's got a face like a rainy weekend," said Mom. "Oh, hold on. That's Lacey."

"She *was* really sulking," I said.

"And who's that on the drums? In all the black, floppy stuff? She looks like a bat."

"Mad Jaz."

"And that's you, Amanda?" said Mom. Honestly, she was looking at everyone except me.

"That's my foot," said Amanda, looking at me rather sourly, even though it wasn't my fault she'd been cut off. Nicole had been the one holding the phone, not me.

The on-screen Katie was just getting into "*I'm the big bad apple on the family tree,*" and for once, it sounded as good as it had in my head.

"We weren't quite together there, were we?" said Adrian. "You came in a bit sooner than we were expecting, Katie."

"I dropped a beat," said Amanda.

"That's Katie's timing," said Adrian. "Don't worry. We can work on that."

"Oh, can we?"

"Absolutely. That and your breath control. See how you run out of air on the ends of lines?"

"That was on purpose."

"You need to be thinking about your diaphragm. Breathe from your stomach, not your chest. Nice finger work there, Amanda."

"Thank you. Although I'm surprised you can hear it. The drumming's insane."

"I like the drumming," I said, even though she was right—it was insane. "I think the drumming's the best thing about it. And I'm okay… Aren't I?"

"What you need to do, Katie, is push the air out from under your rib cage. Put your hand on my stomach while I sing, and you'll feel."

There was literally no way I was going to put my hand on Adrian's stomach, which was currently bulging away beneath an ancient red T-shirt with Oasis printed across his chest.

"Go on."

"I'm all right, thanks."

"Just put your hand there."

"Maybe another time."

"Just here."

"It's fine, really."

"Katie, put your hand on my stomach."

I put out my fingers, the very tips and nothing more, onto the T-shirt and pressed. I'd expected it to be squidgy, but he felt completely solid.

"Baaaaaaaaah. Can you feel what I mean?"

My hand was on the part of him that had pressed up against Mom when she and him… Ugh. Ugh ugh ugh. Anything to make this stop. "Yes, I can."

"Then there's your diction. If you're going to sell the song, then you need to be thinking about—"

And just like that, I'd had enough. "You know what? Why can't you just say you like it?"

"We do like it," said Mom.

"Instead of being all 'Katie, this' and 'Katie, that' and 'Katie, you can't breathe' and 'Katie, your timing's off,' why can't you just say good job?"

"Constructive criticism," said Adrian. "No one's perfect."

"Four hundred thousand people seem to like it," I said. "Four hundred thousand people seem to think my breathing is excellent."

"You have to remember that Adrian was in a band," said Amanda. "He knows what he's talking about."

"Maybe we should be listening to his stuff, then," I said. "Maybe we should turn off your phone and spend the rest of the evening enjoying Adrian's clear diction and excellent timing."

I meant it sarcastically.

So you can imagine how I felt when that is exactly what we did.

Adrian's band was called Vox Popular, and, as he told us—a lot—"It was in that lull between eighties synth and Brit pop, like an electro Blur but pre-Blur."

Not my kind of thing at all.

I turned the record over, and there were two guys on the sleeve. One had dark hair and a stonewashed denim jacket and eyes that were sort of sleepy. And the other one was Adrian, who was about a million years younger, with all this hair on his head, wearing a leather jacket, but a much smaller one, cut tight around the top of his jeans. I caught myself for about a microsecond thinking that he'd been pretty good-looking.

Yikes. *Katie, you need to wash your brain out with soap and water. And maybe some fire just to be on the safe side.*

"You can really play," said Amanda, the big suck-up.

"And you can *really* sing," said Mom in a way that made me cringe so hard I was genuinely in danger of bursting a kidney.

"Well," said Adrian, lifting up the needle so we could listen to it all over again, "I dunno about that. God, I haven't played this in years."

Interesting then, I thought, that in a house of complete chaos, he knew exactly where to find it. It was suspiciously undusty too.

I noticed there was a moment of a silence. Clearly, I was supposed to say something pleasant.

"How many did you sell?" I asked.

"Altogether?"

"Altogether."

He fiddled with an invisible piece of something off the table. "We…we didn't. We cut the single, but before it came out, we split up. Creative differences."

"So you didn't sell one? Not a single single?"

"Never had the chance," said Adrian.

"And I've had four hundred thousand people listen to my song."

"Katie!"

"I'm just saying."

Mom and Amanda both started talking at once, presumably in some kind of race to see who could tell me to shut up first, but before they could, Adrian held up a meaty hand.

"She's right, she's right. Tell you what, K. Want me to put in a call to Tony?" He pointed down at Sleepy Eyes. "He's still in the industry, got his own label now. Top Music."

That Adrian knew anyone in the music business was doubtful. That the dude in the denim had his own label was incredibly unlikely. And that this man would have any interest in me seemed beyond impossible.

I opened my mouth, but Mom was ahead of me.

"Absolutely not."

"But—"

"Katie is not going to follow in her father's footsteps," said my mother, and I hadn't seen her so upset in a long time. "I don't mind this as a…hobby. But that's all."

"It's just a video," I said.

"And that's fine. That's terrific. But don't start getting ideas."

If someone tells you not to get ideas, it's a guaranteed way to start getting ideas. Really. They should stick it at the top of our creative writing papers in English.

"But if Adrian can—"

"Nope," said Mom.

"Can we at least watch it again?" I asked.

And so we did.

Chapter Twelve

"LACEY?"

It was first break, which I always think is a really bad name for what is basically a massive dash to hit the bathroom, the vending machine, and the lockers, all in fifteen minutes. Hardly a break. Even basketball is more relaxing.

I'd sacrificed my morning Mars Bar in pursuit of my best friend, who'd burst out the door the second the bell rang. She tore off down the stairs through this huge, scary crowd of senior boys, and even though I was a little afraid my hair would get caught in a clump of bad stubble, I had to follow. It was like one of those films where someone's chasing their true love through an airport, only instead of customs officials and passport control, there were backpacks and a boatload of Axe body spray.

I cornered her in the stairwell, small and pale and angry, like when our old next-door neighbor's rabbit got trapped behind the dryer in our garage.

"What?" she spat.

"I just…" *Next time*, I thought as Lacey stood there glaring at me, *I will definitely decide what I am going to say* before *I start running*. Thinking ahead—I'd never truly appreciated its importance until that moment. The good thing, at least, is that I was going to take something from this, to learn, to really grow as a person—

"*What?*"

"I just thought we could have a talk. About everything."

She folded her arms. "Okay. Let's have a talk."

The sight of Lacey standing there with a white face and a stance that can only be described as confrontational gave me complete conversation paralysis. Even her elbows were giving me evil looks.

"Um," I said.

"*I've got mad beats! I've got mad moooooooves!*" This was being sung by a teeny-weeny girl I recognized as the school chess champion. And I did not want to get down on her. Being chess champion, she clearly had enough problems already, but this just wasn't helpful.

I grinned in a way I hoped would shut her up. Instead, she saw Lacey and started bashing an imaginary tambourine.

"*This is what my life is like now,*" said Lacey, and she did not seem happy about it.

And that was too bad, really, because the chess

champions of this world must have it pretty tough. It was probably nice for her to feel like there was someone even lower down the pecking order to laugh at, to give her a taste of what it's like not to be at the bottom of the popularity pile.

I explained this to Lacey.

"So you're saying that you think it's okay for that little idiot to basically *bully* me?"

"No. Yes. But it's not bullying exactly—not really."

"Last night we went to the gas station," said Lacey, her elbows angrier than ever, "and the man behind the counter started singing it."

"At the gas station?" I said, trying to decide whether I was pleased at the idea that now completely random people were watching. "Which one?"

"I don't know!"

"The one on the main road? The one by the co-op? Or that one up past the church? Or the one by the fish and chips shop—"

"Stop listing gas stations!"

"Sorry. I just want to know what he said."

"That his little sister has listened to it a hundred times, and now they can't stop singing it even though it's really annoying." She said that last part with a relish that I found inappropriate.

"That's great," I replied.

"I'm glad you think so."

"And then Aunt Rachel phoned from Scotland because she'd seen me in it and told Mom that my bangs looked bad."

"Your bangs look great! They really bring out your eyes."

She smiled slightly. "Do you really think so? You need to get them. I've got scissors somewhere…" She started digging through her bag. So I jumped in before anything terrible could happen.

"Isn't this a little bit amazing, though? That people in Scotland are watching? I mean, I know it's embarrassing that everyone's doing tambourines at you, but isn't it sort of awesome too?"

Judging from the way that Lacey's expression changed, I should probably have just let her give me bangs right then and there. In fact, I should probably have let her shave my entire head.

"Why is it still up?" said Lacey. "You said Jaz was going to take it down. Why hasn't she?"

"I asked her to," I said, hoping Lace wouldn't notice that my left eyelid had started to twitch. Besides, I *had* asked her. It wasn't a complete lie, so long as you ignored the conversation afterward. "I asked, and then I begged, and she just laughed. You know what Jaz is like. She's crazy."

"Ask her again."

"I will. But...I sort of worry that the more we ask her to take it down, the longer she'll keep it up there."

Lacey sighed. "Yeah. There is that, I guess. Kit Kat?" She snapped off a finger and waved it at me.

"Sure."

Thank the Lord we were finally having a proper conversation. Because it hurts, having your best friend turn on you. It's like being attacked by your pillow or something.

"I'm sorry it's so embarrassing for you though," I said.

"Aren't you embarrassed?"

"My bedroom's a disaster, isn't it?" I admitted. "And I wish I'd worn more makeup."

"Yeah," Lacey agreed. "You do look pretty awful."

"Huh."

"And that thing you do with your nostrils on the high notes is so bizarre!"

"Um."

"It's like your whole face goes into this *spasm*."

"Er."

"It's a good thing you sound nice. They were playing it on the TV this morning and—"

I grabbed her by the shoulders. "Seriously? That's huge."

"Yeah," said Lacey sadly. "A bunch more people to laugh at me."

"Lacey," I said, trying to be casual, "can I look at it on your phone? Just for a sec?"

She fished it out of her pocket, still talking about how the guy at the gas station had been asking where he could buy the single and how should she know, and then as I was about to check in on my numbers—

"I'll take that. Thank you, Lacey." McAllister materialized in front of us. "No phones in the hallways."

"But—"

"And Katie, I have a message for you from the principal. She wants you in her office now."

"But—"

"Now," said McAllister, who is basically Professor McGonagall only evil. So I left Lacey fuming and phoneless and went upstairs.

♪ ♫ ♩ ♫

The principal lives in this little office right at the front of the school where she can look out over the playground like a sort of God. I say she lives there even though I don't suppose she sleeps there, but I can't imagine anything else. She wears a wedding ring, so there must be a Mr. The Principal out there, but I can't imagine him either. Some people belong where you find them and nowhere else.

Anyway, I turned up at the office and hung around by all the glossy posters. These had really impressed Mom the first time she came in until Amanda and I explained that they're only glossy so you can peel the chewing gum off them without causing any damage. They didn't laminate the first set, and I think they lasted about a day and a half.

So I pretended to admire a poster about how many different types of vegetables you can get in our cafeteria (a very exciting four) until the school secretary looked up and saw me and shook her head in a sort of general disapproval at my existence, following it up with, "Wait here please. There's a bit of a line today."

At which point I looked across at the sofa to see the line, which consisted of Mad Jaz.

"What are you doing here?" I whispered.

"The usual," said Jaz, who apparently had a usual. "You?"

"I don't even know," I said. Then because I was clearly in enough trouble that it didn't matter if I got into more and the itch to find out how the video was doing was unbearable—worse even than when I'd broken my arm and had to use one of Grandma's knitting needles to scratch inside the cast and then got it stuck in there, and a doctor had to pull it out again, and when she did, it was covered in pieces of fluff and skin goop—I asked, "Can I borrow your phone?"

"Yeah," said Jaz. I found myself slightly wanting to hug her. Jaz was turning out to be a pretty decent pal after all.

She dropped it into my lap, and I pulled up the video: 808,266 views.

"I know," said Jaz, hearing me sigh. "You really need to start turning this into money."

"Katie."

The principal was peering down at me. She always looked a little like an owl, but today she was particularly owlish, all round glasses and long stares down her pointy, little nose. I tossed the phone back into Jaz's lap.

"Please come in."

Believe me when I say that I'm not a regular in the principal's office. The very few times I'd been in before were due to extreme misunderstandings and were in no way a reflection of my personality, which is to never break the rules unless absolutely necessary.

"Now, Katie." The principal was watching me closely as though she was seeing all this other stuff instead of just my face.

I tried to look innocent. And academically minded.

"I've had some calls. Quite a few calls. About this video."

"I'm sorry," I said.

"Don't be. You're not in trouble."

"I'm not?"

"A number of journalists want to speak to you."

"What, like, from the *Harltree Gazette*?"

"One of them was from the *Harltree Gazette*, yes. And one of them was"—she cleared her throat, this delicate little *ahem*—"from the BBC."

My knees started to shake, and I had to sit down in one of the principal's special chairs.

"Now, you don't have to if you don't want to, but we just wondered if you *did* want to speak to them, whether doing so from here might be...fun?" said the principal. "We could set you up with a little table in front of the trophy case."

"Won't we have to win some trophies?" I said. "Because that might take a while. Especially the way the basketball team's been playing lately."

"We, er... We do have some backups that we could put in there," said the principal. "Mr. Griffin has just made an emergency visit to the engravers." She twiddled a pen. "You don't have to, of course. But if you did want to mention our music program and the outstanding teaching you've received here..."

Hold on, was the principal asking *me* for a favor?

"If you like," I said.

She looked very, very happy. "You'll be in your school uniform, of course." She peered at me. "Maybe not that particular version of a school uniform. We'll find you something that's ironed. If you can just wait a few minutes, I'll let them know."

"Wait, let who know?"

The principal raised her window blinds, slat by dusty slat.

A row of cars, big ones, were parked along the no-parking area at the front of the school. And there was a van with satellite dishes on its roof.

"I'll tell them half an hour, shall I?" said the principal. She must have caught a whiff of my panic. "Go get yourself a glass of water. And tell Jasmine she should come back at the same time tomorrow."

I escaped back into the lobby to find Jaz picking holes in the seat of her chair and pulling out the stuffing. She'd gotten about four fluffy caterpillars' worth and had them lined up next to her.

"You've been freed for twenty-four hours," I told her.

"Why?"

"Because I've got… This is so… Because I'm about to have a press conference. Jaz, what will I say? And what do I even look like? I haven't got my makeup with me!"

A smile spread across Jaz's face.

"Let me help you with that," she said.

Chapter Thirteen

RIGHT, HERE WE GO," SAID the principal, full of energy. "Come this way—oh. Oh my goodness."

"Is it all right?" I said. "I was thinking that I ought to fix myself up a little if people are going to see me."

"It's…your choice, I suppose," said the principal, handing me a new sweatshirt with its tags still on.

I should note here that the principal wears no makeup whatsoever. I thought that was the only way to explain her very extreme reaction to Jaz having given me the tiniest bit of eyeliner.

"It's all very nice," said the principal. "And I'll be next to you." She led me down the faculty hallway and into the faculty lounge. "Don't forget to mention our music program. You've found it very helpful."

And then she opened the door onto a scene of complete chaos.

On the one hand, it was just the faculty lounge. So

even though someone had put in some effort with a school banner and a nice arrangement of desks and a suspiciously full trophy cabinet, it was still just a stuffy corner of the school that smelled like the teachers' coffee.

On the other hand, it was kind of a portal to a brand-new, super weird world. The room was absolutely full. On one side were all my teachers. On the other were a bunch of people I'd never seen before in my life.

"One at a time," said the principal. "If you're ready, Katie."

"Not really," I said, and they all laughed as though I'd made a hilarious joke. I noticed several cameras pointing straight at me.

"Becky Haddon, BBC *Look East*. How does it feel to have a million hits?"

"I…I don't know," I said.

There was this awkward silence. It occurred to me that maybe this wasn't the answer they'd been hoping for.

"Okay. It feels like…" I thought for a second. "You know those dreams where you're standing in a very, very, very small room, and you feel like you're kind of safe? I guess it's probably a womb thing—that's what my friend Lacey says. Her mom's really into all that stuff. So you're in the room, and you're feeling like you're being held and snug, and then one by one, the walls drop away, and you're actually standing on top of a mountain with the wind whipping around you. And when you look down, instead of the usual mountain stuff like trees or snow or…goats… it's, like, just people, all watching, and then you realize you've got no clothes on. It's sort of like that."

Big silence.

"But in a good way," I added.

"Katie loves our music program," said the principal. "She's found it very helpful."

"Mmm," I said. "Very."

"Alex Hayward-Bradley, the *Harltree Gazette*. Tell us about your influences."

"I've got this major thing for Björk," I told him. This was easier than I'd thought. "Even though she's obviously out there. And Kate Bush, who is also pretty wacko. Then there's Amy Winehouse, which is just basic, and Lily Allen. Remember her? And for pure pop, anything by Cathy Dennis. Lately, I've been in kind of a country groove, which started with early Taylor Swift and then got completely out of control, and now it's all about Dolly Parton, Emmylou Harris, and breakthroughs like Caitlin Rose."

"Katie has been very influenced by our music program," said the principal.

"I have," I agreed.

"And what's next for you, Katie?"

I had to think about this one. "Geography."

When I finally got done, it was lunchtime. A minute before, I'd been feeling almost sick, but one sniff of the cafeteria, and I found myself really hungry for a chicken pot pie. And I don't know whether the principal had left a secret message, but as I came through with my tray, everyone else sort of melted away to let me pass. I didn't have to wait in line at all.

"Katie!" Sofie was waving at me, so I took my lunch and joined her.

"Hello," I said.

"Is it really true that you just did a press conference?" she asked.

"Yup."

"What did you say?"

I thought back to what I had said. "Just…stuff. It was a pretty crazy."

"And you did it looking like that!" said Sofie.

"The principal gave me a new sweatshirt," I said, and then looked down and saw I'd already spilled pie on it.

"No, your face," said Sofie.

"What about my face?"

Paige suddenly appeared and shouted, "*Your face! Katie, what happened?*"

I felt it over with my fingers. Everything still seemed to be there. A nose, two eyes…

"She's making it worse," said Paige. "Katie, stop smudging it."

"Smudging what? Will someone please give me a mirror?"

Someone gave me a mirror, which made me immediately regret having asked for a mirror.

It also made me regret giving Jaz a liquid eyeliner pen and full, unsupervised access to my face.

"It's like you've got spiders instead of eyes," said Paige.

"It's like you put your makeup on in a car," said Sofie.

"A bumper car," said Paige.

"I cannot believe I did a press conference looking like this!" I screamed, at which point the whole table laughed so loudly that we got yelled at by the lunch lady.

"I cannot believe you are having the pot pie," said Savannah, joining us with her plate. "It's cruelty plus calories. You have to go vegetarian, Katie. It's the only feasible option."

"But you're eating a burger," I said.

"Yes," said Savannah as though she was explaining something to a particularly idiotic child. "But it's a chicken burger."

"Chicken is meat," I said.

"Er, no," said Savannah. "I mean, yes, it might be meat in the scientific sense, but it's not meaty-type meat."

"She's right," said Sofie. "It's not."

I'd never eaten lunch with Savannah and her crew before. And it was kind of interesting, being this close to the action. Even if the action was currently picking the bun off its burger and saying, "I'm not feeling the carbs today."

"Katie had a press conference," said Sofie. "That's why there were all those vans outside."

Savannah's blue eyes slid up and focused in on me, and suddenly, I knew how it felt to be a chicken burger.

"You did?"

I nodded.

"Katie," said Savannah. "I have been thinking. A lot. About you going viral and my party. And how one affects the other."

I waited.

"There's this thing called the butterfly effect," said Savannah. "How if a butterfly flaps its wings in Japan, there's an earthquake in New York."

"Right."

"And I was thinking that our situation was sort of like that. Only you're the butterfly, and your video is the flapping, and I am New York. Mmm?"

"I'm sorry," I said. "I'm having trouble following you."

"What I'm saying is… Would you like to come to my party?"

"Oh!" This was big. "Yes, please! Thank you!" *Don't sound so grateful, Katie.* "I mean, if I'm free." *Don't sound so ungrateful, Katie.* "Which I will be."

"We should go shopping for something to wear," said Sofie.

"You do not want to shop with Sofie," said Paige. "Like, H&M is fine for some people, but not for girls like us. Come with me to Zara. My sister works there. I get a discount."

"Please," said Savannah. "If Katie's shopping with anyone, it's going to be me."

Chapter Fourteen

Y OU KNOW THOSE GREAT BIG groups of glamorous girls you see out shopping sometimes? All legs and big hair?

I was part of one!

And not on the outside either, tagging along, trying to keep up. I was right there in the middle.

"So, Katie, help me out here. I'm playlisting my party, and Paige and Sofie are worse than useless."

We were trotting along the main road into town after school, Savannah managing to walk surprisingly fast given the height of her heels.

"Well," I said a little bit breathlessly because really, going at that speed is unnecessary, even if the shops are closing soon, "I guess it depends on what kind of vibe you're after."

"It's going to be totally vibing," said Sofie.

"Shut up, Sofie," said Savannah. "Katie is trying to speak. Also, vibing is not a thing."

Amazingly, Sofie didn't seem to mind being told to shut up. And Paige didn't look especially bothered about being called worse than useless. I guess you must develop a thick skin after an extended period of being around Savannah.

"If you want people dancing, then some proper disco would be good."

"Mmm," said Savannah. "Complete yes. Make the list and send it to me. Okay?"

I spent a moment trying to decide whether I enjoyed being Savannah's DJ and then decided that I did. Maybe she'd have those cool big headphones for me to wear.

I smiled, turned around, and froze.

Lacey was standing with her mom outside the supermarket. When she saw us, she turned away, but her mom waved to me.

Which was bizarre, because Lacey's mom? I don't know why, but she's never been my biggest fan.

I guess it might have had something to do with the time I gave Lacey mega eyebrows with a black Magic Marker. Which turned out to be permanent. The day before her brother's wedding.

Or maybe it was from when Lace and I were pogoing to Rihanna, and Lacey fell through a glass table and had to get eight stitches in her wrist at the emergency room.

Or it could have been from when I was showing

Lacey how to turn pants into pedal pushers, and I accidentally cut up her mom's work suit. The designer one. From Chanel.

If she did disapprove of me, it was probably fair enough.

Only, today at least, it seemed that hostilities had been suspended.

"Katie! Sweetheart! You're sort of a celebrity at the moment! Love the video. It's just a shame that Lacey couldn't have looked a little more cheerful, isn't it?"

Lacey kind of growled.

Hmm. Maybe not *all* hostilities.

"Are you out shopping? Lacey, you don't need to be hanging with me. Go. Go!"

Lacey did not look especially pleased to be joining us, but she stepped into place behind Paige.

"Enjoy yourselves, girls!" said Lacey's mom, heading toward the shopping carts.

"This is fun," said Sofie. "Where should we go, Savannah?"

"Cindy's," said Savannah.

Cindy's is the one good shop in Harltree, and by that, I mean it is expensive. They stock Miss Sixty and DKNY and Michael Kors.

People like me don't go to Cindy's.

"We are so going to Cindy's," I said.

"Fabbo," said Savannah. "I'm searching for party

dresses. I need to find something that really honors what it's like to be me at my party."

"But of course."

"And you need to be thinking more about your look, Katie. Like, don't take this the wrong way, but right now you are so icky."

"A million people like my look!" I said, feeling a little bit offended.

"A million people have seen your look," said Savannah. "That does not mean they like it. And I am saying that as your biggest fan."

There were two pieces of information there. I decided to concentrate on the second.

And yes, I was absolutely aware that Savannah was probably not my biggest fan, seeing as how she had only begun to notice me at the point where the video had happened. Still though. You have to take your kicks where you can, and right then I was out shopping with a Harltree A-lister, going into Cindy's, and being greeted by a woman who was very probably actually Cindy herself and being offered a free glass of Perrier.

What wasn't to like?

"Darling Savannah," said Cindy, whose face was as tanned as it is possible to be before becoming an orange. Then, "Oh my goodness! You're her!"

"She is," agreed Savannah.

"I am," I said. "Sorry, just to check, 'her' being…?"

"In today's paper," said Cindy, spreading out the *Harltree Gazette* on her wooden counter. And there was a picture of me, right on the front page, with my crazy Jaz eyeliner and the headline:

HARLTREE GIRL HITS ONE MILLION

I showed the article to Lacey, who skimmed down and said, "Why are you talking so much about our school music program?"

And when I read it myself, it did seem to be mainly about that. There was a nice part about me and my influences though, and actually, even the eyeliner looked okay, sort of rock and roll.

Savannah had gone off with Cindy to see some important new jeans, and Lacey said, "Look, are you sure you want me here?"

"We're getting a taste of the high life," I said.

Lacey looked a little worried.

"It's just for now," I said. "Then we can go back to being the lowest of the low."

"Speak for yourself," said Lacey.

"Katie," said Paige. "What do you think?" She was

holding up a black dress so small that for a second I thought it was a top.

"Wow," I said. "Well, you could try it on, I guess…"

"It's not for me!" said Paige. "It's for you! I'm trying this on." She held up something gold and sparkly and about a sixteenth the size of the black minidress.

"That is gorgeous," said Savannah.

"So nice," said Sofie.

"It's very Paige," said Lacey, which made me giggle, which made her giggle.

This was going to be fun.

And it was. Even when I got stuck in the minidress and Cindy had to come and cut me out of it, which we all blamed on a faulty zip and not the fact that Paige had clearly picked out something that was two sizes too small.

"You're so humble," said Cindy. "I'd have expected you to be this little diva, but you're not."

"Mppppphhhhhhhh," I said, still inside the dress.

"A million people," said Cindy.

"Mmmmmmphhhh."

"And here you are in my little shop."

"Mphhhh—oh, that's better, thank you," I said, crawling out onto the floor and sucking in lungfuls of delicious, delicious air. "I thought I was going to die in there."

Lacey, meanwhile, wasn't taking any of this even slightly

seriously and had used the time while I'd been in a Lycra prison to pick out a selection of things for me to try on that were completely absurd like a green Lurex jumpsuit and a leopard-print cape.

"Er, really?"

"Really," said Lacey, looking longingly at a particularly bizarre ensemble. "At least try it on."

"I don't think so," I said.

Normally, I would have done it. Lacey and I were very good at wearing silly outfits. But not here, not in Cindy's.

"But—" Lacey began.

"Katie," said Savannah. "Listen to someone with taste for one second, please. Like, I know you have this whole floppy, baggy thing going on, but you are not actually *that* fat."

"Er, thanks."

"That's okay," said Savannah. "I mean, you could be way thinner if you just stopped with all the junk and found your inner model. She's completely in there somewhere. But in the meantime, you should find your not-terrible parts and emphasize them."

"My not-terrible parts."

"Yes. Respect your waist, Katie."

"Let me get this straight, Savannah. You are telling me to respect my waist?"

"Yes, babes." She took a dress off the rack. "With this."

This being a floor-length navy-blue dress with clever straps that twirled around the shoulders and across the bodice in a way that I could already see would give me what Grandma would call "a proper bust."

"That is so my party," said Savannah. "Go try it on."

I checked the label. "It costs a fortune," I said.

"So?"

She looked at me, head cocked to one side, and I realized she wasn't quite seeing straight. I mean, she was seeing the me that had a million hits. The me that deserved nice things. The me that was going to her party.

What she *wasn't* seeing was the other me. The me that didn't have the money for this dress. The me who lived in a falling-down house and had been known to eat pizza for breakfast.

"I can't afford it," I said.

"Ew," said Savannah. "That is so upsetting."

"Sorry, Savannah." And I found myself feeling the tiniest sliver of sadness. I don't know why. I mean, I'd never spent that much money on a dress before. I'd never considered that I might. I'd never even considered considering it.

People who spend lots of money on clothes are idiots. Lacey and I have always been extremely clear on that. It's way more fun to go to secondhand store on a Saturday morning and find something weirdly wonderful and take it home and cut the sleeves off and take the hem up and wear it loud and proud.

Except that standing there in the shop with Savannah looking at me all pityingly and the dress resting in my arms, all shimmery and clean smelling, I was starting to think that maybe it wasn't more fun to go to a secondhand shop. That perhaps it *was* more fun to be Savannah.

I knew I had to get out of there.

"Oh, is that the time? I need to be back for dinner," I said.

"Call me, yeah, babes?" said Savannah, who surely hadn't seen my phone recently because otherwise there is no way she'd have allowed anything so hideous to know her number.

"Will do." Before anyone could say anything else, I bolted from the shop with Lacey just behind me.

"What the—"

"Wait!" I told her, holding my hand up until we were around the corner. "It cost a small fortune!"

"Where does she think you'd get that kind of money?" asked Lacey. "Seriously, she is so on Planet Savannah. She forgets the rest of us exist. Want to get a Dove Bar?"

We went and got a Dove Bar. I let Lace have most of it. I was feeling kind of unsettled.

"Ooh, look! This charity shop is still open!"

"Is it?" I said. "Actually, I do sort of need to go home. I should send Savannah that track list before I forget it all."

"Great," said Lacey. "Just me in there then. Whatever I find, I keep!"

"Okay."

"Even if it's really amazing."

"Fine."

"Even if it would actually look better on you."

"All right."

"Katie! Can you honestly believe I'd do that to you?"

Which brought me back down to earth, and I smiled. "You wouldn't dare. And I'll come with you next week once I've got my allowance. Got to get a party outfit, don't I?"

"It's a date."

But still. I couldn't help but think that once you've been to Planet Savannah, even though it's weird and scary and incredibly expensive, you wouldn't mind going back.

♪ ♫ ♫

So I was walking home toward the main road through a particularly sad part of town. Once upon a time, it must have been all right, since the road had cobblestones in places, and some of the buildings had beams and those nice windows you push up with both hands that sometimes drop and try to snap your fingers off.

Anyway, because it was also Harltree, there were fried chicken containers and beer cans lying around, and the shops were the kind I wouldn't even consider going into: a rundown newsstand, something to do with secondhand computers, and—

Oh no.

Amanda was just closing the door to Vox Vinyl. Adrian's place. Which was not where I'd planned on ending up. Not now or ever.

I turned around, but then I heard, "Katie! Over here!"

"Hey, Mands."

Her shoulders had been slumped, but now she was hopping around like a kite in a hurricane. "You came!" she said. "I'm sorry. You should've texted or something. Another five minutes, and I'd have been gone."

"I didn't know I was going to be here until now. Mands, the video! It's had a million hits! One million! And I'm in the paper!"

"Great," said Amanda, clearly not listening at all. "Are you coming in, then? There's lots to show you. I've got this bulletin board going—local bands can advertise gigs, look for new players. I've set up some cool lighting, and—"

"Maybe another time," I told her.

"We're not in any rush."

"Actually, now that I've run into you, I wouldn't mind a ride back. I want to tell Mom about the hits. All one million of them. A million, Mands! A million people watching me! Us!"

Amanda slowly digested the news that I hadn't, in fact, come for a magical mystery tour of Adrian World and set off toward the parking lot. "That's crazy," she said.

"Are you saying I don't deserve it?"

She shot me a sharp look. "Calm down, Miss Sensitive. I didn't say that. Did I?"

I scurried along, trying to keep up. "You're leaving early," I said.

"I guess so," said Amanda.

"How come?"

"Adrian just told me I could go home, okay? God, Katie, why are you making such a big deal about it?"

I hadn't been making a big deal of it. But I would now.

"Did you do something wrong? Hey, you didn't steal anything, did you?"

"What? No! Of course not!"

"Were you rude to a customer?"

She looked at her hands. "I didn't exactly get the chance."

This was not right. "I can't believe he doesn't let you talk to customers! You know everything about everything.

Seriously, there's not a band in the world you can't go on and on about, and you're really nice. He can't stick you in the stockroom like you don't exist. Do you want me to talk to him? I'm going to talk to him." She unlocked the car, and I slid into the passenger seat. "You left a perfectly good job to go and work there. The least he can do is let you wait on the customers."

"You are not going to talk to him, all right?"

"Oh, and you're just going to roll over and take it?"

There was a short pause while Amanda swallowed an imaginary something. "The reason I didn't get to speak to a customer isn't because Adrian wouldn't let me. It's because there aren't any customers."

"Ah."

"Yeah."

"Well, he did sort of say not to give up the café—" I stopped when I saw her eyes begin to glisten.

"You can't say anything. Not a word. Mom's got enough to worry about."

"We'll talk about my million hits instead, okay?"

"Good plan."

Then she turned on the radio, and we sang along to Adele all the way home.

In Honor

You said you were the one with taste
You said I should respect my waist
But I think taste is a thing you eat
And my waist says I need a treat

Gonna honor my hips
And honor my thighs
With ice cream, chips,
And cakes and pies
Cakes and pies

You said being thin's a doddle
You said to channel my inner model
How did that model end up in here?
I guess I ate her for my dinner.

Gonna honor my hips
And honor my thighs
With ice cream, chips,
And cakes and pies
Cakes and pies

And come next week
I'll have a stew
With extra mash
In honor of you

MOM!" I WAS OUT THE car and running up the road, my feet smacking the sidewalk, *smack thump smack*. I felt simultaneously as old as I'd ever been and also about six. "Mom! Moooom!"

She was still in her uniform. "Yes?"

"It's had a million hits! I'm in the paper! How cool is that?"

"It is very cool," said Mom, reminding me that Mom shouldn't really use words like "cool." It sounded almost as bad as the one time she said the word "sexy," which still haunts me to this day. "We should celebrate. Let's celebrate!"

"Yes! How?" I thought of a Savannah-style festivity with champagne and toasts and probably a firework display.

"Chinese?" said Mom.

"Takeout?"

"No, ready meal. Adrian got them on sale at the store."

I told her about the press conference and being invited

to Savannah's party and how we'd been shopping and I'd seen a dress I liked, because you never know.

"That is a disgusting amount of money," said Mom.

Okay, sometimes you do know.

It was still pretty nice though, especially with the smell of the black bean sauce leaking out of the oven and Amanda humming "Just Me" to herself as she got out the knives and forks.

"And let's have real Coke," said Mom.

We sat down at the table, the three of us, and smiled at one another.

"They played parts on the radio," said Amanda. "The announcer was telling people to go find you online."

"The director's daughter says to say hello," said Mom. "Apparently they're all big fans."

Maybe fireworks are overrated.

"Evening, all." Adrian came in and looked at the table. "Enough for one more?"

There wasn't, but he sat down anyway and started digging into Mom's portion.

"Ade! We're celebrating. Katie's had a million hits!"

"Probably more by now," I said giddily. "Probably quite a lot more."

"Let's see then," said Mom.

Amanda looked down at her phone. "One million two

hundred thirty-seven thousand, six hundred and twenty-six," she said.

"I can't even slightly picture it," I said.

"I think there are about a hundred thousand people living in Harltree," said Mom. "So I bet everyone in Harltree's seen it. I mean, everyone."

I imagined the guy in the cell phone store and all the other guys who worked in the cell phone store. And all the customers in the cell phone store. And everyone in all the other stores up and down Main Street. The women with the strollers and the babies in the strollers and every single person going in and out of the parking lot. All the streets, all the houses between there and here, the ones I'd driven down, the house with the funny turret thing and the apartments they'd built in that old primary school and the fancy houses with the great big gardens. And all the roads I'd never even gone down, probably never would go down, and the roads that led off those roads and the roads that led off *those* roads and each of them lined with houses and in each house, people—all those people, every single one of them, watching me.

"Now times it by eleven," said Mom. Then, after a few seconds, "I know."

"You have to remember this feeling," said Amanda. "Forever and ever."

It was then that I noticed Adrian was shifting about in his seat. And I kept noticing him, picking at invisible things on his jeans with those sausage fingers, rumpling what was left of his hair up and down and twiddling one of his supersized earlobes.

"So," he said.

"What?" I replied through quite a lot of beef chow mein.

"What are you going to do?"

"Remember this feeling," I said. "Forever and ever."

"After that," said Adrian.

"Er, I don't know."

He was really rocking around now, so much so that I thought he might break the chair. "This kind of thing, it just doesn't happen. You get record labels trying to break people for years, spending all this money, touring them, and nothing. And then in just a couple of days, you've got the kind of following some bands, even pretty big ones, can only dream of."

I honestly didn't know what to say. "So…?"

"So I think this is an incredible career opportunity. And you have to take it."

This was completely unexpected. Not just for me but for Mom too, who looked about ready to punch him.

"This isn't what we discussed."

Wait. There'd been a discussion?

He looked at the table. "No, it isn't. But—"

"But nothing. Katie is finishing her education, and then she is going to get a real job and, unlike *some people*, lead a decent and responsible life. She's got the brains to do so much more with her life than this pointless—"

"My music is not pointless!"

"It's a hobby!" said Mom. "And that is what it will remain!"

"Is this about Dad?" I said.

"It is about taking responsibility!"

"I'm a teenager! I don't have responsibilities!"

"You have the responsibility to finish school," said Amanda in a way I don't think any of us found very helpful. "And work hard and clean your bedroom and—"

Oh, please.

"I hear what you're saying, Zo," said Adrian. "But that doesn't change the basic fact that what Katie has here is something really incredible, and in my opinion, she needs to embrace it."

"*In your opinion*," said Mom.

"Yeah. And I've been making some calls—"

Mom's face turned purple, which sounds like an impossible exaggeration but isn't. "Have you?"

"Yeah. And my old bandmate Tony, he's still in the business, and he'd like to catch up and meet Katie. Talk to her, find out what she's all about—"

"Since when did I give you permission to start phoning people about my daughter?"

"That's not—"

"And how dare you send her off to one of those places on her own? She's a child. She can't be expected to make decisions like that—"

"Which is why I'll go with her!"

"Who said you could do that? I know how this goes. First, it's a recording here, a quick gig there. 'Just a one-off, Zoe, and the money's great.' And then suddenly they're running here, there, and everywhere, and you don't see or hear from them in months. And then everything that was good, everything important, it gets…it gets… My family comes first, Ade. Before anything else."

He held up his hands. "I was only—"

"Before *anything*."

"All right!"

She hadn't seemed especially interested when I'd basically come straight out and told her I couldn't stand the guy. Now that he was offering to do something nice for me, she was going nuts.

I do not understand my mother at all.

♪ ♫ ♫

Back upstairs in my room, I could still hear the shouting going on, little snippets drifting up the stairs like balloons, if the balloons were filled with misery. I heard "You do not go behind my back" and "There is nothing more important than her education" and "This is Benjamin all over again," which was not good news, considering what Mom thinks of Dad, and Dad almost certainly being the Benjamin in question.

I shut the door and turned it over in my head. The facts were as follows:

1. "Just Me" had more than a million views.
2. Adrian could get me a meeting with a record label.
3. Mom did not want me to meet with a record label.
4. I had lied to Lacey about taking down the video.

That seemed about the sum of things, although it didn't factor in Mad Jaz. But some things aren't ideal for lists.

Discounting number four, because really, I couldn't do anything about that right now, I was left with a sort of empty feeling inside. I could pretend all I liked that I didn't care about my song. Only, I did. I cared a huge amount.

They'd played "Just Me" on the radio. My words, straight from the heart, out there in the world, doing their thing, getting into other people's lives. As though I'd cut up pieces of my soul and sent them over the airwaves like confetti.

And people liked it.

But Mom didn't care. Even Amanda didn't seem especially bothered. How bizarre that the only person who seemed interested in my future was the one person I wanted out of it for good.

Still, if Mom said no, then that was that. I knew from experience that arguing with her wouldn't help. Once she'd decided something, she never changed her mind. No amount of begging or pleading or leaving articles about nursing jobs in California lying around would alter things.

The only thing I could possibly do was go to meet this Tony guy without Mom's permission.

But if I did that…

Then I'd be, as McAllister would say, crossing a line.

A line with signs all along it saying things like "Are You Sure?" and "Danger!" and "This Could Get Everyone Into Some Pretty Serious Trouble."

There was no way I'd do that.

"Adrian?"

"Katie!"

He was downstairs in the den, a bowl of chips balanced on his stomach. I tried to think where I'd seen someone do that before. Then I remembered—it was a photo of Mom, when she'd been pregnant with me.

I suppressed a full-body shudder and went in.

Adrian had taken over the room next to the garage and called it "the den." Meaning, I guess, for it to be this kind of awesome chillaxing zone as though we were in some American sitcom. He'd even stuck this ugly, old beanbag in one corner. It was made of brown corduroy and didn't have enough beans, sagging there like a giant used tea bag. Then there was an ancient TV, not even a flat-screen, taking up most of one corner, and a sort of fake leather chair thing with a piece that flipped out for your legs. The walls were painted this nightmare toothpaste green, and the back wall had mushrooms growing out of it. So it was hardly surprising that the only person who ever did any chillaxing in there was Adrian.

"I just came to say thank you," I said. "For helping me with my song. It's kind of incredible to think how many people like it."

"Yeah, well. When I was in the band, we had sort of a moment like this. We'd just recorded the single, and we got booked to play on a late-night talk show. It was big. Prime-time TV. We nearly… We might've…"

"Why didn't you?"

"The band split. That afternoon."

"Creative differences." I remembered.

"Yeah. Well, no. It was me. We were in the studio, doing the dress rehearsal, and…I freaked out. Lost it. Told Tony we should cancel the gig, that this wasn't for us. He didn't take it so well. Said I was crazy. And maybe he was right." He took a handful of chips. "And I said it would come around again, that I was talented, the opportunity would be back. And I waited. And…and here I am."

"Here you are," I said.

He seemed to sort of wake up. "But you don't need to listen to me. You're young. You'll have plenty more chances."

There was a very long silence.

"This Tony," I said. "Are you really still friends?"

"He sounded pleased to hear from me. Which was kind of a surprise, given how we left things. Why?" He was looking at me, really looking. "You still want to go and say hi?"

"Maybe," I said. At which point I had this feeling like I was walking over the edge of a cliff or something.

If Mom found out…

It would be bad.

Really bad.

This could even split them up.

No more Mom and Adrian.

Was I the sort of person who would do that?

"Yes," I said. "I want to go and say hi."

Apparently, I was.

God.

He broke my gaze. "I don't know."

"Sorry," I said. "I know it's a lot to ask."

"You know we'd have to…keep it to ourselves." I nodded. "It's a heck of a risk to take. And for someone who doesn't even like me."

So he'd noticed.

"I think you're great," I said, trying to look into his eyes so he wouldn't know I was lying, but I found that I couldn't. Maybe if I just kept talking instead…"I'm sorry if I've been grumpy. It's just, the move and school and the divorce… It's been very hard." Which, come to think of it, was true. It had been.

He nodded. "Maybe we just need to get to know each other better. A trip to London could be just the ticket."

Stay calm, Katie. Stay calm.

"Yes," I said. "It could be. We could hang out, maybe get some food, meet this Tony guy…" My voice was so high I sounded like a chipmunk. I tried to lower it, to regain a little sophistication. "It would be pretty cool."

"Okay," he said, hesitating. Then, as if he'd decided—truly decided—to go for it, "Okay! I'll tell him."

He watched me doing a sort of dance of excitement, and his face…

Well… It made me stop. "Are you sure about this?" I said.

"I guess…I don't believe in regrets. I want you to feel like you gave this a shot. So if it doesn't work out, you don't spend the rest of your life wondering what might've happened."

And for a second, or maybe even less, I understood what Mom saw in him.

Chapter Sixteen

I DIDN'T SLEEP WELL. IN FACT, I slept incredibly badly. Worse even than when I was little and trying to wait up for Santa Claus or the nights after Dad had cooked his beef thing with all those peppers.

Because the opportunity was there. This huge, glittering *thing* that I didn't even know I wanted because I'd never thought I could ever have it.

I mean, I'd be lying if I said I hadn't ever imagined people singing my songs or yelling my name, but it was in the same way that I'd imagined waking up and finding I suddenly had the ability to fly. People from Harltree don't get famous, except that woman eight years ago who got knocked on the head and suddenly started speaking Chinese.

To think that after all the hideous Mom-and-Dad stuff and Amanda and Adrian and the bus and school, there was a way to turn my life into something new…into something good.

It was amazing, like a dream—ironic, given that I hadn't slept at all.

"Morning, morning," said Adrian. "I'm frying eggs. Who wants a fried egg? Katie? Nothing like a fried egg, yeah?"

There was no way he could have been more suspicious, short of wearing a giant hat that said "I'm hiding something" across the front.

Incredibly, no one else seemed to have noticed.

"You all right to open up on your own today, Manda?"

"What? Oh my gosh!" She flushed a deep rose color. "Are you sure? That's such a responsibility."

He grinned at her and tossed a huge bunch of keys down onto the table. "You'll be all right."

"I'll do my best," she said, all earnest and sincere. "Thank you."

I couldn't help rolling my eyes just a tiny bit. Only then I felt bad because Amanda bit her lip and looked down at her cinnamon squares. But not in a hungry way. She just looked sad.

"Fried egg, Katie?"

"Yuck, no." At which point I remembered my new pro-Adrian status. "Oh, all right. Just one."

He leaned in to plop an egg onto my plate, all wet and glistening and eggy, and as he did, he whispered, "End of the road, ten a.m."

"What? Ten a.m. today?"

He was already back at the stove.

"What's today?" said Amanda, looking up from her cereal.

"Oh, just…this…thing…I've got. With…Lacey." When it comes to lying, I'm not the best.

"Adrian, can I play the new Michael Kiwanuka EP? Or would you rather I stuck to the official playlist?"

"Play what you like," said Adrian. "I mean it. You've got great taste."

She practically danced on the table.

Meanwhile, I headed upstairs, wondering why Adrian wanted to meet me at the end of the road like we were in a spy film or something. What with daydreaming and wondering and not being able to find any clean sweatpants, I didn't make it to the end of the road until nearly ten thirty.

Adrian was hanging out his car window. "Quick! Get in! We're going to be late."

His car smelled a little bit of mints and a lot of cigarette smoke. This was because just as I'd arrived, Adrian had been smoking a cigarette, which he threw away the second he saw me. Mom has strong opinions on smoking—these opinions are that me and Amanda never ever do it, or she'll kill us. This translates into everyone we ever meet also being banned from doing it, which I don't understand at all. Does she think we're really that easily influenced? Also, if I'd ever wanted to smoke, which I don't, the sight of Nose Hairs taking a drag would be a pretty effective deterrent.

"Late for what?" I asked.

"Top Music."

"*What?*" By now I was in the passenger seat; otherwise, I might have collapsed.

"I fired off an email last night, got a reply straight back. He'd love to say hi. Of course, this is just a first meeting, so don't get too excited. These things take time. Lots more meetings. But it'll be interesting to hear what he has to say, yeah?"

"But, but…it's a Saturday. I thought people didn't work on Saturday." I was staring down at my beat-up sneakers and flaking nail polish. "I haven't even brushed my teeth!"

"We'll get you some mints at the station."

I took a quick look at myself in the passenger mirror, then wished I hadn't. Maybe we could find a drugstore, and I could do my face with the makeup testers.

"So, Tony started Top Music a few years ago now. And I think it's doing pretty well from what I can tell. Doesn't surprise me. He always had that kind of drive. Much more so than me."

"And he's nice, right?"

"He's in the music industry," said Adrian, doing a

three-point turn in the middle of a really busy traffic. "What do you expect? In fact, let's go over our nonnegotiables. It's good to be clear on this kind of thing from the beginning."

"Clear about what kind of thing?"

"Not missing school."

"But—"

"You know what your mom thinks."

"Dad wouldn't mind," I mumbled. "He'd let me miss school if it was important. This is."

"I'm not taking parenting lessons from a man who leaves his kids to go and live on the other side of the world," said Adrian, which was the most he'd ever said about Dad. "No missing school."

I shoved myself down low into my seat. "It's not going to be a very fun meeting, is it? If you go in and basically start telling him off."

"Katie, I'm on your side."

"But I can handle myself," I told him. "I'm really very organized."

We passed a sign for the station, and it occurred to me that I was on my way to London to meet a man at a record label.

"Katie, are you all right?"

"*Mnnnrg.*"

"You don't sound all right."

"*Uwuuuug.*"

"Do you want me to pull over? Breathe, Katie. In out, in out. There you go."

"Sorry," I managed. "It just occurred to me that I'm on my way to London to meet the head of a record label. *Woooooah*—it's happening again."

"In out, in out," said Adrian. "And look, it's exciting. But it's not *that* exciting."

"What do you mean?"

"He's not going to offer you a deal on the spot if that's what you were expecting. You weren't, were you?"

"N-no."

"Good. These things take forever—weeks of negotiation. They'll want to hear you play, maybe see what you're like in front of an audience. And that's even if he wants you for the label, which he may not. Most likely it's just going to be a friendly chat so he can keep an eye on you, watch what you do next."

"That's still cool," I said bravely.

"Don't be upset. That's more than most people get in a lifetime!"

Which was true.

Well, at least the hyperventilating had stopped.

London's fantastic. It's basically everything that Harltree isn't. It's so big that even familiar places aren't familiar really—at least not in a Harltree way, where I know the exact location of every last puddle and the last major event was when they opened the new supermarket.

There's just this...feeling about London. It's only a few miles from home, but really, it's another planet. London is dirty and dangerous and exciting, and stuff happens there. Which is to say that even though I don't ever really relax when I'm on the subway and I can't figure out how anyone knows how to take the bus anywhere and when I get home and blow my nose, my snot's gray from all the pollution, it's still my favorite place. It makes me want to write songs like "Warwick Avenue" or "Waterloo Sunset." It would be crazy and happy-making and have a racing beat with the kind of hook that makes you jump in the air and scream.

In fact, I got so caught up in thinking about how the chorus would loop into the verse and back that I'd sort of forgotten what we were doing there in the first place. It was only when we got to what had to be the biggest building on earth that I remembered again.

"Wow." Adrian looked up at this kind of infinite

glass-roof thing that reflected us into a billion chopped-up pieces. "Tony's done well for himself." He glanced at the massiveness all around us, and it was as though he was literally shrinking. "We were pals," he said like he was trying to convince himself it was true. "He was a good guy."

I tried to imagine Adrian being pals with someone like I was friends with Lacey. Tried to picture him talking to them late at night on the phone, but I just couldn't. Possibly because cell phones hadn't been invented then. Maybe landlines hadn't either. He was pretty old.

"Are we going in?"

"Yeah," said Adrian, fumbling his way through the revolving door and tripping over his own feet.

I followed him in. The walls were made of this kind of ripply, shiny stuff, and there were TVs inside the tables and on the pillars and basically all the places you'd least expect to find a TV. They probably had them in the toilets too.

It looked like a film set—one where the movie was all about a billionaire who lived in the future. On Mars.

We stood frozen for a second.

"Well?" I said.

"I haven't seen him since that afternoon," said Adrian at last, and he looked down at the floor, which was glowing. And at the table covered in glossy magazines. "We didn't leave on the best of terms."

"Chill," I said. Not that I was feeling especially chilled.

At which point he took a big breath and went up to the reception desk.

"Hi, there. I'm Adrian Lambeth, and this is Katie Cox. We're here to see Tone."

"Tone?" said the lady, who might have been a cyborg.

"Tone. Eee. Tony Topper."

"Of course," said Robo-Woman. "Take a seat."

We went and sat down, and I watched the different TVs playing Karamel videos.

"They what you listen to at school?" Adrian asked, nodding toward the screens.

"I'd rather saw off my own ears," I said.

He tried to take his big jacket off and got an arm stuck, and seriously, it was the most embarrassing thing in the world.

"So," I said quietly, "I was thinking maybe you could wait out here."

"What?"

"I'll give you a complete rundown of everything he says." Then, because this didn't seem to be going down too well, I said, "I've got a really good memory. Not in a photographic way, but I'll definitely be able to tell you the gist of the conversation, and—"

"*Ade!*"

The voice boomed across the reception area, echoing up into the glass ceiling.

"T-Tony? You all right? It's b-been a while."

"Buddy! I didn't think you'd make it! How've you been?"

"This is Katie."

"Hi, Katie. Boy, it's been forever, Ade. How many years? Come through, come through. So, you married yet? Gemma's always asking about you, you old dog…"

London, Yeah

Trafalgar Square and then Big Ben
Bond Street and Covent Garden
Greenwich and the Cutty Sark
And a really massively big Primark

Put your hands in the air
For London, yeah

Camden Town and Kensington
Notting Hill and Wimbledon
Leicester Square and Regent's Park
And a really massively big Primark

Put your hands in the air
It's London, yeah

Take me to the bridge
London Bridge
Or the Millennium Bridge
Either is good

Put your hands in the air
For London, yeah

Put your hands in the air
It's London, yeah

[repeat until exhausted]

Chapter Seventeen

TONY WAS ABOUT THE SAME age as Adrian—whatever that was—and the same kind of build too, sort of fleshy, with a big face.

Which sounds like they were really similar, but they weren't at all. Because this guy, he was *rich*.

There are people at school who clearly have more money than me. You can tell because they come back from Christmas vacation all tanned. And they have designer bags and clothes and will not stop talking about them. I know more about Savannah's Juicy Couture jeans than I do about some of my cousins.

Tony was different though. He seemed rich all the way through. I'd hardly looked at him, but I could see he had the sort of ripped, rumpled clothes you only get if you spend zillions on them, stubble far too exact to be an accident, and teeth so white it was bananas. Like he'd put some fake ones into his mouth and then coated them in Wite-Out.

"You look great," said Adrian. "Seriously, buddy."

"I'm just back from the Caribbean. You should've seen me before I went. Kurt, from Karamel—you know Karamel, right?—he was telling me I needed to take a break before I dropped down dead. And he was right."

"So you've been busy these last few years," said Adrian as we shot up two floors in an elevator that was all mirrors, giving me a great view my own behind. "Since... since everything."

"Yup, yup," said Tony. "Started the label small, meant to keep it that way, but Crystal Skye went platinum, and then we just had to try to keep up, you know."

Crystal Skye was one of those people you heard *everywhere*—in stores, in cafes, in toilets... Her music was supposed to be relaxing, all plinky-plonky piano and the sound of rushing water. Which, come to think of it, probably explains the whole toilet thing.

"So"—Tony glanced back at Adrian as we swung into a corridor smelling strongly of perfume—"you're not in the industry anymore?"

"No, not anymore," said Adrian, and I wondered if Tony could hear the regret as easily as I could. "Got the shop now. Keeps me busy."

"In town?"

"Little place called Harltree. Not very far from here."

"And are you married?"

"No ring yet, but I've got a great girl—Zoe, Katie's mom. It's not all this"—Adrian waved his hand around as though five fingers could sum up the palace of amazingness that was Top Music—"but I'm doing pretty well, given what happened."

Tony nodded. Then, a second later, he was thumping Adrian on the back and saying, "Good for you, pal. I'm glad it all worked out."

We ended up in the biggest room ever. In the middle was an enormous table with twelve huge chairs all the way around. On the wall behind each chair was a big black-and-white photo: one of Karamel, one of Crystal Skye, and in the middle of the biggest table in the world was a really small plate of cookies.

"Take a seat, take a seat," said Tony waving his hand, which I think might have pretty recently had a manicure.

I sat down as near to the cookies as I possibly could, but even then they were still way out of my reach.

"So, Katie, here's my card—let me tell you a little about us. We're Top Music. We've got some of the UK's biggest artists—"

"Wow," I said, turning the card over in my hand. It said, "Tony Topper, CEO, Top Music." There was a phone number and an email address. In gold.

"We're doing great things, Katie, and we've seen your video. And we love it."

So it turns out that dreams *do* come true. And not just the one where everyone in my class is laughing because Devi Lester has squeezed mustard in my hair.

"You do?"

"We do."

"Really?"

"Yes!"

Adrian cut in. "What do you like about it?"

Tony looked me in the eye. "You're so real, Katie. It *is* just you—your bedroom, your talent. We love it. Everything's so overproduced these days."

"By you!" said Adrian.

Tony held up those well-groomed hands. "Guilty as charged! But then, you haven't heard some of our guys in their raw state." He leaned in, and I caught a whiff of musky aftershave. "Crystal Skye can't sing at all."

I found myself giggling. "She can't?"

"Nope. But you...you can sing."

"Um, thanks."

"So tell me—where do you see yourself going? Creatively, I mean."

I leaned over and took a cookie. No one had ever asked me where I was going creatively. No one had ever cared.

"Er. Well, I've got lots more songs. I've been keeping them in a lyric book. Lots of lyric books, actually, because I've been writing songs for years and years."

"Not planning on giving up anytime soon, then?"

"No! In fact, I think I've got one in my bag somewhere… Hold on." I dug through my backpack. There was my English folder, a charger for my old phone, my sunglasses case, several pens, some broken headphones wrapped around my sunglasses, and…there it was. With half a Mars Bar stuck to the front.

I picked off the Mars Bar and placed the book triumphantly onto the glass table.

"May I?" said Tony. He flipped through it.

"Most of the songs are ready to go," I said, shoving my English folder back in again and managing to flip the rest of the bag's contents onto the floor. "There's 'Respect Your Waist,' which is about body issues and stuff." I retrieved a balled-up tissue from behind Tony's chair. "And this one's called 'Mobility Scooting on the Pavement.' It's about, well, mobility scooting on the pavement. I'm sorry, I've gotten lip gloss all over your rug."

And while I wouldn't have chosen to pitch my future career while on my hands and knees scrambling through a pile that included a broken necklace from Mango and one of Amanda's socks, it did at least feel quite authentically me.

"These look great."

"So, okay, 'Respect Your Waist' starts with a kind of strumming thing, just a few bars, then drums, one, two, one two three, and then the melody kicks in—"

"You're like a young Crystal Skye," said Tony, closing the book and placing it back down on the table. "So much energy. This is just like the conversation I had with her all those years ago."

"Thank you," I said.

Tony glanced up at Adrian and then smiled. "Katie, how would you like to join us at Top Music?"

"Hold on." Adrian was leaning across, reaching for my book. "Don't you want to hear any of this?"

"No need. I think I've heard more than enough. Katie?"

"That's… Sorry… I'm just a little overwhelmed. Um, maybe a cookie would help?" He passed me the plate, and I ate three to calm my nerves. "So what does that mean? Like if I go with you. Not that it's an if. I mean, when. When I do, what happens?"

"You go into the studio and lay down 'Just Me.' And then we start thinking about a tour, build up your fan base as soon as possible, an album…and then if it all goes well, you, Katie Cox, are a superstar!"

A tour. An album.

"When can we start?" I said.

"We'll have to think about all this," said Adrian. "Won't we, Katie?" Then, to Tony, "This is all going faster than we'd thought. Decisions like these can't be made in a rush. We'll go home, talk it through"—he threw me a panicked glance—"really think about what's right. And Katie's not going on tour while school's in session. That's nonnegotiable."

"What? We can totally negotiate!" I said.

Tony spread his hands on the glass table. They were even more perfect than Savannah's, and she gets her nails done every Saturday morning in town. "There's no hurry. You take all the time you need."

"Thank you," I said, casting a triumphant look in Adrian's direction.

"Although I would say that we shouldn't wait too long. I had a look at your analytics, and your hits are still going up, but not at the same rate they were even a day ago. You can't afford to lose momentum on this. And of course, we need to strike before the backlash."

"Backlash?"

"It's inevitable. There'll be haters, trolls, maybe someone will send you a teddy bear cut in half or something—nothing to worry about. The important thing is to have a new story ready, regain control of the conversation…"

Adrian was tilting his head in a way that meant, *Let's*

talk about this outside. I pretended not to notice. And when that became impossible because it started to look like he was going to break his neck, I pretended I didn't get it. There was just no way I was going to leave the room. I mean, there are times you can go off into the corner to have a quiet talk about stuff, but while someone is offering you the chance of a lifetime is really not one of them.

"Do you mind if I just borrow Katie for a minute?" said Adrian.

"Sure, sure," said Tony.

Adrian didn't ask if *I* minded—he just yanked me out the door, Tony politely pretending he hadn't noticed that I was being pulled along by the back of my jacket.

Only, because the office had a glass wall, even once we were outside, we were still basically standing next to him.

"Come here," said Adrian, heading back toward the elevators. We went and stood next to an indoor palm tree, which wasn't the most private place in the world, but hey.

"I'm not sure about this," said Adrian.

"*I know*," I said. "Next time you want to talk to me, can you please not semi-kidnap me first?"

"I mean, with him. In there."

I didn't think Adrian was as a complete idiot, just a

partial one. Even so, I decided I would have to spell it out. "He is offering to record 'Just Me.' He wants me to make an album. How is that not right?"

"It's too fast. It's wrong. We should be having a longer conversation. This is… It's not…"

"So you think that me being offered a record deal is wrong?"

Adrian leaned against the palm tree, which wobbled. "No. Yes! I think this deal is wrong. We should've approached a few other places, waited… Don't look at me like that. This is only because I care about you."

"Thanks."

"All I'm saying is that we leave it for now, go home, talk it over, and go from there."

"But you heard what Tony just said. There's no time for that! He wants to make me a superstar, but if we don't start now, then it's over!" My voice cracked. "Before it's even started."

"You have the rest of your life to write music," said Adrian.

"What, like you?"

Even I knew that was harsh.

I guess that's why he didn't reply but just looked down at his feet as I turned around and went back into the office, where Tony was waiting for me.

He smiled like everything was fine. And it was, I told

myself. Just because Adrian's having a freak-out. It doesn't mean anything.

"One thing," said Adrian from behind me. "Just let me ask: what's the catch?"

"There isn't one," said Tony.

"Of course there's a catch, you old dog," said Adrian. "I know you, Tony."

It was one thing to say all this while hiding behind a fake palm tree. It was another to say it to the man's actual face—and after he'd been so incredibly nice and basically offered me my dream on a plate. As well as a plate of really excellent cookies. I felt like one of those old-fashioned tea-kettles. You know, the ones that shriek.

Tony leaned back in his chair. "Do you ever think about the old days, Adrian?"

"Nah," said Adrian. "I mean, yeah, a bit. A little bit. Yeah."

"Me too," said Tony. "We were something, weren't we?"

"Yeah," said Adrian. "We were."

"I meant to say: I loved your work on Katie's video. Are you sure you haven't been doing a few gigs over the years?"

"Ha!" said Adrian, looking away. "I might've done the odd folk night down at the pub. But—"

"Because your technique—it's old school. You're the real deal, Ade. You could show those Karamel boys a thing or two."

"Well…" Adrian was grinning, even while trying not to. "I guess I could give them a lesson."

"I was thinking more about some session work on the album. Their new single has a retro vibe I think you'd really like. We could make a big deal about it. Feature you in the next video. Maybe not a bad idea to give the moms a reason to fork out some money for their little darlings too. You would be building a whole new fan base."

"I'm in a very steady relationship," said Adrian, but I could see he was pretty flattered.

"Well," said Tony, "just something to think about. Maybe while you're thinking about Katie."

"I don't know," said Adrian.

I must have sighed or made a little noise or something because something inside of him seemed to collapse, and Adrian said, "It's your call, Katie."

Tony turned to me and held out his hand. "So do we have a deal?"

I had this very, very strange feeling.

That if I said yes, I could stop being the girl who had a half-eaten Mars Bars shoved into her bag. Who had pimply skin and a messy room and a brick for a phone, who had to save up if she wanted to buy new strings for her guitar. The girl with big thighs who'd never been on a trip farther than Plymouth. I was about to burst free from her, leave her behind like an old skin.

Which should have been a happy thought. So I don't know why I shivered.

Actually, yes, I do. It's because I was afraid. Afraid that this wasn't really *me*. The me that Savannah had sneered at, the me that got told off by McAllister, who missed her dad and was losing her best friend…the true me—she'd vanish. The me who wrote silly songs about the way she was actually feeling—she was going to disappear. And yes, she wasn't that cool or exciting, but she was real.

And I didn't know if I was ready to leave her behind.

Then I thought, *Don't be so stupid. They're going to make you a star. This is your dream. It's* everybody's *dream.*

Who even was the real Katie anyway? Just some girl with chipped nail polish and a songbook full of scribbles.

And so I shook his hand and said, "Yes."

Chapter Eighteen

AND THEN ADRIAN AND I were back out in the street, both of us with hot, red cheeks, panting like we'd run a race.

"Is this really happening?" I said. "I'm recording a single *next weekend*. In a studio. A real recording studio. I cannot believe this is happening to me!"

Adrian smiled and shook his head.

I couldn't seem to stop talking. "I can't believe… We were just playing in my bedroom…goofing around… and now…"

"I know!"

I was spinning, whirling about, bouncing off the cobblestones like my feet were springs.

The sun's rays had gone golden and slanty, and Covent Garden was full of amazing-looking people jamming the sidewalks outside every pub or hurtling toward the subway, and some guy with dreads was playing the saxophone, and I just didn't want to go home. Not yet.

"I was thinking we could go walk for a while?" I said. "Since we're here."

"Fair enough," said Adrian.

Maybe he had a little of that sunshine inside of him too.

It would explain why he let me go into H&M, which had way better stuff than the one in Harltree. I had real trouble deciding between a turquoise belt and a bracelet, and when I eventually came back from the register with the bracelet—which was the wrong decision and something I still regret—I found him all worked up.

"There's a place just round the corner that sells Fenders. Have we got time?"

Then we were in this guitar shop, and when he heard my news, the guy behind the counter didn't mind that we clearly weren't going to buy anything and let me play "Just Me" on this Ovation in the most gorgeous deep orangey red.

It somehow *sounded* orangey red too, or maybe that was just the feeling I had inside of me already, leaking out through my fingertips into the strings.

After that, Adrian played a vintage Schecter and then a Coronado semi-hollow. And then my stomach rumbled so loudly you could hear it even over the 1965 Gibson acoustic.

"Do you want to get a sandwich?" he said. "Or a pizza? Let's get a pizza!" He checked his wallet. "Or maybe a sandwich."

There was a Pret a Manger in Covent Garden, and we sat up on those high silver stools while the world flowed around us. I was like an island, surrounded by a churning sea of people. An island eating a falafel wrap followed by a chocolate brownie. Followed by another chocolate brownie, because we were celebrating after all.

"You want this?" said Adrian, seeing me eyeing his muffin.

"Are you offering?"

"No! But go on."

We munched away in this happy silence for a while as the couple next to us had a humungous fight in what I think was Japanese.

"Maybe I'll go to Japan," I said. "Can you get wraps there?"

The man next to us stopped arguing and turned and looked at me. "Of course we have wraps in Japan," he said. "Aren't you that girl from video? 'Just Me'?"

"Yes!" I said. "I am!"

"I love that," he said. "It stay in my head. I got mad beats!"

"'Just Me'!" said his girlfriend, who had green-striped hair and was, for some reason, dressed as an old-fashioned maid with a hat and frilly apron. In Harltree, she'd have probably been beaten up, but here no one seemed to even notice. "We do selfie?"

"Of course," I said. "Of course!"

They each did peace signs while I plastered on a huge smile. It was only afterward that I realized my teeth must have been full of chocolate brownie.

Adrian was checking his watch. "Katie…"

"Ten more minutes," I pleaded.

"We have to go home," he said.

He didn't sound quite like he meant it.

"When you were in your band," I said, "what was it like?"

He chewed a chip, thinking, "A pain in the butt, mostly. We argued over everything. And the way it ended—I wouldn't wish that on anyone. But…I've never been closer to anyone than I was with Tony. I still miss that."

"Not even with Mom?" I said.

There was a moment when he was clearly deciding whether or not to be honest. Then he took another chip. "When I was in that band, it was us against the world. With Zoe, however close we get, you and your sister will always come first."

♪ ♫ ♫

He dropped me at the end of the road, then went off to the fish and chips shop, leaving me to bounce up the lane on my own. It was the last part of the day, the blue of the sky fading into a faint, purple blush. I used to have some eye shadow that exact shade. The one time I wore it, Lacey asked me if I'd been punched.

The memory of it made me laugh, and then I was running, skip-hop-jumping, getting little pieces of dirt in my shoes, and sending a fat bird squawking up out of a bush and twirling into the trees as though someone had gotten halfway through blowing up a balloon then let it go, only with feathers and a beak.

Everything was so sharp and clear and still. There was no breeze, and the yellow field seemed to be on pause, more like a painting than a place. I could hear every crunch of my shoes on the lane, the muffled drone of traffic from the highway, and my own fluttering breath, in and out, in and out.

It's a secret, I said to myself. *No one can know. Not yet. You've just been in town with Lacey. So calm down. Look normal. Be normal.*

In fact, I remembered Mom was working a long shift that day, so there wasn't any need to sneak around. It was only Amanda at home, and Amanda never noticed anything.

"Hey, Katie." She was curled up on the sofa, watching TV.

"Hey, Mands. How was the store?"

"All right."

"Busy?"

"Not especially."

I hung around in the doorway, thinking I should go upstairs.

Amanda hunkered down as though she was trying to disappear down between the cushions. Which was not a good idea. I'd seen what was in there when I'd helped carry it in for the move. Let's just say I put those cushions back in place and resolved never to pick them up again.

"So has anyone else said anything about the video?"

She didn't even look away from the TV screen. "Who?"

"I don't know. A customer?"

"No."

"Oh. Okay."

A very annoying woman with too many teeth pranced around on the screen trying to sell us some laundry detergent. Amanda even seemed to be listening. Take it from me, it's a sad day when color-safe bleach is more interesting than your own sister.

"Wanna come upstairs, play some bass?"

"Maybe later."

I should have left it at that. Why didn't I leave her there? Instead I said, "So, Adrian took me to meet a record label today."

"*What?*"

At least now she was looking at me.

"And it was brilliant, Mands. It was this huge building in actual Covent Garden, and they had pictures of all their acts up, even yucky Karamel and the guy, Tony, he was so nice, and basically, he offered me a record deal there on the spot, and I said yes! And I'm going to record the single next weekend! How cool is that?"

"No *way*! That is *amazing*!" she said, and now she wasn't curled up anymore. She was on her knees on top of the cushions, then tumbling onto the floor, then up on her feet. "*Amazing amazing AMAZING!*"

"Isn't it?"

"So Mom changed her mind? Katie, we've got to get you into the store for a gig. You could sign stuff—"

"Mom didn't change her mind. Mom doesn't know."

Well, that threw a damper on things, I can tell you.

"Then why are you telling me this?"

"Because it's exciting." *Because you are my sister.*

"You know what Mom said. We both heard her."

"Yeah, but—"

"So why were you and Adrian sneaking off into London anyway? Wait"—she held up her hands—"don't tell me. I don't want to know anymore. I don't want to be a part of your…thing."

Then, I got it. "Oh. You're jealous."

"No, I'm not."

"You are," I said. "You're jealous because it's my song and I'm going to be a real musician."

"I couldn't care less."

"And because I spent the day with Adrian, not you."

"You have no idea, do you?"

"Well, I'm sorry to have intruded on your love-in, but don't worry. You can have him back once the single's finished."

The light seemed to dim, or maybe it was just because the commercial was over. "You know they don't agree about that. And you made him take your side, and now what's going to happen? We have a home now."

"A ridiculous home."

"A *permanent* home," said Amanda. "I thought you wanted that? And you're putting it on the line…for what?"

"I'm not putting anything on the line. Stop being so melodramatic."

"But if Mom finds out—"

A thought gripped my neck with icy claws. "You…you won't tell her, will you? If you tell her now, it'll all be over before it's even started. You only get one chance, Mands. That's what I've realized, and if I don't take it—"

"This is a bad idea," said Amanda.

I waited. And waited.

"Fine. You win. I won't tell her, all right? But when this comes out—and it will—I am not getting involved."

"Fine. I didn't need to tell you. I just thought you might be pleased."

Her eyes were back on the television. And then I thought of the other thing I'd come in to say. And that I probably should have mentioned first.

"Um, Mands. Can I borrow your phone? Sorry, I know it's not… Only I haven't checked my views on 'Just Me' since yesterday, and since my new phone isn't—"

"Get lost."

"Okay!"

So I went upstairs and brushed my teeth, which felt kind of pointless so late in the day, but they were feeling pretty gross. Then I lay down across my bed to try to get my mind around everything.

I had a record deal.

I was going to record a single.

And Mom was going to be fine with it.

The very second I got around to telling her.

That Belt

That belt
That belt
That turquoise belt
Six ninety-nine
And it could have been mine
With sparkly stones and pieces of felt

Would've matched my leotard
Popped against my hot-pink sweater
Here's the thing, that belt rocked hard
It would've made my whole life better

That belt
That belt
That turquoise belt
Six ninety-nine
And it could have been mine
With sparkly stones and pieces of felt

Can only blame myself, it's fine
'Cuz when I went to pay for it

I had to stand in a great, long line
Got distracted, bought a bracelet

That belt
That belt
That turquoise belt
Six ninety-nine
And it could have been mine
With sparkly stones and pieces of felt

Would've made a whole new me
Could've been a fashion riot
But sadly it will never be
Because I simply didn't buy it

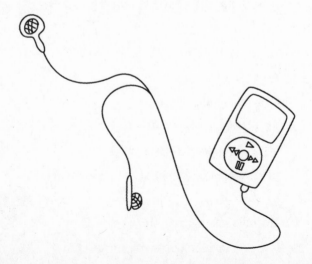

Chapter Nineteen

I LOVE LACEY'S HOUSE. I REALLY do, though I have to say that I find being there a little tense. Everything's so clean and nice and not broken. She's got a tank in her kitchen with all these tropical fish swimming around in it, like jewelry with fins, and fluffy carpets and a kitchen with drawers that close themselves. And a special faucet that has boiling water come out of it and another one that makes ice cubes. And an ice cream maker and a white sofa without any stains on it whatsoever. Which I find really stressful to sit on, but Lacey doesn't.

I want to be the kind of person who can drink Coke on a white sofa without having a mental breakdown.

And that gave me the upsetting thought that even though I hated my stupid, new, falling-apart house, maybe it and me were meant for each other.

"Just relax," said Lacey, who is completely aware of my sofa issues, even if she doesn't support them.

I gripped my Coke can.

"It's really not going anywhere," said Lacey, seeing the metal start to sink between my fingers.

"But suppose I throw it in the air?" I whispered. "Suppose I just toss it everywhere?"

"Why would you do that?"

"I don't know!"

Then Lacey's mom came in with—oh *man*—two bowls of spaghetti bolognese.

"Er, would you mind if I ate it at the table?" I said.

I know Lacey's mom isn't sure about me at all, but this seemed to make her happy. Very happy. "Maybe you do have some manners after all! We're watching *Alien* later if you girls would like to join us?"

"Katie can't watch *Alien*," said Lacey. "It freaks her out. She'll cry and spill popcorn everywhere."

"We can't have that, can we?" said Lacey's mom, glancing down at my bolognese bowl.

Then she guided me over to a table with a perfect white tablecloth and white cotton–covered chairs.

"And I've got you chocolate ice cream with chocolate sauce for dessert."

I wondered if it would be weird to ask her to put some newspaper down. Or if I could have mine in the garden.

Lacey put me out of my misery. "Can we eat upstairs?"

We took our bowls up to Lacey's bedroom, me sitting at her desk with my jacket spread out underneath, just in case.

Lacey ate sitting cross-legged on her white duvet cover, and she didn't spill even a dot of sauce. I know this because she went off to the bathroom and I checked.

"Okay, how weird was shopping with Savannah?" said Lacey. "What is this world that she lives in?"

"She needs to come with us to a secondhand store."

Lacey sat up, and if she'd been me, she'd have spilled her dinner. "You haven't invited her, have you?"

"No! Of course I haven't! Can you *imagine*?"

We imagined and laughed.

"So here's what I don't get," I said. "How does a person be Savannah? Because I got a close-up look at her in the locker room, and she is flawless."

"What do you mean?"

"She's just perfect. All of her. I thought she'd have some monster birthmark or pimples in her armpits or something, but she doesn't."

"Pimply armpits?"

"Yeah. From shaving them. Maybe I'm not doing it right." I showed Lacey my armpits. "See?"

"Yuck!"

"That is not how they look in magazines. Can I look at yours?"

"No."

"Please?"

"No!"

"I've shown you mine!"

"Did I ask to see your armpits?" said Lacey, who, to be fair, had not asked to see my armpits.

I sighed. "Just think if Savannah had done the video. She'd probably have had three times as many hits as me."

"From perverts," said Lacey. "How is that thing even still up?"

"Erm." I'd been thinking that I'd really quite like to watch it again on her computer and see how the hits were doing, but maybe that wasn't such a good idea.

"Maybe *I* should be talking to Jaz," said Lacey. "Perhaps I should offer her money or something."

"Or you could just support it," I said.

"Huh?" She nearly dropped her fork. Nearly, but not quite.

"Look," I said. "Jaz isn't going to take it down. We know that. And a lot of people are watching it, and they seem to like it, and I know it's embarrassing for you, but for me…it's kind of incredible. Like, the best thing that has ever happened to me. And you're the best friend who has ever happened to me, and I'd just really like it if you could be…okay."

Lacey started to speak and then stopped.

"And yesterday," I went on, thinking it was now or never, or anyway, now or very, very soon and so it probably had to be now, "I did something incredible. Me and Adrian, we went to see a record label."

"*What?*"

"It's called Top Music. They do Karamel and Crystal Skye."

"You hate Karamel. You say they are overproduced and have stupid hair."

"Yes, but that's not the point."

"That's not you, Katie. You're, like, all individual and bad makeup and split ends-y."

"I do not have split ends! Well, I do, but that's not the point. Which is…" I had to stop for a second to think what the point was. "The point is that this is a really big thing for me. And I'd like it if you could be happy."

"I am happy!" said Lacey.

She did not look happy.

"Okay then," I said.

We ate for a while, and then my bowl was empty, which was a shame, both because it meant I didn't have an excuse not to talk and also because Lacey's mom is a good cook—one of those good cooks who believes in small portions.

"The best thing," I said quietly, "is that he wants me to go into a studio and record 'Just Me.' As a single. I'm going to have a single, Lacey. Me."

"Seriously?"

"I've never been more serious. Well, okay, I *have*"—I was thinking of the time I stepped on a sea urchin on vacation, which had been very, very serious—"but…yes. I mean it."

"What was it like? At the label?"

"Bizarre. In an amazing way. Glass everywhere and the receptionist dressed all in black with the most perfect lipstick you've ever seen. And security guards on the doors and an elevator with a huge mirror in it, so you can make sure you look all right before you get out. And they had really nice cookies."

"Did you see anyone famous?"

"Only their pictures. But honestly, it was the most exciting thing. Like, the opposite of Harltree." I tried to put into words that feeling I'd had, taking the subway to Covent Garden, how everything had been so *alive*. "I wish I could always be there. It makes here seem so boring and pointless."

"Here?"

"Not your bedroom. I mean this town. This stupid, pointless town."

"I like it here," said Lacey. "Anyway, London's scary."

And that is when it came to me that of course, Lacey liked Harltree. She never complained that our Topshop was too small or that there wasn't anything to do on the weekend other than sit in the park or pay too much money to see things exploding at the movies.

Lacey was content. She'd probably stay in Harltree forever and marry Devi Lester.

Huh.

"I'm moving to London the first chance I get," I said. "Maybe it'll be soon. Maybe once my single's out…"

"I don't think it's legal until you're sixteen," said Lacey.

"Fine. I'll wait until I'm sixteen, and then I'll get this big apartment with a TV that slides out of the end of my bed and a grand piano that sits in the middle of the room and a huge walk-in closet."

"It sounds nice," said Lacey.

"Will you visit me? We'll go for ice cream. And rides in my helicopter."

"You'll have a helicopter?"

"Yeah! Parked on the roof! And the propellers will be made of gold. Wait—maybe that's a little trashy. I'll have them in platinum; it's a little more subtle."

Lacey was wearing a thoughtful, complex sort of an expression. It reminded me of something, and for a moment I couldn't think what. Then I remembered, it was the face the next-door neighbor's cat used to make just before it threw up on our carpet.

I got ready for some hair holding because I know that's what you're supposed to do when a friend is sick. Although I have to say the thought worried me a little because I'm really not good at all around vomit, and you'd have to be close to it to hold up the vomiting person's hair. What if it was all so disgusting that instead of being a helpful hair holder, I ended up puking onto her head?

Then Lace swallowed and said, "Okay then. When are you recording?"

"Next Saturday."

"Ah," said Lacey. "That might be a problem. I've got basketball. Do you think you could do it Sunday instead?"

Which made no sense at all.

"Um, why does it matter that you've got basketball?" I said.

"Well, I can't exactly be in two places at once, can I?" said Lacey.

She turned a very bright red as she said it, meaning that it was significant in some way. Only I couldn't see how. I mean, it was *basketball*. And Lacey played defense, which involved standing around for most of the game and then watching helplessly as someone taller than her shot the ball through the hoop. Just what did this have to do with my recording career?

Oh.

"Can you make it Sunday? I can definitely make it Sunday. Mom wanted us to go and see Auntie Lou, but I'd much rather go up to London. Auntie Lou always makes me play with my cousin Andrew, and he's at this funny stage where he just wants to list types of dinosaur."

The wind blew rain against the window. Maybe it had been doing it for a while, but this was the first time I'd noticed.

"Lacey," I said, trying to think of a sensitive way to phrase it, "you're not… There's no reason for you to be there."

"No reason for me to be there?"

"Well, no."

Lacey looked around as though she was trying to drum up some support from her bedroom furniture. "That is *my* tambourine on the original."

"What could I do?" I asked. "Say I wouldn't do it without you?"

"Yes!" said Lacey.

I'd been pretty patient. But *really*.

I couldn't put my one big chance of giving my life some kind of meaning on the line in order to include someone who didn't want to be in the original video anyway and had spent the last few days asking me to get it taken down.

There was just no way.

It was so obvious that it didn't even need explaining.

Except, apparently, to Lacey.

"Look," I said. "I'm sorry. But this is about being professional. And—"

"You don't think I'm professional?"

"Not at playing the tambourine, no."

"Well, you're not a professional singer," said Lacey.

"I'm about to be!"

"You wanted me to support you," said Lacey. "This is me being supportive."

"Which is…terrific! And I'm so happy," I said, trying to sound so happy. "And I'll include you—of course I will. I was planning to…thank you in the liner notes! Yes!"

"Great."

"Great!" I was pleading now. "So we're okay then?"

She sighed. "I guess so."

"Does that mean we can watch *Mean Girls*?"

"I don't think I'm in a *Mean Girls* sort of a mood," said Lacey. "I'd like to go downstairs and watch *Alien*. Okay?"

"Um, okay," I said, trying not to shiver. "Let's do that."

She got up off the bed. And then, at the same moment, we both saw, smack bang in the middle of her carpet, a big splodge of bolognese sauce.

Chapter Twenty

So the whole Lacey thing—and yes, I will admit that it had now become a real actual thing—wasn't the best. Luckily, I had a million hits behind me; otherwise, I might have been seriously upset about it all.

"Look," I said to Jaz. "It's gone up again—1,327,888."

"Yes, but have you seen my video of Nicole drop-kicking a brick?" said Jaz. "She nearly broke her toe, but it was so worth it."

"Has it had a million hits?" I said.

"No, but we only put it up last night." She unlocked her phone and turned away. Conversation over.

Which left me free to sit back and enjoy the ride.

I have to admit the bus ride was starting to lose its excitement, which is saying something because it hadn't ever been exciting in the first place. At least it had been a little interesting though to look out of the window and be driven past places I hadn't known existed, even if those places were just houses and the occasional row of shops with a run-down newsstand or a greasy-looking chip shop.

Now, I knew every road and every stop and was even starting to recognize the non–school bus regulars: the veiny man who kept remembering to hate me, the woman with weirdly huge boobs to the point where it was possible she had some kind of syndrome, and the young guy who looked like he'd once been a full-scale emo rock singer but was having to scale it back that now he had a job but couldn't quite let go of the eyeliner.

And I wasn't interested in them much either. I wasn't really interested in anything except when I could escape back to London with my guitar.

Adrian had said it was all moving too fast. If this was too fast, then normal speed might actually have killed me.

We got to school a little bit earlier than usual so the corridors were still pretty packed with the preassembly crowd, a bunch of sixth-graders here, a clump of seventh-graders there, a slew of seniors blocking the way like a mountain range. I kept my eyes down, knowing they'd be watching, and blocked my ears with headphones. A bunch of people singing "Just Me" was the last thing I needed.

"Katie Cox," said the principal, who had chosen that particular moment to walk past.

"Yes!"

Knowing there would probably be more press stuff on the menu, I'd gotten into the bathroom before Amanda could hog it and did my makeup.

There'd been an exfoliating scrub, then a ten-minute mask. Then more exfoliating scrub, partly because there was still some left in the bottle and partly because the mask seemed to have embedded itself into my pores and my cleanser hadn't been able to clean it. All this had made my skin kind of red, which meant I'd had to use plenty of Amanda's moisturizer, and this had given my cheeks a sort of a sheen, so I'd whacked on plenty of powder to finish with. And I have to say, I didn't look actively worse than when I'd started.

"Would you like me to talk to the papers again? Say some more about the music program?" I said. "Because I can. I don't think I completely covered everything the other day, but I figure I could do it way better this time. I can work it in with my guitar playing and song writing and stuff. Make it feel really organic, you know."

"Katie," said the principal, "no earphones in school."

"Oh." I took them out. "Sorry."

And no one was singing "Just Me." Or at least, I'm sure they were, but not at that particular moment.

Phew!

So I managed to get through all that, just about, but

there was still homeroom to navigate. Which was definitely going to be tricky and embarrassing. Especially when I saw everyone was huddled around Savannah's phone and smiling and pointing.

"I know," I said. "Another hundred thousand hits. That's the entire population of Harltree all over again. On top of all the people who are already watching. Eek."

"Oh, hey, Katie," said Paige.

Lacey did a sort of mini wave.

"Dreamy, yes?" said Savannah.

"I've never seen anything more delicious," said Sofie.

All right, maybe there was a *chance* that they weren't watching me.

"I want to lick the screen," said Savannah.

More than a chance.

"Something more exciting than my song?" I said jokingly. "This had better be good!"

"It is good," said Sofie. "It's Savannah's birthday cake."

"Not the actual cake," said Savannah. "This one doesn't have a waterfall. But they're going to add that when they make it. Dad made them promise before he paid the deposit."

I shuffled in between Lacey and Paige to see the screen. "I was just wondering if you guys were thinking of another trip to Cindy's because I'm still considering that dress and—hold on, that thing is a cake?"

"Five tiers," said Savannah.

"It has lights!"

"I know," said Savannah.

"How can a cake have lights?"

"It plugs in." She gave the screen a little kiss as though it was a picture of her latest boyfriend.

Come to think of it, a cake boyfriend would be amazing. You wouldn't have to worry about what it tasted like when you kissed, and if you ever split up, you could eat it.

Was that too weird to be a song?

"I might write a song about that," I said.

"So it's five flavors, obvs," said Savannah. "The bottom layer is red velvet."

"Would you be okay with it being a song?" I said.

"Sure, babes. Then rose and pistachio."

"I mean, a lot of people might hear it."

"And then cherry vanilla swirl."

"Because," I said loudly, "of how I'm going to record a single! I have a record deal, and I am going to record a single. Me!"

Well, that shut her up, and with two tiers still to go.

"For real?" said Sofie, and finally, it seemed like I'd pulled her attention away from Savannah's catering arrangements.

"Totes," I said, which is the first time I've ever used that word and also, I expect, the last. "I went into Covent

Garden, and I met with the head of Top Music. They do Crystal Skye and Karamel and stuff."

Savannah perked up.

"Can you get us free Karamel tickets? A backstage pass would be the most perfect birthday present."

"I bet I can," I said.

Savannah smiled the first genuine smile I'd ever seen from her. I know it was genuine because her forehead scrunched up and you could see her gums. Savannah *never* showed her gums when she smiles.

"Babes, if you can do that, then I will… I will…" She searched around for the most grateful, the most amazing, the most generous thing she could think of. "I will invite you to my party."

"I thought I was already invited to your party?"

"Oh." Savannah was clearly considering uninviting me so that she could reinvite me on the condition that I got her some Karamel tickets.

"I'll definitely get them for you," I said. "I don't know if it'll be in time for your birthday, though."

"Well," said Savannah, looking a little deflated, "late is better than never. Let me know when you have dates, yes?"

"I will," I said. "Savannah, the very second I get Karamel tickets, I will hand them right over. I promise." This wasn't really as generous as it sounded because I would rather lobotomize myself than listen to Karamel for even a minute. At least it was a promise I could definitely keep.

"Thanks, babes."

"So I probably shouldn't talk any more about how the meeting went or anything," I said. "But I suppose, just to finish off—"

"You've genuinely got a record deal?" said Sofie.

"Yes. With the people who do Crystal Skye and Karamel. Yes, I do."

"Even though she hates Crystal Skye and Karamel," said Lacey.

"She hates Karamel?" said Savannah. Then, to me, "You hate Karamel??"

"I hate boy bands," I said. "And Karamel are a huge, great big boy band, so yes. I hate them."

"I still don't get why you'd record a single with a record label when you can't stand any of their music!" said Lacey.

I thought of that huge glass building and the posters and the incredibly expensive cookies. I thought about Tony's eager expression. I thought about that beautiful receptionist with the perfect makeup and Covent Garden and how, even with a million hits, my friends clearly still considered me slightly less exciting than a cake.

"You wouldn't understand," I said. "It's an industry thing, isn't it?"

"If you say so," said Lacey.

"Anyway. The point is, we're recording the single this weekend!" Lacey looked away. "And after that, who knows? I suppose we'll make a video, and then maybe there'll be an album. My album!"

The door bounced open, and there was McAllister, looking mightily annoyed, which is just her normal expression, but still. "Tell me what are we all discussing so intensely when we should be on our way to assembly?"

"Katie's got a record deal," said Sofie.

"That is very exciting," said McAllister, her eyebrows moving fractionally higher in a way that I'd never seen before, which I suppose meant she was genuinely excited. "Now, assembly. Lacey, cheer up for goodness sake. And Savannah, those earrings are coming off right now, or I will take them home and give them to my niece."

Cake Boyfriend

Pat-a-cake
Pat-a-cake
Baker's man
Bake me a boy as fast as you can

Give him fudge for hair
And frosted blue eyes
And finish him off with
Vanilla cake thighs

My cakey boyfriend
Oooh my cakey boyfriend
My bakey cakey boyfriend
Oooh my cakey boyfriend

And when we kiss
It'll be so fun
I'll nibble his earlobes
And bite his tongue

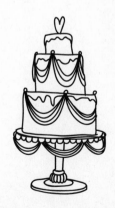

My cakey boyfriend

Oooh my cakey boyfriend
My bakey cakey boyfriend
Oooh my cakey boyfriend

He'll have a sweet boy heart
But if we ever disagree
Gonna cut him into slices
And have him with my tea

My cakey boyfriend
Oooh my cakey boyfriend
My bakey cakey boyfriend
Oooh my cakey boyfriend

And when he's gone
It won't much matter
You can bake me another
From the leftover batter

My cakey boyfriend
My cakey cakey boyfriend
Oooh my cakey boyfriend
My bakey cakey boyfriend

[repeat to fade]

Chapter Twenty-One

IT SEEMED LIKE SATURDAY WOULD never get there, but then luckily it did, or I might just have exploded through an excess of nervous energy. Even things that normally made time go really fast, like watching TV and sleeping, felt slow and draggy as though the world knew I wanted to hurry up and had decided to go secretly into rewind.

Like I said, though, Saturday did eventually put in an appearance. It began, as all Saturdays did, around the kitchen table, with Mom cleaning up mouse droppings from the floor and saying, "I'm going straight from the hospital to karaoke…if that's all right?"

We all said it was.

"Anyone doing anything fun today?"

"Well," said Amanda. "I am going to run the store. Adrian's store. I will be running it."

"Good for you, my love," said Mom. "So you're not working today, Ade?"

"Thought I'd take Katie out for the day," said Adrian. "Get to know each other a little. Yeah. Mmm." He was such a bad liar. I had to take over.

"We decided we'd do some bonding," I said. "Go for a drive, maybe get some lunch or something."

Mom looked from me to him and then back again. Of course she didn't believe us. We were so blatantly lying. I braced myself...

"Finally!" said Mom. "Two of my favorite people in the world have started to get along."

"Er," I said. "Kind of."

"What are you going to do?" Mom said. "Tell me. I want to be able to picture you together."

"Just go into town," I said.

"Town!" said Mom.

"Eat a pizza?"

"Pizza!" She went to her wallet and dug out a twenty. "Spend it all."

"It's really not that big a deal," I said.

"It is," said Mom. "If I could've had one wish in the world, it would have been for the two of you to be friends. Now, I'm going to have a shower. If anyone touches the hot water faucet, I will personally come and drown them."

She went, humming the chorus of "Natural Woman," and, after a moment, Adrian followed.

"If they are getting in there together…" I began, my hand heading toward the kitchen sink.

Amanda's nails dug into my arm.

"You have to stop this."

"The shower? I know!"

"The lies to Mom."

"I told Tony yes," I said.

"So tell him you've changed your mind. Or tell her. Tell her right now and see what she says."

"You know what she'll say. She'll say no. And…" I was surprised to find I was on the verge of crying into my Pop-Tart. "I want to see what happens. It's exciting. It's the most exciting thing that'll ever happen to me, and if I pull out now, that's it. Over. Finished. Just the whole rest of my life with nothing to look forward to. Just like everyone else."

"That is a really unhealthy way of looking at it," said Amanda. "Honestly, Katie, you can't pretend your life is already over. You haven't even finished school."

"*Fine*." And now I wasn't sad anymore, just angry. "I want to do this because it will be *cool*. All right? I want to sound amazing and look amazing and for people to buy my album and listen to my songs and think, 'These are amazing.' Because I am a selfish, horrible person. And maybe you think I ought to be content with riding the bus to school every day and having my best friend ignore me and my bra strap pinged and egg mashed into my hair and listening to Savannah's party plans. But honestly, I think I might be happier at least taking a chance on something else."

Amanda put down her mug and left. But I knew she wouldn't tell Mom. So I guess I should have felt good about our little talk.

Somehow, I didn't.

♪ ♫ ♫

"I'm a star," I said to myself. "I am an artist. I am going to record my single. Like Prince and Rihanna and Jessie J. I'm doing this. It is real. This is me, on my way to London. To sing."

I kept this up in my head all the way there, and I was so hyped by the time I got to Liverpool Street that I could feel my fingers trailing fairy dust all over the turnstiles.

Adrian, on the other hand, seemed edgy, and every time he opened his mouth, a downer dropped out.

"There'll be a lot of people from the label there," he said. "I know you liked Tony, and he seemed laid-back, but take it from me, the studio's very different from the office."

"Huh," I said, not really knowing what he meant and not much wanting to think about it.

"See, they'll have their own ideas," said Adrian. "And sometimes that's great! A collaboration!"

"Okay," I said, navigating my way past a woman with a suitcase who was completely blocking the way onto the Central Line.

"Sometimes, though, it's not so good. You don't want them to overcommercialize your sound. I mean, a little smoothing out, that's all well and good. But…"

"But what?"

"You're *you*, Katie. And that's not very Top Music."

"What are you trying to say?"

"You're special. Don't let them make you into something you're not."

"Which is?"

"Slick. Auto-tuned. You know."

"Maybe I'm okay with that," I said. "Seriously, what is it with people thinking I don't deserve the full treatment?"

He stopped. "Is that what you think? That you don't deserve it? The point is that you don't *need* it. Katie, maybe you don't know it, but there's no one out there right now even half as good as you. You know why people keep clicking on the video? Because you're Katie Cox! So enough with trying to be someone else, all right?"

"Oh," I said, swinging my guitar straight into a living statue. Living statues, it turns out, can be really grumpy.

After a few minutes of apologizing, which didn't work, and some cash from Adrian, which did, we got far enough away for me to say, "Look, I get that you're worried. But let's just see how it goes, okay?"

"Yeah."

"But…"—and I had to glance down at the sidewalk because it was difficult to say—"I appreciate that you care."

"Nice one, Katie," said Adrian, looking like he might be about to go for some kind of hug, and then, thank the Lord, we reached a small doorway with a line of buzzers, one of which said "SQ Studios." The conversation was over.

♪♫♫

Despite what Adrian had said, it was just Tony who was there to meet us, rising up out of a chair shaped like an egg to grab my hand and tell me how excited he was.

The whole place was smaller than I'd thought it would be. Down at the end of a long flight of steps, there was this strange sealed-in world without windows, sort of shabby and worn with things stacked up against other things and peeling-back carpets. And while I could mainly smell Tony's aftershave, there was just the faintest tang of mold like dark clouds lurking on the horizon at the end of a sunny afternoon.

Just nerves, I told myself, noticing how dry my mouth had become and giving my throat a very subtle clear—and then another one and another until Adrian handed me a bottle of water.

"Takes me back," he was saying, nostrils flared as though he was sort of inhaling the scene. "Hey, Tone, maybe it's my mind playing tricks, but isn't this where we recorded back in the day?"

"It is," said Tony. "The very same studio. I thought it would be…poetic."

Which explained why everything was so dark and dingy when I'd been expecting more of a Top Music reflective-surfaces vibe.

"What sort of stuff were you planning?" I asked. "Because I don't want fifteen backing singers or a violin quartet or anything." I could see Adrian nodding.

"Right now, it's just you and your guitar," said Tony, motioning me down yet another set of stairs. "We can always put more on later."

"Or not," I said. "If it doesn't need it."

"It's entirely your call."

"That doesn't sound like you, Tony," said Adrian, but I guess his words got lost in a bunch of doors opening and closing because he didn't get a reply.

Then, we were in a room with a glass wall where a man

sat at a desk covered in knobs and dials and lights and slid-ing things.

"How does it feel, Katie?" Tony's smile split his face in two. "How does it feel to be recording your first single?"

"It feels…" I tried to put into words the electricity sparking down into my fingertips, the way my stomach felt as though I was just getting to the top of a roller coaster, the smile that kept tugging at the corners of my mouth.

"Don't tell me. Tell Adrian. He's the one responsible for all this."

I turned wordlessly to Adrian, and Tony said, "Look at her, Ade. Remember that feeling?"

"I do."

"I have to take a selfie," I said, getting my phone out. "The girls at school will lose it when they see me in here." Then I remembered my stupid phone didn't have a camera. "Adrian…your phone…can you?"

"What's a selfie?" said Adrian, and I decided to leave it.

"Never mind." I looked around for somewhere to put my water bottle and settled with the top of a speaker.

"Careful," said the guy sitting at the desk in a quiet way that suggested he was trying very hard to be polite while actually being quite worried.

It was a voice I recognized well. Mom used it pretty much every time I borrowed anything of hers, even though the incident with the skirt and the nail polish remover was years ago. I'd said I was sorry about a million times, and I'd have bought her another one if the store hadn't stopped making them.

"Katie?" said the desk guy, while simultaneously pressing some of the buttons on his desk. "I'm Moe. Want to go tune up? It's through there."

I unzipped my guitar case. Having it in my arms felt easier. *I can do this*, I told myself. Moe came in and started fiddling around, putting headphones over my ears and making the microphone stand higher and lower and then higher again.

"Happy?" He looked at me like he felt sorry for me. Like how Savannah looked at me, only his eyes were kind.

"Yes, thank you, Moe."

He looked surprised.

"What?" I said, thinking that my big, flappy mouth must've gone and offended him.

"Not usual for the artist to remember my name," he said.

"What artists have you had?" I asked.

"Recording here? A few biggies. Kylie did some things. Elbow, they were a laugh. Lorde, we loved her…" He touched my shoulder. "Relax. You're going to be fine."

He was gone, shutting the door behind him. The room was now very, very quiet. Not the deep silence of the countryside at night or the scratchy hush of exams. This silence was flat and complete. As if someone had turned off my ears.

Through the glass Moe mouthed something at me. I thought that maybe this was what it was like to be one of Lacey's mom's tropical fish.

"Katie? Can you hear me?"

This time the words came through the headphones, but honestly, it was as though they had been injected straight into my brain.

"Yup."

My voice had never been so clear. I could hear every last part of it, all the little creaks and clicks, the slight wet noise my tongue made against the roof of my mouth. I'd always thought of it as smooth, something that flowed, but now, close up, it was like wood—grainy and knotted and full of splinters.

"Katie, hi?" Tony this time. "Ready to try it?"

I strummed a quick chord and then another.

"Let's do a quick run, see how it works out, okay?"

Then my fingers were moving of their own accord, scattering notes this way and that as the tune rose up in my throat.

"I got mad skin,
I got mad hair…"

When Adele had started out, she'd have been just the same as I was now—standing in a studio, full of music.

And call me crazy, but it was as though they were all there, my idols, lining up just behind me, cheering me on— Kate Bush, her arms wrapped around Amy Winehouse's teeny-weeny waist; Dolly Parton, all boobs and hair; Joni Mitchell and Taylor Swift; Björk, who was for some reason dressed as a swan…

Adrian winked at me through the glass, and as he did, I felt my heart leap.

"I got mad love,
I got mad hate,
I've got all my life to come, and I just can't wait
And here's the thing, I think you'll agree,
We're all in this together. It's not just me."

Chapter
Twenty-Two

LATER—MUCH, MUCH LATER—I WAS BACK in my bedroom. My bones were still vibrating with the memory of it all, so much so that I couldn't quite seem to sit still and kept pinging between my bed and my desk and the window and the floor, around and around and around.

There was the same tangle of clothes at the end of my bed, the same weird stain on the ceiling, the same old plate of pizza with its ever-increasing mane of green fur. Nothing had changed, but somehow everything had. Which I guess is what it will feel like when I actually have my first kiss, an event so far away that they will probably get a man on Mars before I manage to plant one on my mouth.

I so wanted to tell Lacey about the day. How Moe had clapped me on the back and said that I'd played brilliantly. How they'd asked me if I was hungry and bought me a chicken wrap when I'd said I was. How they had a big jar of pencils on the desk with SQ Studios all written on the side and how I'd snuck a couple at the end, one for me and one for her.

But that was old Lacey. It would take more than a pencil to get her to like me again.

Still, she'd come around. And the pencil would keep.

How long until a pencil doesn't work?

There was at least one person I *could* tell. One person who was scheduled to talk to me, who would be obliged to ask me how my day had been and listen to the answer.

I looked at the clock again, and again and again and again until finally, *finally*, it was time to talk to Dad.

"Katie!"

And oh, but it was good to hear his voice. Like buttered toast on a cold Sunday afternoon. Like a hug. Like…Dad.

"So, my little pop star, I've been hearing great things! *Let's all sit down and have a cup of tea!*"

"You've seen the video, then?"

"Have I seen it? It's all I see! I turn my email on, I get links to you. And people asking about you. Did I know my Katie was all over the Internet? What do I think? Can I get her to sign stuff for the girls at the store?"

"People are listening to me in California? I can't believe it."

"You'd better believe it." He inhaled. "And that's Adrian, huh?"

"Yup."

"Kind of a sloppy pianist, if you ask me."

"He's all right."

But Dad was still going. "Nah, he's rotten. And his fashion sense isn't much better. I'd have thought your mother might have gone for someone a little more… Well, a little less…"

The way Dad goes on about his new girlfriend, I couldn't resist taking the opportunity to getting back at him just a little bit. "He might be doing some session work on the new Karamel album."

"No way!" Dad sounded genuinely upset.

"It's true."

"I can't remember the last time I worked with anyone under the age of twenty-five."

"Come back here, then," I said. "I'll talk to Tony, see if he can get you in on it as well. I'm sure you could stay on the sofa."

"Ah, you know, I said I'd help Catriona set up her new studio. Seriously, though, that Adrian guy, he's a piece of work."

"But you thought *I* was all right?" I asked. Which was fishing, I know. But…

"Katie, you were wonderful."

At last, a family member who appreciated me. It put me in such a good mood that I even asked, "So how is Catriona?"

"She's great! She's just started two more classes, so she's incredibly busy but good busy. And she's been making me these terrific hot chocolates, sweetened with this stevia stuff. It's like sugar, only it's not sugar—"

This went on for a while. And reminded me why I don't normally ask.

"So, you should know," I said, "I'm going to release the song as a single."

"One of the girls was saying that's exactly what you should do. Everyone's doing it these days. Apparently it's really easy. Just a few clicks, and maybe I won't have to send you all that child support money. Joke!"

Let's be clear: Dad has always paid his child support on time. But, oh boy, does he go on and on about it.

"Ha-ha. No, it's with Top Music. They're a real record label. We went to London today to record it." I had this sudden flash of fear, that maybe he wouldn't be okay with it. That he'd freak out, break his code of silence with Mom, and—

"That is fantastic news! *Fantastic!*"

"You think so?"

"Of course! Top Music? They're huge!"

"You're not worried? You don't think that it's basically a bad idea?"

"Of course not. Stop being so negative!"

"Just, Mom's been a little, er, funny about it. Mom and Lacey, actually. And Adrian's been going on and on about how they were going to make me miss school and change my sound and how stressed out I'd be and that the whole thing would be a fight. But it wasn't like that at all! Tony, he's the head of the label, he's been really nice, and he let me record it exactly how I wanted. I did it in three takes. Literally!"

"Of course you did."

"So you're not going to jump on a plane and ground me or anything?" I said.

"Katie," said Dad. "You're happy, right?"

"Very."

"Why would I mess with that? You go out there, do what you want to do, then make sure you get on the phone and tell your old dad all about it."

"Okay!"

Clearly, this was the correct reaction. The normal reaction. The reaction of someone who cared about me.

We talked for a while after that, about a scorpion Dad had found under his car and the ins and outs of opening a Pilates studio in a neighborhood that already had three Pilates studios.

And I told him how great our new house was and how much I was enjoying the bus ride to school and how everyone was getting along so well. By the time I put the phone down, I was exhausted with the effort of smiling so hard. Because of recent Wi-Fi restrictions, it was a smile that Dad couldn't even see.

"I'm glad you guys are doing so well," he said. "When I was around, everything seemed so hard. But you're making it look easy!"

For a second I faltered. And for some reason, Adrian's words came back to me: *I'm not taking parenting lessons from a man who leaves his kids to go and live on the other side of the world.*

"I wish you could come and see us," I said. Then, quickly, before I could change my mind, "It's just, I miss you so much."

"You don't need me," said Dad. "I'd just get in the way of this new career of yours."

"Um, okay."

"Bye, Katie. Talk soon."

"Talk soon, Dad."

♪ ♫ ♫

There was something wrong with Amanda. I could tell because she wasn't eating her toast and because she hadn't bothered to get dressed. Oh, and because she was crying.

It wasn't obvious crying, like the sort I usually do, which

is supposed to make people come over and ask what's the matter. For example, after Paige whacked my chest in a particularly vicious game of hockey. I try not to do it too much since I'm not pretty when I cry. My eyes seem to drill themselves back into my head and my nose turns into this giant strawberry. A strawberry that emits snot.

Amanda's crying is much prettier, so she could absolutely use it to get as much sympathy as she wanted. Only, being a better and nobler person than I am, her tears are generally reserved for Really Bad Things Happening In The World, like wars and famine and fluffy animals getting eaten in nature programs.

Now, I want to cry at those things too. Really, I do, because I factually know that a whole city being bombed is worse than a chest whacking, even when the chest whacking was definitely done on purpose.

Only the message never seems to make it through to my tear ducts.

Anyway, Amanda was doing some serious breakfast table crying. The sort where tears leaked in little streams down the sides of her nose. What's the word we used in English the other day? Rivulets. Baby rivers of sad.

"What?" I said quite quietly. Then, when she didn't reply, "What?"

"There's just no point," she said.

"What do you mean?"

She looked around. "Just…this. I don't know." We both went quiet as Mom bumbled over to the back door, doing something with a load of plant pots. Once she was safely outside, Amanda wiped her nose on the back of her hand. "Don't you ever feel like things are just kind of hopeless?"

"This isn't like you," I said. She shrugged. "Come on, there's lots to be happy about! The sun's shining. And we live in a world of opportunity. Anything can happen! Seriously."

I was feeling it too. I'd just recorded my first single in an actual studio with an actual record label. Everything was basically awesome and would be from now until the day I died.

And when I did die, they'd know what to play at my funeral. So even if people weren't crying because I'd been a good person, there was a fair chance they'd cry at my amazing music.

Result!

"Anything can happen?" said Amanda slowly. "Anything?"

"Miracles are possible. I am literally proof of that. Two weeks ago I was nobody. And now…"

"You are the exact same person that you were two weeks ago," said Amanda. "Just more people have seen inside of your bedroom, which, by the way, is a health hazard."

Arguing with her was clearly not going to get me anywhere, so instead, I said, "Has something upset you, Mands?"

"Yes. Yes, actually, it has."

I waited, but all I got was more sniffing. "Is it me?" I said, dropping my voice so that there was no way Mom could hear, even though she was safely at the back of the garden. "Because I'm going to tell her. I just want to wait a little longer, just so she can hear how amazing the single is and be proud of me, and then maybe she'll understand. That's all."

It wasn't helping. Watching Amanda weep and weep made me feel so terrible that I was on the verge of getting up and fetching Mom and telling her everything.

Only then she said, "It's the store."

"What, Adrian's Disaster Emporium of Hopelessness?" I laughed with relief. "I mean, seriously, what is with that place? Who even goes into a shop and buys music any-more?! It's like he's literally trying to go broke."

"*Shut up, Katie.*"

That was unexpected.

All the softness had gone from her expression. In fact, in maybe a millionth of a moment, she'd gone from teary big sister to red-faced, spitty-mouthed monster.

"The shop *is* going broke. And Adrian won't tell Mom because she's so into the idea that he's head of this retail empire."

"But…can't you…just…"

"You think you know everything just because you've been going up to London. You know nothing. Nothing. Okay?"

I just stared. Maybe my mouth flapped open and shut a few times.

"Because I have *tried*. That store was *my* dream, K. You know about dreams, right? I thought, maybe if it was run by someone who was really passionate about music, who could talk to customers about bands, play them stuff they'd love, then maybe it could work. That I'd have unsigned groups do new act nights, and a noticeboard where people could sell secondhand guitars and get new drummers, and we'd have regulars who'd buy up all the rare vinyl, and maybe we'd arrange bus trips to festivals, and do a podcast of things we were enjoying, and yes, Katie, I *know* no one buys music in a store anymore, but I thought maybe I could change that. And now Adrian's business is going to go broke and that's my dream over. Done. Finished."

"But you never know," I said. "Anything is possible."

"We had one customer yesterday," she said. "One."

"Which is better than nothing!"

"She didn't buy anything," said Amanda. "She wanted directions to the train station."

"But everything you just said, they're all great ideas. It deserves to work. I mean, you do. It sounds like you're being brilliant. Incredible. He's lucky to have you."

"Maybe," she said, and now the tears were back. "But it's not enough. I'm glad you're getting to live your dream, Katie. But it doesn't mean I will."

Chapter Twenty-Three

T HERE'S A PATCH OF GRASS around the back of the school labs that's supposed to be a wilderness garden.

I've never quite known what a wilderness garden ought to look like, but I'm fairly sure no one meant for it to turn out how it did, which was this dark, damp corner of the school with moss instead of grass and a big row of recycling containers. Once, Lacey swore she saw a bluebell growing there, but it was so obviously wishful thinking on her part that I didn't even consider believing her.

Being totally honest, things between me and her were not good. Just how not good, I wasn't sure, since she wasn't really talking to me. I don't think she was actively *not* talking to me because she answered my questions and replied to my texts. But ever since Aliengate, I had been aware that if someone came and tested our friendship levels, they'd have found we were running pretty low.

So I'd brought her outside in order to try a little of

BFF-style bonding. To really talk about our feelings, get close, and open up to each other in that way only besties can.

"Um," I said.

"Mmm," said Lacey.

"Er."

"Oh look," said Lacey. "There's Savannah. Should we go and sit with her?"

"But, but…" I began. Then, because Lacey was already parking her behind on the grass, "Okay, then."

The Savannah-Paige-Sofie beast had found the one patch of sunshine in the whole area and had stretched out its six very long, very brown legs.

Come on, Katie. Spread the love.

"Hey, everyone. Mind if me and the very awesome Lacey Daniels sit with you? She's so great."

Which earned me some very strange looks.

"We're party planning," said Sofie.

"How much planning can one party take?" I asked.

"Just because *your* parties are three people dancing to an ancient NOW album doesn't mean everyone else's are," said Lacey in a way that, frankly, sounded a little critical.

"Mellow down, girlfriend," said Savannah. Then, to me, "Have you got my Karamel tickets? How was the recording? And have you got my Karamel tickets?"

"Sorry, no tickets yet," I told Savannah. "But the recording was amazing. It was in this little studio in Soho, and I did it in three takes."

"I bet you have the most amazing pictures," said Sofie.

"It's annoying, but actually, I don't. Stupid Neanderthal phone. But it was so interesting down there. They had all these framed platinum albums on the walls and a signed photo of the Rolling Stones. I mean, I'd have paid just to look around, and there I was actually getting to record my own music." I shook my head. "It blows my mind."

"Amaze," said Savannah, wiggling her perfect little toes. I noticed that each nail had been topped with a sparkly stone. "You know what? Even though you don't have any Karamel tickets for me, I think we should play your single at my party."

"That would be pretty groovy," I said, which was supposed to sound casual and laid-back and super-chilled but didn't, due to my using the word *groovy*. I mean, who says that? Other than me? "I'll send you the MP3."

"Can we hear it now?" said Paige.

"I haven't got it yet," I said. "Sorry."

"But I thought it was all recorded?"

"These things take time," I told her.

"So you don't know when it's coming out?"

"Er, no. They didn't say. Soon though. Because of momentum."

"But it'll be ready for the party?"

"Definitely." Then, because we seemed to be straying quite a long way from my original purpose, "I missed you at the studio, Lace. It's like, where was my entourage?!"

"Lacey didn't come to the studio with you?"

"She had basketball," I said.

"Which we won," said Lacey.

"Well, that's good!" I said. "Classic Lacey! You are a total winner! Hey, we should do something to mark the occasion! What are you doing tonight? Let's celebrate!"

"Calm down," said Lacey. "It's not that big a deal."

"It is. You won! You were the winning team!" I shook my invisible pom-poms. "Go Lacey! Go Lacey!"

"Katie, are you okay? Is Katie okay? She looks like she's having an epileptic fit."

I looked down from the top of my imaginary cheer-leading pyramid to see—oh no—Mad Jaz, who was suddenly just *there*. Maybe she'd always been there. Or maybe she'd materialized, like a sort of a demon. She was dressed quite demonically, her school uniform accessorized with an enormous black velvet scarf and ripped lace gloves.

"I was just cheering for Lacey," I said. "She's the best."

Jaz's head swiveled from me to Lacey and back again.

"The best," I repeated. "I cannot imagine having a better friend."

And maybe it was my imagination or did Jaz look just a little put out? Come to think of it, it was probably my imagination. That plus Jaz's face permanently looks a little put out.

"So, back to my party," Savannah was saying. Only, Jaz wasn't listening.

"I just came over to tell you that your video has had one and a half million views."

"Honestly," said Lacey. "Can we please stop talking about that stupid, embarrassing video? It's old news."

"I've been thinking again about the lighting," said Savannah.

"Not that old," I said. "One and a half million? That's amazing! When you think of it in terms of the population of Harltree it's…loads!"

"Yup," said Jaz. "Bet you're glad you didn't take it down now."

"More like *you* didn't take it down," said Lacey.

"Only because Katie told me not to," said Jaz.

Oh no.

"And whether I should have different colors for different areas," said Savannah.

"Katie asked you to take it down," said Lacey. "Because of how embarrassing it was for me."

"That is the most selfish thing I have ever heard in my life," said Jaz. "It's lucky that she changed her mind."

"No, she didn't. She wanted you to take it down, and you said no."

"I never said that," said Jaz, who, to be fair, had never said that. Except in my version of events.

I was beginning to realize I'd made a fairly serious mistake. Or several very serious mistakes.

"Er, Jaz, don't you remember how I said could you take it off the Internet, and you said you wouldn't?" I gabbled. "Maybe not. Oh well, moving on…"

"I do remember. You said you wanted it to stay up," said Jaz.

"Did I?" I said.

"*Did you?*" said Lacey, getting to her feet. "Because that's not what you told me. That's not what you told me at all."

Even Savannah had stopped talking.

"You…lied to me," said Lacey. "I know you're friends with *her* now. But I can't believe you'd actually lie."

"I never thought of you as a liar, Katie," said Savannah, looking very severe but still pretty. "Because if we can't believe you about this…"

"I'm not a liar! I mean, technically, in this one particular instance, then yes, I am, but just this one time. I mean, honestly, Lace. This is the best thing that's ever happened to me. I couldn't take it down just because you found it very slightly embarrassing. Could I? I mean, really?! Come on."

"I just wanted the truth," said Lacey, teetering on the edge of tears and then going over the edge altogether.

"I'll make it up to you, Lace," I said, as Savannah, Paige, and Sofie went into a whispery cluster. "When I get famous, which will be incredibly soon, I'll get you concert tickets, and if I get any clothes, they're all yours—as soon as I'm done with them, obviously. I mean, just because they'll probably be giving them to me for a photoshoot or a concert, but if that happens I'll have them dry cleaned. I'll do…whatever you want, Lacey."

Lacey snuffled.

"Lacey, babes," said Savannah. "Come sit with me a moment, okay?" She patted the grass next to her.

Something about Savannah's words worked where mine hadn't. Lacey sat back down again. Now it was the four of them, in the sunshine, and me and Jaz in the shade. It couldn't have been more symbolic if it tried.

"Want to know what I'm thinking?" said Savannah.

Lacey did a little shrug.

"It'll cheer you up. Promise."

Then Savannah said something into Lacey's ear, probably about how much of a loser I was or that I was looking especially chubby today or something. Whatever it was, Lacey's eyes widened.

"Of course," she said, and she did look happier. Much happier. It was kind of good but also, if I'm being honest, a little disturbing how quickly she'd cheered up. Then, "It's fine, Katie. And I cannot wait until your single comes out. I really can't."

Paige smirked.

"What?" I said.

"Nothing," said Sofie.

At that moment, the sun went behind a cloud, the bell rang, and lunchtime was over.

And on the way back inside, I saw a clump of bluebells.

Chapter
Twenty-Four

EVERYWHERE I WENT, PEOPLE WERE talking about
Savannah's party. Even Mad Jaz wasn't immune.

"It's going to be the worst party anyone has ever had,"
she told me as the bus fought through the morning traffic.
"There won't be anything decent to drink, and Fin says
that she's going to have *relatives*."

Jaz managed to make the word "relatives" sound like a
stomach flu.

"So you're not going to be there tonight?"

Mad Jaz looked at me as though I was mad. "Of course
I'm going."

"She invited you?"

"No."

My understanding of the inner workings of Jaz was still
at the beginner level.

"And Nicole's bringing this home brew she made with a

recipe from this iffy Spanish website. It's got stuff in it that you should in no way ever drink."

"Er, great." The bus went around the corner by the garden center and did this sort of lurchy, belchy thing that sent a backdraft of fumes up and into my lungs. I tried not to breathe and failed and felt a little sick.

"It will be." Jaz looked pleased. "If anyone can create something insane, it's Nicole." She scrolled down on her phone. "Hey, so apparently she tried to give herself a hickey last night. She'd read you get a good one if you suck really hard, so she used the end of a vacuum cleaner."

"I might not have any of Nicole's home brew," I said. "I probably need to protect my voice, what with my single coming out soon. They'll be needing me to do some live gigs."

"Oh, right," said Jaz, peering at her screen.

"I know, isn't it incredible that I have a single coming out?" I said. Then, because the sixth-graders were shouting about something and Jaz didn't seemed to have heard, I said it again. "A single coming out."

"Good." She was still looking at her phone.

"Um, what time are you getting to Savannah's?"

"Around eleven."

Eleven? Eleven was when I would be going home. I tried not to let this show on my face as I said, "Okay, cool, yeah. I might be there a little earlier, but not much. Late nights and pop stars don't mix."

"Yeah they do," said Jaz.

"Just, you know, with the single coming out and everything…"

Jaz did this epic sigh. "All right, fine. Play it."

Another corner, and now we were on the fast part of the road heading up to school, where all the trees hang low over the road, and three years ago a piece of the bus roof got caught on one and came off. There were pictures all over the *Harltree Gazette*. I hadn't thought about it at all since then, but I did now. Because presumably I'd be on the front of the *Harltree Gazette* again soon. I was just as exciting as a low tree. Maybe even more so.

Except…

"They still haven't sent it to me."

"Why not?"

"I don't know," I said, wishing I'd had the idea to ask at the time. "I'm probably going in again soon though, to talk about the album and the tour and everything. They must be waiting for that."

"When?" Funny how when I wanted Jaz to listen, she never would. But the very second we got into stuff that I would rather have left alone, she grabbed and hung on and wouldn't let go, like when the next-door neighbor's dog got under the fence and dug up the body of Amanda's hamster.

"They haven't said. Soon. It's got to be soon. At the meeting, Tony said time was really important. We have to keep up the momentum. You know how it is."

And then we got to school or, to give its real title, Savannah's Pre-Party Warm-Up Zone.

And if I'd had someone to get ready with later, then maybe I'd have been excited too.

Me and Lacey were so good at getting ready for parties. The getting ready part was always the best part too. Having Lace do my liquid eyeliner with flicky bits curling up at the ends and me gluing fake eyelashes onto her and once pretending one was a spider so she screamed and covered us both with a bowl of veggie chips. Trying on every last thing in whoever's house we were at, or dancing to Beyoncé in our heels and tights.

I wasn't going to let this…thing go on any longer, I decided. Being a celebrity was a lonely business, and I didn't want to end up in a humongous mansion all on my own, collecting shoes I couldn't walk in and probably having a ton of plastic surgery because there wouldn't be anyone around to tell me I shouldn't.

I'd figure it out at the party. Whether she wanted to or not.

♪♫♩♫

As it turned out, I did have someone to get ready with. A brown furry thing that came scuttling across the floor while I was trying to squeeze myself into Amanda's green dress. For a second, I thought it was a huge spider, and then I realized it was either a mouse or a baby rat and that this was both better and also worse. Especially when I then saw a spider two minutes later hanging next to the door.

I pulled on my sparkly tights. It certainly was quicker, getting ready this way. Even the curly eyeliner worked on the first try. I hadn't gotten to the end of "Single Ladies," and I was hot to trot.

Then, because it was still only seven thirty and Jaz had made it clear that arriving at a party in the first hour is literally the most embarrassing thing anyone can do, I sat back down on my bed and contemplated going downstairs for something to eat. There were definitely fish sticks in the kitchen, and I thought I remembered a half dozen eggs too. Not quite the chocolate fountains and cotton candy and personalized pizzas that the rest of my classmates were currently enjoying for dinner. But then, like Jaz said, you don't go to a party to eat. Or have fun.

Exactly what you *do* go to a party for, she hadn't said.

I emptied out my backpack and started pouring it into my evening bag, which was by far the best thing I'd ever found in Harltree's secondhand store. A little, black, shiny leather purse with a real metal chain, far too small to take anything more than my phone and wallet, which made it completely impractical but also really lovely. I was just pushing everything else into a pile when I saw some gold writing. A piece of card. Tony's card. With his phone number on it.

And then the feeling that had been nagging me since my conversation with Jaz came creeping back.

Why hadn't Tony sent me my single? Especially when playing it at the party would make everything work out right, once and for all.

All right, not quite everything.

But most of the important stuff.

Well, it would make me look cool, and really, everything else was just details.

Could I ring him and ask for it on a Friday night?

A little much.

But then, this *was* an emergency.

Then—of course—I knew what to do. I wouldn't do anything stupid, like wait until Monday.

I'd send him a text!

Hey Tony, it's Katie here. I was just wondering if my
single was ready because if you could maybe send it
to me I could play it at this party I'm going to tonight.
Thanks! Katie xo

The reply took forever to come. Long enough to decide
that the xo had definitely been a mistake. Long enough for
me to pluck my eyebrows, then overpluck my eyebrows,
then draw them back in again with an eyebrow pencil.

Finally, when my lower forehead was at pretty much
the limit of what it could take, I got a response:

Katie, good to hear from you! Sorry, it's still being
mixed at the moment. Sounds terrific though. You're
going to love it. T

Well, it was something. Straightaway, I texted back.

I don't mind playing whatever version you have!
Also, you said I was touring soon…? Where? Want
to invite my friends! So excited! Kx

Another eternity, this time long enough for me to apply
nail polish and let it almost dry and then check to see if it had
dried with just the lightest touch of my thumb and ruin it.

Will be in touch about that soon. Got some great venues lined up. Madison Square Garden. The Hollywood Bowl. And heard of a little place called Wembley?

The spider-mouse-rat finished doing whatever it had been doing down under my bed and zoomed off back across my rug.

"Amanda?" I shouted. "Manda, are you there? I have news. Manda?!"

Nothing. Just the *drip-plunk* noise of the hot water tank filling up.

I looked in the mirror and said, over and over again, "You are going to be a star."

Somehow, I wasn't quite feeling it.

♪ ♫ ♫ ♪

In the end, I got to Savannah's at nine thirty. Which was interesting, because I've never turned up late to a party before. I've only ever seen the late turner-uppers, who've always seemed just awesomely cool.

Maybe I wasn't doing it quite right, or maybe I simply wasn't cool enough, because turning up late wasn't as much fun as Jaz had made it sound.

The tent was off the chart, of course, completely enormous

and taking up most of Savannah's massive garden, almost like a real room with lights and speakers and everything.

Only it wasn't quite a room. The air was simultaneously cold and hot and smelled of trampled grass. There was a small tree in the middle, which someone had covered with pink crepe paper to try to disguise the fact that it was a tree. And you could hear the generator even over the stereo.

Plus, for all her catering talk, Savannah's not the biggest eater, and she'd clearly hugely underordered. The chocolate fountains had run dry, the cupcakes were gone, and there weren't even any chips left.

Now, here's the thing.

According to every movie and TV show and article ever, it's stupid to feel ugly and awkward at a party. Because everyone else there might *look* as though they are having a great time. They might *seem* as if they are confident and relaxed and gorgeous and happy. But, deep down inside, they're completely miserable and insecure and not enjoying themselves any more than you are.

I'd always been a little suspicious of this.

And I have to say that Savannah's party proved once and for all that it is *a complete bunch of lies*.

I know this because I spent a full fifteen minutes closely observing everyone in that tent, and they were all having the most marvelous time. Ignoring me.

After an infinity of staring at Sofie's streakily self-tanned back, I gave up trying to penetrate Savannah Circle and went and stood next to Devi Lester and his friends. He, at least, would be grateful for a little of the Katie Cox stardust.

"What?" said Devi, after about twelve minutes of talk about Star Wars.

"Nothing," I said, going back to the food table in case there were any chips that I hadn't spotted the first time around. There weren't.

There was Lacey though, coming in from the garden with the canal crowd. Wearing a purple top I'd never seen before. She *had* been to the secondhand store—*without me*.

"Helter-skelter!" she was saying. Everyone in the vicinity cracked up. She turned to me. "Katie!"

"Hey, Lace! Ha-ha!"

"Why are *you* laughing?"

"Because…it was funny?"

"You missed the beginning," said Lacey, her eyes shining with a very particular kind of cruelty. "You don't know what we were talking about."

"Sorry," I said, simultaneously wanting to disappear and die. You don't point that kind of stuff out when people can hear. Especially not to your best friend. Even to your ex-best friend.

"So what's been happening?" I said in this super casual way.

They all stared at me, then started giggling.

I was starting to think that this evening might have been a mistake when—

"Katie, have you got a lighter? This is, I don't know his name. He was outside the liquor store. Boy, this party sucks."

Jaz was in this humongous black ball gown, slashed up the legs to show all this red netting stuff, and she had about six chokers around her neck. One was a pair of interlocking hands, which made it look like she was being strangled by her own jewelry. Plus, she seemed to be wearing all the makeup in the universe. Really. It was a miracle she could keep her eyes open. And the strange thing was that she still managed to look incredibly messy, what Grandma would call "slovenly," as if she'd sort of fallen into her clothes, even though getting that outfit together must have taken forever.

"Hi, Jaz. No, sorry, I haven't got a lighter. I find them a little frightening, actually. Mands has them for burning incense, and I always worry she'll set fire to her fingers."

"Well," said Jaz, looking at me with disdain through about thirty-seven coats of mascara, "it was a long shot."

"Hi, Nicole," I said. "And hi…you."

The guy Jaz had brought shuffled and took a swig from a small bottle.

"How's your, erm, hickey, Nicole?"

Nicole answered by pulling down the neck of her polo shirt and showing me. I sort of wished I hadn't asked.

"Whoa," said Jaz's guy. "That is blowing my mind."

"I know," I said. "I'm probably going to have nightmares about it later. Nicole, should you maybe put something on it? Or go to the doctor?"

"Not that," said Jaz's bloke. "*That*."

I followed his eyes to the middle of the dance floor, where two people who I assumed were either Savannah's parents or her servants (or, from their exhausted expressions, possibly both) were unveiling the world's most ridiculous cake.

It was five tiers high, kind of like a wedding cake, if a wedding cake had been pimped so hard that it barely stayed up. Each layer was a different color, with gold decorations on it and flowers and candles. And then—

"Darling, lift up your feet?" The man pulled out an extension cord and plugged it into the generator, and then the thing lit up like Vegas, and a literal waterfall started coming down from the top. *Sploosh sploosh sploosh.*

It was simultaneously the best and the worst thing I'd ever seen.

"I *love* it," Savannah shrieked. "I *love* it! I mean, it's smaller than in the picture. But I love it!"

Jaz had now made her way over to the speakers and was

hooking up her phone. Ambient Karamel made way for a *bang-bang-bang* bass overlaid with a man who sounded like he was being burned alive.

"No!" said Savannah, gliding across the floor like a seriously angry swan.

"No offense, Sav," said Jaz, "but your taste in music is garbage."

"Yours is worse," said Savannah.

"I am not staying to listen to that boy band puking into my head."

"Fine by me," said Savannah.

Not quite fine by me though, seeing as how Jaz was the only person at this party who had bothered to talk to me.

"There must be something we can all listen to," I said, searching through her library for some Mad Jaz/Savannah crossover music. A sort of sugar-pop metal hard-house fusion. Oddly enough, there didn't seem to be anything that would even slightly work.

"It's too bad you won't let us play your single," said Jaz. "It's literally the only thing we both want to hear."

"You know I don't have it yet," I said.

"So sad," said Savannah with pity.

Lacey was just coming back in from the garden and even though I waved at her, she looked straight through me. As though I was a ghost. Not even the scary kind that get to star in horror films, but the invisible kind that just trails around after living people, waiting to get noticed for the rest of all eternity.

Wembley Arena though. She'd notice me then.

But by the time I was at Wembley, she'd just be a dot in the crowd. I needed her to see me *now*.

"How about I sing it live?" I said.

The canal crowd came bobbing along behind her.

"You know, unplugged. Acoustic!"

There was no time to think whether or not this was a good idea because right away, Jaz was turning off the stereo, and everyone stopped talking.

A space opened up around me.

Lacey's eyes met mine, and I felt myself go solid again.

This was my chance.

To show her.

To show everyone.

I opened my mouth and in my head the song swelled up behind me, a huge wave, and I let it rise, and rise, until it lifted me. And then I opened my mouth and sang.

"I got mad skin,

I got mad hair…"

And right away, I knew I'd made a truly epic mistake.

Chapter Twenty-Five

BASICALLY, THERE WAS A COMPLETE disconnect between how the song sounded in my head, i.e., magical and awesome and amazing, and how it sounded in Savannah's mega-tent. And that was—and I'm not going to linger on this because it is too, too painful—was not magical or awesome or amazing. It was small and sad and garbage.

I got through the first part though, and while I missed having my guitar there every last second, I was just starting to think that maybe it would be, and if not okay then at least not suicide-level awful.

Only then, while I was singing, that guy, the one Jaz had picked up like the rest of us might pick up a penny, started looking kind of restless, shaking his little bottle, then said in a very loud voice, "What else is there to drink?"

And—total traitor weirdo that she was—Jaz said, "Probably not much. I told you this party would be bad."

I continued on, louder now, and shifted my eyes over to just behind Dominic Preston's gorgeous head.

And Dominic was talking too! Whispering to Devi Lester. Aaaaaargh!

I was still singing, which was my second mistake. If I'd stopped at the end of the first verse, maybe I could have saved myself, pretended I'd always meant to end there, while at least some people were still listening.

No, though. Toothpaste for brains Katie has to plow on through like a sad slug and—

"*Savannah!*" Paige came whizzing in. "Karl is making out with Nicole. In your roses!"

And that was that. The whole crowd relocated itself outside to see Nicole and Karl.

I couldn't join them, since I was trapped in my own song, flailing around somewhere toward the end of the second verse.

Still, at least I didn't have to worry about where to point my eyeballs anymore, because the only person left in the disaster zone was me.

"Oh, Katie."

And Lacey.

I stopped singing.

It was very quiet.

Except for some laughter from outside and then a

double shriek. It sounded like Savannah had thrown Karl and Nicole onto the grass. Savannah is surprisingly strong for someone who makes stick insects look pudgy.

"You poor thing."

Lacey came over and went to hug me. Only, because she was Lacey, she gave up at the last minute and half draped her hand on my shoulder, as though she was patting me and I was an injured horse.

I realized that no one had put their arms around me in a while.

"That was a little embarrassing," I said.

"A little?!" said Lacey, and we both laughed.

"Can we…can we be friends again?" I said. "Because all this stuff is really wearing me out."

"Me too," said Lacey. "It's hard enough having to do the walk every morning on my own, without having to spend all day being upset."

This I did not understand. "But you're not on your own. You're with the canal crowd."

"Who toss my bag in the water and call me 'Lacey with the stupid facey.'"

"Do they?"

"They always did. And they do it even more now that you're gone."

"I thought you were all pals?"

"I have to pretend it's okay," said Lacey, "or I think they might throw me in too." She sighed. "I can handle the occasional dunking. But not every day. Not on my own."

Which made perfect sense. Man, life can be hideous sometimes.

"I'm not much enjoying the bus," I said.

"But you and Mad Jaz are total besties these days." She said it in this flat, sad way and I felt very, very bad.

"We're friends, I guess. Just about. Sometimes I even really like her. I mean, she's funny, and she's exciting and she's…" I stopped, because this didn't seem to be going over so well. "But, Lace, she's like an unexploded bomb. I just never know what she's going to do next and it's really…"—I searched for the right word—"tiring. Like, just now, she was the one who wanted me to sing. And then she talked right through it! You'd never do that."

"No way," agreed Lacey.

We had this nice moment, Lacey blinking at me from beneath her bangs, which were looking pretty good since she'd straightened them for the evening. Which I was about to tell her that when she said, "I missed getting ready with you tonight."

"Me too! Oh, Lacey."

We hugged, properly this time, and it was the best of the best.

"I'm so sorry I lied about the video. I'd do anything for us to be friends again. All I want to do, literally, is for us to watch *Mean Girls* and have pizza. That is my complete vision of happiness right now."

"Mine too," said Lace.

"I need you in my life."

"And I need you," said Lacey. "I hate before and after school now. They used to be my favorite parts of the day."

"And how am I supposed to cope with all this fame stuff on my own? I need our friendship. To ground me. Otherwise, I'll probably turn into one of those crazy people who only eat blue M&M's and won't let anyone make eye contact."

"Katie, just stop."

I was so busy thinking whether it was the blue M&M's I'd eat or whether the orange ones were actually better or whether M&M's were a little too American and it would be more patriotic to have Smarties, in which case I'd definitely go for the orange ones, that it took me a second to realize what she'd said. "Stop what?"

"It's not that your songs aren't good. You know I like them. But all this stuff about a record label—"

"It's called Top Music."

"Is it?" She fiddled with her zipper, then looked me in the eye. And I could kind of see why some celebrities didn't like having friends. "Is that really what it's called?"

"I don't understand," I said, because I didn't.

"You don't need to pretend. Or maybe you do, to everyone else. If you want to stay on Planet Savannah, then, okay. But don't pretend to me. Not if we're friends like you say we are."

"Pretend what?"

"Come on, Katie. There wasn't a recording studio, was there?"

Which is when I began to think that things were even worse than I'd realized.

"Of course there was."

"It's okay. You've let it all go too far, and it's embarrassing to admit it's made up, I know, so I'm not going to make a big thing of it. But I don't get why you need to tell all these…"—and I saw her reach for the word "lies" before stopping herself and saying—"*stories* about a label and a single and a tour and whatever. I think we'd all respect you more if you just told the truth."

"But I did. I was."

"It's over, Katie. You've had your five minutes, and now it's done, and we can all get back to normal."

She said it so kindly. And I did think, as a series of shrieks from the other side of the canvas told me that the tent was about to fill up again, that maybe I could even go with it. I could nod and not talk about it again and wait until the single came out. And in the meantime we could be true friends, like before.

But I mean, really—how could I be friends with someone who thought I was a liar?

Then there was Sofie, standing, framed in lights, the garden dark behind her, shouting, "Look! It's Harltree's number-one superstar!"

And Lacey laughed.

"You don't know anything," I said. "You're the world's most ignorant person. You think I'd make up something like that?"

She stopped laughing, and a distant part of my brain noticed that I was talking very loudly.

"I *have* recorded a single. A real single in a real recording studio. In real London."

"You lied about getting Jaz to take the video down. You wouldn't let me come with you to the studio. You couldn't even get Savannah her Karamel tickets. I mean, you've got literally no evidence whatsoever. Not even a photo. Why should we believe you?"

"Because…" I searched through my head. "They had special pencils, and giant bowls of candy everywhere, and you could have as much as you wanted. And the room was this bizarre soundproofed box and there was a sort of thing over the microphone that looked like a stretched pair of tights and—how can you think I'm making this up? It's true. All of it. I recorded a single. My single."

"Then why can't we listen to it?" said Paige.

"Because it's not out yet!" I shouted. "There is a reason that this stuff takes a while, and you wouldn't understand because, unlike me, you are not in the music industry. But there is a single and I am going on a tour, really, really soon. To Madison Square Garden. In New York."

"Of course you are, babes," said Savannah.

"And Wembley!" I said. Now everyone at the party was standing and staring at me, and a tiny part of my brain chose to inform me that I now had the audience I wanted, just ten minutes too late. "I am playing Wembley Arena!"

"Let it go," said Lacey.

"Fine," I screamed. "I don't even care what you think. Because I don't need you! You're losers, you know that? Boring, pointless losers. And I have integrity and talent and dignity, and I am taking them somewhere else."

I turned around, tripped over the extension cord, and crashed right into Savannah's stupid cake.

Chapter
Twenty-Six

I'VE HAD PARTIES END BADLY before. There was the time when I was seven and we all went to an ice cream parlor and ate ten different types of ice cream, and I threw up ten different types of ice cream all the way home. Or the time I accidentally left in Paige's coat and then had to spend the next semester trying to convince everyone I hadn't been trying to steal it.

Even so, standing outside Savannah's house, wearing her cake, for a full half hour while I waited for Amanda to come and pick me up was a new low.

"What?" she said, as I slid into the seat beside her, dripping gold icing all over the upholstery.

"It's nothing. I'm fine."

"Okay."

She crunched the gears and I remembered, as I only ever do when it's too late, that it took Amanda four attempts before she passed her driver's test, and even then she only scraped by. And then literally scraped through on her way home.

"All right," I admitted. "I'm not quite fine."

Her eyes darted to take in my jacket, which was slathered with frosting. And globs of pistachio and rose or lemon and cherry or diamond dust and unicorn tears or whatever it was that Savannah's poor team of bakers had stuck in there.

I'd eaten quite a lot of it while I was waiting. But that still left most of it.

"Katie, have you been…?" Amanda tailed off. "What have you been…? How have you…?"

"Savannah had a very large birthday cake. 'Had' being the operative word."

"Is that one of those monster ones from the place by the junction? I love those cakes! They were on TV a few weeks ago; they send them all around the country. They have ones with speakers inside them that play music, and they did this one full of live butterflies, so that when you cut into it—"

"You get a load of cut-up butterflies?"

"Yes, it's pretty hard to see how that would work," said Amanda. "But Savannah had one?"

"She did. Until I fell into it."

"God." Then, "It was an accident, I hope?"

"*Of course* it was an accident!"

"It's just…"

I felt the tears start coming. "Not you too."

"All right, all right, I'm not saying you did it on purpose. Don't get angry while I'm driving, please."

I made an attempt at pulling myself together, which meant singing Shania Twain lyrics in my head. I had to do the whole of "Man, I Feel Like a Woman" and half of "That Don't Impress Me Much" before I was calm enough to say, "They didn't believe me. About all the Top Music stuff. They think I'm making it up."

"Really? Even Lacey?"

"Even Lacey," I said.

"But you've got all those views!"

"Apparently that's not enough."

"Well, I guess it's understandable," said Amanda finally, after we'd got through a particularly scary one-way intersection. "I mean, it doesn't seem very likely, does it?"

"Why does everyone think it's so crazy that I could finally make something of my life?"

There was a long part where we just drove in silence. Well, Amanda did the actual driving, but I did quite a lot of pretend steering in my head, especially when we had to go down the narrow section at the end of the main street.

Then, finally: "You *are* making something of your life," said Amanda. "This is your life. Here and now. Your family and friends and school and home. We're not…some waiting room that you have to sit in until you finally get called into the amazing place you think you deserve to be in."

We drove some more.

"They'll see when the single comes out," I said. "I just wish Tony would tell me when that is going to be. And when are we shooting the video? Or will they use the one we recorded?"

Amanda made a noise that somehow told me she didn't know and also didn't care. She was probably still wrapped up in all that store stuff.

Finally, we were at the house. I opened the car door and there was that fresh, outside smell blowing in from the trees and the fields and the sky.

And as we went up the driveway, I saw that the curtains weren't quite shut. There was a slice of light, and in it, I caught a glimpse of Mom and Adrian curled up on the sofa. Their faces were lit gold by whatever was on the TV, and Mom was smiling at something.

And I thought, *At least I'm safe now.*

I'm home.

"Katie, hey." Adrian got up the second he saw me. "Glad you're back early. I was just about to have some nachos. Want to share?"

"Actually," I said, "I'm going to bed."

"You sure?" he said. "I'll put extra cheese on. Just the way you like them. It'll be a one-to-one ratio of cheddar to chips."

My stomach sent me a message to say that a load of squashed icing didn't exactly constitute dinner, so I nodded and followed him into the kitchen. Where he shut the door with an expression that said this hadn't been about triangular chips.

"I wanted to talk to you."

"What about?"

"I was on the phone with Tony, asking about this tour."

Bubbles, gold and sparkly, came fizzing through my chest and out of my mouth in a giddy laugh. The timing could not have been more perfect!

I saw myself unrolling a poster, maybe in assembly, Savannah and co. being nice, Lacey begging to be my friend again, and Jaz... Well, I wasn't sure what Jaz would do. Hopefully something good.

"Oh my God. Oh my God! Because he talked about it

at our meeting, but then I didn't hear anything, and I was starting to worry, but this means it's all about to kick off, doesn't it? Oh my God!"

He put his hand to his forehead. "You can't go, Katie."

"*What?*"

"It's everything we said you wouldn't do. Foreign travel. Missing your classes."

"So? I don't care if I miss some school. I can catch up easily enough."

"No."

"Can't they send a tutor or something?"

"Oh, and you think you'll be able to concentrate on quadratic equations in the back of some bus?"

"I can't concentrate on them when I am at school," I said truthfully. "So maybe a change of venue would be helpful. Worth exploring, anyway."

"No," said Adrian.

"Let me just speak to Tony," I said. "I'm sure there's a way—"

"There's no point," said Adrian. "I told him that it wasn't going to happen."

Chapter Twenty-Seven

"YOU DID WHAT?" I SAID, and if it had been a movie, the music would have gone frightening and slow.

"I told him it was a no-go." His voice was completely certain, but his eyes, they were looking at the floor, the microwave, the unopened bag of nachos—anywhere except at me. "We agreed that you would be responsible."

I hated him, this man, this nobody that Mom had picked up in the pub who was now ruining my life.

"We did not agree," I said.

If it hadn't been for Adrian, I wouldn't be riding the bus. I'd still be friends with Lacey, I'd have a house that wasn't on the verge of falling down, my sister wouldn't be in ultimate depression mode, and most of all, I'd be going on tour with Top Music. Instead, I'm stuck here, trapped, in this stupid house, going to stupid school surrounded by people who hate me, basically just waiting to die.

"We had a conversation, Katie. Don't say you don't remember because you do."

"*You* had the conversation, and *you* told me that I wasn't taking time off from school. I don't remember getting a say."

"You can't just go running off." His mouth had little white blobs of spit in the corners.

"You can't go telling Top Music what I will and won't do. It's not your place, okay?"

"It is exactly my place," said Adrian. "I'm your manager. It's what I'm here for. I'm the one looking out for you here; you've got to see that. I'm in your corner! Record labels, they pretend they're your friends, but—"

"Just because your career was a complete failure, you think mine's going to be too! Well, it's not, okay? And you are not on my side. If you were, then you'd have actually asked my opinion before you said no." The words came tearing out my mouth before I could stop them. "If you were on my side, then we would have Wi-Fi! If you were on my side, then you wouldn't have dragged my sister into your pathetic failure of a so-called store! If you were on my side, then you would leave us all alone!"

"I—"

I must have been pretty loud because in came Mom.

"What?" she said.

He glanced at me, a sad, hopeless kind of a glance.

"Nothing," I said.

"Are you giving Adrian attitude?" said Mom.

"No," said Adrian. "Katie's okay. It's all okay."

"Yeah," I said. "I was just…upset about the party."

"Why?"

Honestly, can't a girl suffer in peace?

"I fell into a cake," I said. Which was enough to send Mom back into the living room.

"Katie," said Adrian. "Katie."

"I am going to bed," I said. "Good night."

"Can we talk tomorrow? We'll talk about this tomorrow!" His words followed me up the stairs, floating up on a cloud of *we're still friends, aren't we?*-ness, so I shut my bedroom door and left them bobbing about in the hallway.

♪ ♫ ♫

There had to be a way of undoing this.

If I really did have an actual tour lined up and ready, and Adrian had only spoken to Tony a couple of hours ago, then maybe there was still time.

I got my phone out, ready for a text from Lacey, maybe, or Jaz. Or anyone.

Nothing.

Fine fine fine fine, I said to myself. *I do not need them. I do not need anyone. If…*

Hi Tony. Heard you spoke to Adrian earlier.

I hesitated.

Ignore him! He's just a stupid

Not very professional. I deleted and tried again.

He does not have the authority to decide my schedule

A little too professional. Delete.

We got the dates muddled up. I can totally do the tour. Excited!!! Kx

I plugged my phone in to charge and then lay on my rug, noticing, in a sort of vague way, that I had stopped noticing the water stains on my ceiling.

There was something hard just under my head, its corner poking at my skull. So I reached back and flicked whatever it was across the floor.

My lyric book.

I hadn't looked at it in days. It was like seeing an old friend. A genuine friend, not a two-faced canal buddy accuser-toad.

The pages were semitransparent, some of them with grooves from the end of my pen, lines of ink running this way and that as the words crossed and scribbled and sometimes fought with each other and sometimes flowed, up the margins and down into corners, around the staples and jumping between lines like when me and Lacey played Ironic Hopscotch.

There were the lyrics to "Just Me" in three different colors of pen.

And then, a blank page.

There were so many things to write about: horrible parties, renegade managers, so-called friends, miserable sisters. A billion songs' worth of stuff.

I sat up, took a pen from my desk, and began…

Then stopped.

I tried again, the tip of my pen sitting on the paper, pouring out an inky blob. More and more blue, until the paper was wet. Until the point of the pen went straight through the page.

And still, no song.

It was all there, inside me, waiting, but for some reason, it wouldn't come out. Couldn't come through. Like I could hear the words in the distance, but whenever I tried to get close to them, I smacked my face into a wall.

My phone buzzed.

> Hi Katie. That's great news but are you sure? Adrian sounded pretty certain.

Tony was there.

> Am sure.

I shut the book, so those blank pages would stop staring at me.

> Can we have a quick talk? Sorry, I know it's late

I'd barely finished reading his message before I was typing.

> Not 2 late.

The screen began to flash. I took a breath, leaned out the window, and cleared my throat. Which seemed to just dislodge a hidden piece of something, meaning I had to clear it again, harder, and again, before I finally gave up and answered.

"Tony, hi!"

"Oh dear, have you got a cold?"

"No," I said, giving my throat another small scrape and half choking. "I'm completely healthy. And really, I mean it about the tour. It was just a mix-up."

"So it's fine for you to miss school?"

"Definitely."

"This is an issue though," said Tony. "Adrian clearly doesn't want you to go. And he *is* your manager."

"Seriously? Me saying this to you on the phone now about my life and my time doesn't count as much as something that Nose—I mean, Adrian says?"

"He's your official point of contact with us. If he says one thing and you say another… Well, you can see that it presents us with a difficulty."

"He shouldn't have said anything to you without talking to me first," I said. "In fact, I sort of think he shouldn't say anything to you at all. I didn't choose for him to be my manager. He chose himself."

"Ah," said Tony. "I see. I wonder…" I listened to him breathing for a few moments. "I wonder whether he's what you need right now. You and he clearly have different ideas about the direction you need to be going in." He paused. "Creative differences."

Of course. *Of course!*

It was so obvious.

How come I hadn't seen it until now?

"I'll get rid of him," I said. "He doesn't have to me my manager. Does he?"

"That's not what I was suggesting," said Tony. "Adrian's a friend. An old friend." His voice crackled, and I leaned out farther into the night.

"No, but that will solve this. Won't it?"

"I want to be very clear. I'm not asking you to part ways with Adrian. I just thought you could sit down and have a discussion about what you want."

"Or I could get rid of him and just get someone who wants what I want. And what you want. What we want!" It occurred to me that I had literally no clue how you find a manager. "Do you know anyone?"

"We can always find you a manager if that's what you decide."

"Then let's do that!"

"You don't want to talk things through with him? I'm sure he has some good ideas."

"I'm not," I said. "Please. Can we get him out of the picture, and then I'll go on tour, and everything will be like it's supposed to?"

"And we'll find someone to look after you. Good stuff, Katie. You'll tell him?"

"I will," I said.

"Then how about you come in tomorrow for a chat?"

Which would mean skipping school. And on a guitar lesson day too. Then again, without Adrian in the picture, it hardly mattered. "Great," I said. "Around lunchtime?"

"As soon as you can get here," said Tony. His voice was so eager, it was like he was reaching down the phone and pulling me onto the train. "We have so much to talk about."

"Yes! Sorry, I know it's silly, but I was starting to worry that… I don't even know what I was worrying about."

"See you tomorrow," said Tony.

We said good-bye to each other, and as I hung up and pulled myself back inside, I thought how much better everything was now. I had my tour and my single. Two really good things.

Yes, I'd have to tell Adrian.

And ideally find a whole load of new friends to make up for the ones I'd lost earlier.

With my duvet pulled up to my chin and the light off so that the ceiling stains disappeared into the blackness, it really didn't seem so bad.

I'd go to London first thing tomorrow. Momentum— that's what Tony had said I had. We'd sit down, make a plan together. Maybe he'd give me a CD to take home.

I'd come this far. Besides, in case anyone had forgotten, I had over a million hits.

It was all going to be completely fine.

Chapter Twenty-Eight

IT WAS A WEIRD SORT of a night, what with knowing I was about to go on this life-changing mega-tour of amazingness and then have a single come out. Every time I got excited, I remembered that I sort of didn't really have any friends anymore, and went a little flat. And every time I thought about not having any friends anymore, I remembered the single and the tour and got excited again.

So, yet another terrible night's sleep.

I was already a fingernail picker, a pimple popper, and a ponytail sucker; insomnia was a habit I could really do without.

I guess I must have conked out at some point, because then the light coming through my curtains was gray and there were birds screeching, apparently right next to my head.

Living in the country is tough.

And there was a tapping noise coming from somewhere. A woodpecker maybe. Or a rat. Or a horse, or—

"Morning," said Adrian. "Can I come in?"

"All right," I said, trying to shake off dreams of crashing cakes and crazy laughter and something that I couldn't quite remember involving a levitating tractor.

"I'm sorry about last night," he said, sitting down on the end of my rumpled bed. "I couldn't sleep because I was thinking about it. And…I just want the best for you. You do know that?"

"I know that," I said. Not that it helped.

"So I thought we'd go back to Top Music and say that you can tour when school's not in session if you want. And if they don't like that, we'll look for another label. And we'll talk to Zoe, be honest with her this time, tell her all about it. We'll make it work, Katie."

"Adrian—"

"Yeah?"

I focused on his huge furry feet. "I don't think you should be my manager anymore."

He didn't say anything.

"I just figure it'll be better for me to have someone else who's a little more in tune with what I need. But thank you for all your hard work. And everything."

He stood up. "You've decided?"

"I've already told Tony," I said. "So, I guess, yes. I officially have."

What was I expecting? Probably some yelling. Definitely a lecture of some kind.

Instead, he simply got up and left.

So I guess he didn't care that much after all.

♪ ♫ ♫ ♫

An hour later, I was all ready for my secret London mission.

Remembering the *just got out of bed and not in an attractive way* look I'd been sporting last time I'd gone to Top Music, I made sure to wash and dry and brush my hair. Then I packed my gray boots with the too-high heels, a black top, and my good denim skirt. Plus, a lipstick I got free with a magazine, to get the look that Lacey called Big Red Mouth.

The twenty that Amanda kept in her makeup bag would just cover my train fare, and I made sure to eat an especially big breakfast since clearly there wouldn't be time for lunch. Amanda gave me a bit of a look as I went for Cocoa Puffs bowl number three, but I just ignored her.

Adrian was nowhere to be seen. Since our early-morning conversation, I'd been braced for the interrogation from Mom, a whole load of "What did you say to him?" and "How dare you, young lady?" In fact, there was nothing. She just got ready for work while we listened to Florence and the Machine on the radio.

Which gave me a good chance to fine-tune my secret plan. Not that it needed much in the way of fine-tuning, seeing as how it was an awesome plan to begin with. Like all the best plans, it was daring and ambitious, and at the same time really simple and hard to mess up.

So long as the world left me to myself, I'd definitely get away with it.

Given that my current friend count was approximately zero, it didn't seem too unfeasible.

Jaz was already at the bus stop when I got there. Funny how she had skipped school most days for the past year until I started riding the bus, then suddenly she'd become Student of the Year.

I nodded in a way that I hoped she'd realize meant, *Please leave me alone.*

Message undelivered.

"You are so crazy these days, you know that?"

Today she was wearing a full school uniform, only with knee-high lace-up spike boots and her hair in a full beehive.

"You're one to talk," I said, thinking vaguely that I'd never have spoken to Jaz like that a month ago.

Her lips twitched, but I couldn't tell whether it was with laughter or something else. "I'm not the one who blew up at Savannah's party."

"That was an accident."

"Same difference."

"Look," I said, "I am not you, okay? I have good reasons for what happened last night. I am about to become a pretty major celebrity and—"

At which point Jaz doubled over with laughter.

"What?"

"You had a tiny taste of fame," said Jaz. "You couldn't let it go, so you're spinning out this fantasy—"

"My record deal is not a fantasy," I said. Then, "I didn't have you down as automatically believing what everyone else thinks."

She liked that, I could tell. "All right. Prove it."

"I'm going to London today, to talk to Tony Topper who is the head of Top Music, which is a huge record label. We are going to discuss my tour and my single. Lend me your phone, and I'll send you a picture from outside the building if you want. Although I don't know how I'll send it to you. I guess I could send it to Nicole or something. Or, actually, I'll just take the photo and then I can give it back to you tomorrow. I don't know why I didn't think of that first."

Jaz's mouth opened like a Venus flytrap that had just finished chomping a fly and was getting ready for more. "You're skipping school to go up to London? Today?"

So much for my secret plan. "Tell the whole universe, why don't you?"

"You think *I'm* mad," said Jaz, "but I've never been to London instead of going to English."

At which, I have to say, I felt a little bit of pride. I'd out-Jazzed Jaz! Or, at least, I was about to.

The bus came, and I sat apart from the others, up at the front, thinking that I'd shared quite enough of today's plan, seeing as how it was supposed to be classified information and all.

Nicole was attempting to wax her nostrils with masking tape as Jaz came and sat in front of me, melting the little man who had been sitting there with one quick blast of her laser stare. Genuinely, I think he just turned into a puddle because one second he was there, and the next it was Jaz, leaning back to face me. She smelled of toothpaste and extremely strong perfume, which surprised me, since I'd always thought she looked like she needed to wash her face a little.

"What time are you going, then?"

"I don't have to tell you," I said.

"No, but you want to."

Correct, as ever. How did she know this stuff? "I was going to change on here, get off a stop early, and walk to the station."

"So not even go to assembly?"

"No. You never do."

Jaz seemed pleased that I'd noticed. "Yeah. If you turn up and then leave, they'll only come looking for you."

"Exactly."

"What time are you planning on getting there?"

"Around twelve, I guess."

"You'll never make it if you walk to the station. Takes way too long."

"Does it?"

She gave me this pitying look.

"So what do I do?"

"Easy," said Jaz. "We'll hitchhike."

"What?" I said. And then, I really digested what she'd just said. "*We?*"

Chapter Twenty-Nine

PEOPLE I DID NOT WANT to come to Top Music with me:

- Adrian
- Ms. McAllister
- Jack the Ripper
- Mad Jaz

Honestly, I tried everything to make her go away. Which included looking awkward, having big silences fall between us, and in the end, literally telling her to go away.

It was like I was speaking French or something. Not only did she not seem to understand, but she also didn't seem to care. That had always been Jaz's attitude to French, and maybe explained why her foreign-exchange partner had to go back to Paris a week early.

To start with, the hitchhiking thing was totally terrifying.

"Jaz, we can't. Suppose we get kidnapped?"

"No one would want to kidnap *you*, Katie."

Harsh. "They might want to kidnap you."

She put her hands on her hips. "There is no way anyone is kidnapping me."

And actually, she was so scary that I kind of had to agree with her.

We went and stood down by the main road, Jaz sticking her thumb out as though she'd done this a thousand times before, and I thought, *This isn't real. I really* am *in a movie*. Which then made me wonder what kind it was. *Thriller? Maybe. Uplifting comedy? Probably not. Disaster movie? Definitely.*

That's when a car stopped and a man rolled down his window.

"Take us to the train station, okay?"

"I'm not going that way," said the man, but by that time, Jaz was already in the passenger seat.

"What are you waiting for?" she asked.

We didn't get snatched in the end. In fact, he was quite sweet and promised he would buy my single for his goddaughter. Although as I said to Jaz, one not-murderer doesn't mean that everyone else is a not-murderer too.

By this time we were on the train, and as I finished

talking the woman opposite us said, in a loud and bossy voice, "Shouldn't you ladies be in school?"

Jaz's reply made it very clear that she was not a lady.

I guess I should have known from our time on the bus that she wouldn't be the most-relaxing travel companion. Her feet went straight onto the seat across from us (which is when the bossy woman gave up and went away), and she played Slipknot at top volume on her phone. Then, when she got bored with that, she went through all her ringtones one by one. I'd have strangled her except that she'd have killed me for it. And all the time, she kept giving me these little glances, like she was challenging me to something— only I didn't know what.

Then we were at Liverpool Street and the subway.

"Covent Garden," I said. "That's the Central Line and then one stop on the blue one."

And then she stopped trying to swipe gummy snakes from this candy stand and stared at me. "You're really serious, aren't you?"

"Of course."

"I thought you'd have given up by now."

"Why would I do that?"

"So…" Jaz couldn't have looked more surprised if I'd grown a tail. "We're going to this music place. To talk about your tour."

"I'm going," I said. "I'd really prefer you didn't though."

"Huh," said Jaz. "You were telling the truth. This is going to be even better than I thought."

♪♫♫♫

The woman at the reception desk wasn't nearly as smiley as last time, probably because Jaz had picked up a stack of magazines and was asking, "Can I keep these?" while I said, "It's me!"

"Who?" said the receptionist.

"Katie. Katie Cox. I'm here to see Tony Topper."

"Is he expecting you?" said Ms. Frosty.

"He said to come anytime today."

"Hold on." She picked up her phone and dialed.

"How come she doesn't know who you are?" said Jaz. "I thought you were their supercool new singer."

"I have a Katie Cox here to see you." The receptionist nodded. "Yes." Then she smiled at me. "Sixth floor."

"Thanks," I said. Then, to Jaz, "See!"

The turnstile opened and we stepped into a waiting elevator. There was a huge mirror on one side, and I couldn't help but notice that my face was completely white with excitement. This was really and truly happening.

I pushed my hair behind my ears. Maybe Lacey had been right about me needing bangs. No. No, she hadn't.

"Nicole? Yeah, it's important. I'm with her. In London. The music stuff—it's true. We're going in now. Tell everyone." Jaz saw me staring and turned around from her phone. "What?"

"Jaz, I'm skipping school. It's maybe best if she doesn't tell *everyone*—"

Then the door opened and there was Tony.

"Katie! Come on into my office. That's right this way…"

"Hi!" I looked meaningfully at Jaz, so that she'd be sure to hear everything we said. "I'm here! To talk about my tour and my new manager and my single and my album and everything."

"Of course!" He looked *so* happy.

"Like you said, keep up the momentum!" I knew I was babbling a little, but hopefully he hadn't noticed. He was looking at something to my left.

"I'm Jasmine," said Jaz.

"She wanted to come," I said, feeling like I should add something but not knowing what. "And now, here she is."

"Here I am," said Jaz, her head swiveling like crazy as she took it all in—the posters, the spotlights, all that glass.

Please don't do anything, I said to myself. *Please, Jaz. Behave.*

"Can I get you anything?" said Tony.

"I'm fine," I said.

"What have you got?" said Jaz.

"Um. The usual, tea, coffee, juices—"

"Can I have a vodka?" said Jaz.

"Er, how old are—" he began, then, looking at Jaz, "A vodka it is."

A very good-looking boy was sent off to get Jaz's vodka, and we sat down opposite Tony and a big, heavy wooden desk. I glanced around. More pictures of famous musicians, a huge black-and-white one of a bridge, an enormous vase holding an even more enormous arrangement of white flowers, and a photo of Tony with his arm around a blond who I really hoped was his daughter because, otherwise, ew.

"Where's Katie, then?"

"Mmm?"

Jaz waved at the posters: Karamel enjoying their antigravity haircuts; Crystal Skye huddling over a piano, all eyes and shoulders, like she'd just come through a famine. "There should be one of Katie."

"I don't want to be on a poster," I said even though I really did.

"If you say so," said Jaz.

"Anyway," I said, wanting to get things feeling positive, "I told Adrian."

Tony smiled and leaned in, looking at me with this intensity that, on anyone else, would have been slightly scary. "What did he say? What, exactly, did he say?"

"Not a lot," I said. "It was fine."

He seemed surprised. "Really? Tell me everything."

"I just told him that we clearly had different ideas about where I was going and that it might be better if I was managed by someone else."

"He must have been hurt though," said Tony.

"Honestly? Yes, I think he was."

"Good," said Tony.

"You're pretty twisted," said Jaz.

I gave Tony a look that was supposed to say, *Jaz is so weird, but don't worry; she's completely harmless.*

"So…my tour, then. How long do you want me to play for? And will I have a backing band because I should rehearse with them, and I guess it'll have to be pretty soon if I'm going off soon."

"What do you want?" said Tony. He spoke slowly, carefully. Like he'd been planning it for a while. "Tell me, Katie. Tell me exactly what it is that you want. Tell me your dream."

"Just…to make good music. To connect with people. I guess."

"There must be more."

"I…don't know."

"Then I'll tell you," said Tony, licking his lower lip, staring at me harder than ever. "You want the whole world to hear you. You want to stand on a stage and play to millions. You want the house and the pool and the cars. You want the girls, screaming your name. You want it all."

"Girls?" said Jaz.

Tony's eyes bored into mine. "You want it all."

"Maybe."

"Say it. Say, 'I want it all.'"

"I…I want it all."

"Louder."

"*I want it all.*"

"And you'll never have any of it."

"Um, what?"

"Remember this feeling, Katie. Because I want you to tell him. I want him to see it in your eyes."

"What's going on?"

And Tony said, "There will be no single. There will be no album. There will be no tour."

"But we recorded… You said… We agreed…"

"How does it feel?" said Tony. "How does it feel to be on the brink of something and have it snatched away?"

And then I knew, and it felt like falling down, down, down. "You can't," I said. "This isn't…right."

"What is going on?" said Jaz.

Tony smiled at her as though she'd asked him for the time. "A very long time ago, I was in a band. We recorded a single. We were going to make it very big indeed. But before we could, someone split us up."

"But you said…you forgave him!" I stuttered. "You said it was all okay!"

"Did I ever say that?" said Tony. "Did I ever say it was 'all okay'?"

And I could see that it really, really wasn't.

My heart was fluttering around in my chest like a trapped hummingbird. Because if there was no single, no tour, no nothing, then what would I tell Lacey? What would I do?

And what had I done?

"I'm not him," I pleaded. "You can't…you can't punish me just because… You can't!"

"You will tell him, won't you? How he ruined your life? I hope you will," said Tony, the base of his neck flushing ham pink. "We were *right there*, Katie. The whole nation was going to see us, and he walks out without a care in the world. Well, this time, this time he'll care."

"He still cares!" I said. "For your information, he's still upset about it now, like, a billion years later!"

"It was *one song*," said Tony. "It was prerecorded. All

he had to do was stand there and mime. But we're in the studio, and the audience is sitting down, and the lights come on, and suddenly he's all 'What are we doing, Tony?' and 'Are we losing our way?' and 'We're a live band, not puppets,' and then he's asking why we were there, what music is really for. And so I told him. It's for making money! And we were about to make more money than we'd ever dreamed of. And then…he just walks off the set."

"I'm glad he did!" I said. "Imagine if he'd spent the rest of his life with *you*!"

That got him. The hairy part between his open collar turned the color of minced beef. "That useless piece of… What's he made of himself? Nothing! Just some pointless little store in the middle of nowhere, never married, beer gut like a—"

"*Leave him alone!*" I screamed.

"Oh, now I will," said Tony, suddenly calm as anything again. He picked up a phone. "Security?"

"But…he said you were old friends. He was at your wedding…"

"Yeah," said Tony, as two men in dark jackets appeared behind the glass doors.

"It's my song. You can't just—" Then one of the men had his arm around my shoulder.

"Come on," said the security guy.

"Tony!" I shouted, then, to the security guard, "Get *off me!* Tony? Tony!"

He was standing, watching me, his arms folded.

"Take it easy," said the security guy. "Let's get you downstairs."

So I turned around. Which was a real shame, since I missed Jaz throwing the vase of flowers into Tony's face.

♪♫♫♫

And then we were back outside, with the rest of Covent Garden carrying on as if no one's life had been ruined.

Jaz checked her watch. "It's still early," she said. "Let's go steal stuff from Zara."

I was scrolling through the contacts on my phone, up and down, up and down. Not Amanda—I'd only get a lecture. And not Mom—no, no. Not Dad either—he'd probably start telling me the latest about Catriona's Pilates studio.

I went right the way back around until I got back to *A.* Adrian.

Adrian would figure it out.

He was on my side. He'd know what to do...

Only his phone went straight to voice mail. I went to redial, and as I did, I saw I had a text from Amanda.

WHERE R U??? Skool called. Ur in LDN???
And Mom found out about record deal.

My hands were shaking as I typed my reply.

Record deal is off. R u with Adrian? Need 2 speak 2
him ASAP

A second, standing outside the tube, with all of London whirling on by, and then—

Mom and Adrian split up.

Chapter Thirty

S O I'D GOTTEN MY WISH.

Adrian was out of my life.

The house would go too, I guessed, what with it being half his. Another home gone. The third one in a year. Surely some kind of record.

I was facedown on my bed when Mom came in. If she noticed I wasn't in my uniform, she didn't say so.

"Katie, love, please don't cry."

I started making this scary whooping, howling noise, and she held me and rocked me, and when that didn't work, she got me a glass of water. You can't drink water and howl at the same time. When I got to the bottom of the glass, I still wasn't feeling any better, but at least I'd stopped sounding like I needed to be in a mental institution.

"Mom," I said. "Oh, Mom." My head found its way onto her shoulder, smelling that familiar mix of the special detergent she used for her uniform and Elnett hairspray.

"We're better off without him," she said.

"Are we?" I couldn't see her face, but I felt her body go stiff.

"A man like that…"

"Like what?"

"Forcing you into a career to make up for his own failures…"

"It wasn't—"

"Knowing you weren't sure, knowing I didn't want you to have any part in this. And then, when I confronted him, you know what he said?"

"No…"

"He told me he couldn't do 'family stuff.' That he'd come to it too late in life, that he'd tried and tried, and he knew you'd never accept him. Where did that even come from? Sounds like a coward's way out to me. Which I told him."

Or, I thought, feeling another howl making its way up through my body, *the perfectly natural reaction of someone who'd just been informed by his potential stepdaughter to leave her family alone.*

And he'd been right about Top Music. He'd been right all along.

"Mom," I said. "It's not… It's not just him. I wanted to do the record-label stuff."

"But he pushed you—"

"I pushed him."

"He lied to me—"

"I made him lie."

She drew back. "How?"

What would I have given to leap out of my body and into someone else's? I'd have done anything not to be me.

And yet there I was.

Mom was waiting. "How could you *make* him lie?"

"By…by saying that I'd start being nice to him. He was so desperate for us to be friends. And, and we were, we were hanging out and going to London together. Only then, last night, I was horrible. I said some bad stuff."

Mom was standing away from me now. "What did you say?"

"I told him to get out of my life. But that was only because he'd been telling this record label that I wouldn't go on tour during school—"

"Of course you're not going on tour during school."

"And he kept saying that something was wrong. And he was right! He was completely right, and I should have listened to him, but I didn't."

I was crying all over again now, but this time it was clear that there'd be no more hugs from Mom. Not now, maybe not ever.

"So you're telling me that Adrian is not the villain here. That the villain is you."

I nodded and sobbed.

"That you forced him to go against my will, against his own better judgment, just so that you could get what you wanted."

More nod-sobs.

"That a good man came into our lives and you, Katie Cox, drove him away."

I couldn't even say I hadn't meant to—because, honestly, I had.

My eyes were firmly pointed into my lap as I said, "We don't need him, Mom. We don't. He's got us living in this awful house—we don't even have Wi-Fi!—and his store's a disaster. Poor Mands is really upset about it, and that isn't fair because it's not her fault. And it's not my fault this happened. It's his, for introducing me to Top Music in the first place!"

"Enough."

"But…we can do better! You can do better! You're a strong, confident woman, and you could have any man you wanted. All right, maybe not a Hollywood film-star-type man, unless he was pretty old. But most of the other ones. Because you are really not bad-looking, you know. And anyway, you don't need a man to complete you! I was thinking, we could use this time to do some family bonding, maybe. That we could maybe even do a quick trip to California and see Dad. That maybe—"

"*Enough.*"

I raised my head and looked into Mom's eyes.

And oh God. What had I done?

She turned to go, unhappiness sort of swirling around her in an invisible cloak. Then she said, "We do have Wi-Fi. It was the last thing he did before he left. The man can't afford a new pair of shoes, but he got you back online. The password"—and she hesitated, just for a second—"the password is 'superstar.'"

It took a while before I was anything like together enough to open up my laptop.

But then, eventually, I did, and there was "Just Me." With two million, one hundred and seventy-three thousand views, and pages and pages and pages of comments.

Need MORE said 49robep49

Cant live without her said Trouteyes

Feels shes like 1of us said PussInBo0ts

yes!!!!!!!!!!!!!!!!!! said f862fg

Do u think shes 4real??? said NodgetheSplodge

yes!!!!!!!!!!!!!!!!!! said f862fg

She is true said J8nny. **That's why I ♥ her**

yes!!!!!!!!!!!!!!!!!! said f862fg

This went on and on and on. I read how brave I'd been to show everyone my bedroom. How great it was that I was so ugly (why, thank you). How my lyrics were honest and how you could really see that I was close to my family and my friends. That they'd wanted someone who was good and real. How that someone was me.

If I'd been feeling bad before I'd logged in, well, now, I felt like I'd gone through bad and out the other side into a new place where bad was actually pretty good.

Back at the top of the page, Past Katie was singing as though nothing had happened.

Even though everything had happened.

I reached for a tissue, because, you know, unhappiness makes for mucus, and managed to knock the box down the side of my bed. A quick flail for it and I put my hand smack bang into the middle of that old pizza, which by now was doing something really interesting, meaning I needed a tissue even more. So I got down and reached carefully, and my hand closed on the corner of something hard.

Only it wasn't the tissues. It was the little box Lacey had given me on our last walk together.

Very carefully, so as to avoid smearing it with pizza

slime, I opened it. On the top, a pair of Dove Bar sticks, tied together with a piece of ribbon.

And then I knew what I had to do.

What I wished I'd done in the first place.

I took a deep breath.

And then I texted Jaz.

Please take the video down. It's all over. K x

Then I shut the laptop and turned off my phone.

It was so still, and the house was so quiet. A light rain was falling from a heavy, gray sky, more mist than droplets. And I so wanted to hide or to run away.

Only, all the grim stuff, all the misery—it was me. Wherever I went, it would still be there.

And then, I looked across my bedroom and saw it.

Propped up behind my door, like it had been waiting for me to notice it, was my guitar.

Chapter Thirty-One

WHAT DID AMY WINEHOUSE DO when she split up with her husband? She wrote "Back to Black." When Dolly Parton's guy started messing around with this girl who worked in his bank, she wrote "Jolene." And when Morrissey was upset, he wrote pretty much all the stuff he's ever done.

What I'm saying is that there's a rich history of miserable people writing really amazing music.

Not that my music was anything even close to amazing. Now that the Top Music fantasy had gone, I could see that. All the dreams about Wembley and the single, they'd melted away like snow in the sun, and I don't know how I'd ever thought any of it was real. No way was I a star or anything like one. I was just some pimply schoolgirl who liked to play and sing. Savannah, Paige, and Sofie knew it. Lacey knew it. And now I did too. I wasn't the next Amy Winehouse. I wasn't even the next Crystal Skye.

But I certainly had enough heartbreak to join the club.

I picked up my guitar and it fit so nicely under my arm, a missing piece of the Katie jigsaw. Then I flicked open my lyric book with my other hand and wrote,

> I was wrong. So wrong.
> Wrong about my life,
> Wrong about my song.

Then I sang it, and let the notes work themselves free, feeling the music ripple from under me, the hard catch of the strings and the way they bit into my fingers. My calluses were going. How long since I'd practiced?

> Wrong about you,
> Wrong about me.

And so I sang and scribbled and played, as outside the streetlights came on, and the world kept turning. Until it was finished, and I knew where I had to go and what I had to do.

♪ ♫ ♫ ♫

Harltree High Street is not somewhere you want to be after dark. What with clubbers staggering in and out of bars and the kids that sit on the steps by McDonald's, it's all pretty edgy. Like, okay, no one's got a gun or anything, but you can do some pretty serious damage with a bottle of Smirnoff Ice.

As I passed the main group, a girl was screaming something, and for a second, I considered getting myself safely back home again. Then I saw that it was Nicole fighting with another girl over a shoe.

Deciding that more information would not necessarily make me feel better, I picked up the pace, until I was off High Street, down past the shopping center and into the row of charity shops and places selling pieces of Tupperware and cheap wrapping paper.

Vox Vinyl was the last one before the shops ran out altogether, and the shutter was down. I'd failed. I—

No, there it was, along the pavement, a needle-thin sliver of yellow.

I thumped on the cold metal, once, twice, thrice—whatever the word for four times is, I did it. And I shouted, "*Hey! It's me! Open up!*"

After a couple of minutes, I heard a shuffling and then about thirty different bolts sliding open before the shutter *thunk-click*ed upward, and Adrian was unlocking the door.

What I saw was so surprising that I actually forgot why I'd come.

Because it was just lovely in there. Every last inch of the wall was covered in posters, and fairy lights were strung around a little wooden platform, stacked high with shelf upon shelf of vintage vinyl. The record racks were labeled with these awesome fluorescent signs that said things like, "Groove Is in the Heart" and "Dance Baby Dance" and "In the House" and someone had done a huge mural on this monster speaker of instruments and microphones and notes and hearts all twined together.

It was cozy, and it was cool.

Vox Vinyl was *ace*.

He watched me stare. "Your sister did all this. We were just this scuzzy record shop before, but she completely transformed the place. Look at that!" He waved at the fairy lights. "She's even made a little stage so we can do live stuff!"

"I bet everyone loves it."

"I'm sure they would…if they just knew about it."

A clubber staggered past, thrown out of Heaven, and by the sound of it was on his way down to hell.

"Come into the back," said Adrian. "I'll make you a cup of tea."

I followed him through a door behind the counter and into what must normally have been the stock room. Not tonight, though. Tonight, the boxes had been shoved to one side to make room for a drum kit, stacked precariously in the corner, a keyboard, a couple of guitars, and, on the tiny area of floor that was left, a sleeping bag and our spare duvet. The one used by Auntie Jean's dog.

"Can't really afford a hotel," said Adrian. "Thought I'd sell my instruments to tide me over for a while, but no one wants them. I've made sort of a mess of things, really."

Hearing him say it just made things worse.

"*I've* made the mess," I said, hearing how lost I sounded. "You were totally right about Tony. He didn't want to make me a star. He just wanted revenge on you."

Adrian had been looking pretty bad to start with. This didn't help. "The old—oh, Katie. Katie, I'm so sorry."

"And now my music career is over. And I don't care, really, only I've made Manda hate me, and I've lost all my friends and…"

Credit where it's due, he didn't put his arm around me, and he didn't tell me it was okay. He made some tea and then listened while I told him about the conversation in the office and Jaz tipping a vase of flowers over Tony's head.

"Good for her."

"Yeah," I said, smiling at the memory of Tony blinking pieces of wet leaf from his eyelashes. "I sort of wish I'd done it."

We both laughed.

"Are you sure you don't care about a music career?" said Adrian. "If I were you, I'd be pretty upset."

"No. Not really. I mean, I get scared when I sing to more than three people at a time, and I haven't done any real playing in ages. No. I'm glad it's over. I'm glad the video's gone, and I don't want to go on tour. It's a relief, really. I'll just go back to school and forget this ever happened and—"

And then I surprised myself by bursting into tears.

"What?"

"It's just…it was *my* song. And people liked it… And I was so proud. And now it's ruined."

"Are you sure?"

I thought of everything that had happened. "Yeah," I said. "I'm sure."

"Well. You'll write more."

"I guess so."

Somewhere upstairs, a toilet flushed. And outside, another set of clubbers staggered off to find the taxi stand.

"You'll have more chances."

"And so will you," I said.

He laughed in that way people do when something is the opposite of funny.

"I mean it," I said.

"I don't think so," said Adrian. And from the way he spoke, I could tell we weren't just talking about his music.

If I'd felt bad when I'd arrived, well, now I felt bad times one hundred. Times one thousand.

I'd had lots of worst moments recently. This, though, this was the worst of worst. It was even worse than that encounter with Mom, which is crazy, because she was Mom and he was just Adrian. Adrian, who had a creaky leather jacket and hairs coming out of his nose.

It was worse because at least, when all this was over, Mom would have me and Amanda.

Adrian wouldn't have anyone.

"I'm sorry," I said. "If it wasn't for me, you and Mom would still be together."

He did this little twitch. The very tininess of it showed me just how much it hurt.

"I should never have made us go to Top Music behind her back. I knew it would drive her bananas, and I did it anyway."

"But I let you," said Adrian.

"Still," I said. "It really was my fault. And I know you won't be able to forgive me. But at least…at least I've said it."

He was smiling, very slightly. "I can forgive you."

"I don't deserve it."

"Probably not. But I'll do it anyway."

The fairy lights shone and suddenly it was like

Christmas. Hope was swooping through me like birds, and if we'd been in a movie the soundtrack would have been rising as I said, "I've talked to Mom already. She knows it was me. She's pretty angry at the moment, but she'll get over it. At some point." I knew I was babbling, but honestly, I couldn't help it. "So, if you really can forgive me, and if Mom understands that this was really nothing to do with you, then…then…"

"Then what?"

"Then you and Mom can work things out," I said.

He put his head in his hands. "I don't know."

"But it's way obvious! You should be together!"

His face told me that maybe the soundtrack wasn't raising in hope but had faded into sad, slow chords, falling like the misty rain. "Your mom and me… We're not some loose end to be tied up, just like that." He stared at me over the edge of the mug, dark hairs curling over those thick fingers, his chin prickling with specks of black and of gray. "I'm not an idiot, Katie. I know you think I haven't noticed you rolling your eyes at me and telling your friends that you can't stand me."

"No—" I began.

"I've lived alone my whole life. I liked it. Doing my own thing, you know? Everyone paired up except me, and for a while I wondered what I'd done wrong. And then they started divorcing, and I realized I was fine on my own. Always thought I'd be on my own until your mom turned up. And it was good, for a while. But it's difficult, being in a family. Especially when that family's not yours."

I wanted to tell him that he was wrong. But I couldn't. It was the three of us and him. It wasn't the four of us. It never had been and maybe never would be.

"I'm sorry," I said for about the billionth time.

"It's not your fault," said Adrian, sounding very, very tired. "But it is…hard. And it's late. You should be getting home. I'll call you a cab."

"You're not coming too, then?" I said hopelessly.

"Not tonight, no. Maybe I'm not supposed to be happy. Maybe Tony was right."

It was then, as I was going back into the shop, that I noticed the sign behind the counter. The sign that said "CLOSING DOWN" and all the other signs, saying things like "BUY ONE, GET ONE FREE" and "EVERYTHING MUST GO!", which is also the name of an album by the Manic Street Preachers that I'd been meaning to get. Adrian was probably selling it cheap, but somehow I didn't feel like asking.

He saw me take it in. "Yeah. Gonna shut the doors at the end of the week. Bank account's empty."

"But…I'll tell people at school to come. Everyone

loves a bargain, and maybe you could do one of those gigs Amanda was talking about, or—"

"Katie, I don't want to do this anymore. Any of it."

And that was that.

Chapter Thirty-Two

WHAT COULD I DO?

I wrote.

I wrote and I played and I played and I wrote.

When I wasn't with my guitar, time ran slow, and it was like even the air hated me. It was only the music that made things, if not okay, if not even bearable, then kind of maybe exist-able. Maybe.

I played from when I woke up until it was time for breakfast, spreading butter on my toast with sore fingers, and it didn't matter when no one spoke to me in school because the songs were talking in my head. My phone stayed switched off, and my curtains were drawn, and if anyone was worried, they didn't mention it. Probably they didn't even care. Amanda sat with Mom in the kitchen until late every night, but I didn't know what they were talking about since every time I came close, they stopped talking. And in the mornings, we all three moved through the house like ghosts.

"Aren't you going to work today?" I asked Amanda, finding her slumped over the kitchen table, stirring some soggy cereal around and around and around.

"I don't think it would be appropriate. Do you?"

"I don't know," I said.

"And anyway, even if it was, it's too late. The shop's finished."

"It's not! I saw how cool you'd made it in there. You've done amazing things. I bet if you went back in this week and did a really big push, you could get people back in, turn it all around…"

"Too late," said Amanda, more to herself than to me. "Too late."

You wouldn't have known anything was wrong with Mom, not unless you knew what to look for. She was like a TV that had been set up very slightly wrong, her eyes too dark and her smile too bright. Her expressions didn't stay on her face but sort of twitched across it like she couldn't bear to hold the emotion for more than a second or two. I'd seen her like this before, in those weeks after the divorce. I did not want to see her like that ever again.

And me? I couldn't shake off the feeling that I'd been given something rare and special and that I'd thrown it away. As if they'd discovered one last dodo in the world at the exact moment I was eating it for dinner.

So I wrote about it. I wrote about everything—Mom, Amanda, and Adrian. I wrote about how alone I was, on the bus, in art when we had to get into groups and everyone had someone except me.

If living was difficult, the writing was easy. All those words and notes came rushing up to the surface, like the fat goldfish in the school pond, until my lyric book was full, and I was writing in Amanda's old address books and on Mom's bank statements and on the back of the wallpaper that had flaked off in the hall.

"I want to apologize for trashing your cake," I told Savannah. "It was an accident. But I'm really sorry. And I know I basically shouldn't have shouted. It was a disrespectful thing to do."

"Babes," said Savannah, "it's fine."

Was she saying she'd forgiven me? "Are you saying you forgive me?" I asked.

"Meh," said Savannah, as though there was a patch of sticky stuff on the table in front of her, and she'd accidentally put her hand into it, and the sticky stuff was me. "Katie, you are so not even on my radar right now."

Lacey wasn't much better.

"I've, um, look, I know that I've sort of been a bad friend," I told her, having gotten the early bus so that I could corner her as she came across the field.

"Yup," said Lacey.

"Screaming at you was way out of order. I do care what you think."

"Okay," said Lacey.

"So, look, can we be friends again?"

Lacey stopped to think about it, the wind ruffling her bangs. "The thing is, Katie, all we've done since you started riding the bus is fight. And I don't want that anymore. So, yes, we can be not enemies. But it's just easier for me if you do your thing and I do mine."

It was as though some invisible wall had come down between me and the rest of the world. And whatever I said, the words wouldn't get across. Like words weren't enough.

"Yeah, well," said Jaz when I told her in PE, supposedly fielding during softball, "Anyone can say anything. McAllister can fly. I'm the president of China. You have a weird nose."

"Do I?"

"The point being, whatever," said Jaz. "Why should they care what comes out of your mouth? Why should anyone?"

Sometimes Jaz really bleaks me out.

"I just wish Lacey would understand," I said, watching as, in the far distance, Sofie chopped at the ball and then ran smack into Devi Lester. "If she could just hear how I feel, she might get a tiny part of what's in my head. I've been writing all these songs and she won't listen to them."

"Why not?"

"Jaz," I said. "You were at Savannah's party. I am not just going to whip my guitar out and start serenading her in the middle of math."

"Where?" said Jaz. "And when? I want to be there."

"Um, that would be never," I said. Lacey was standing in the batting lineup now, laughing at something Kai was saying, then bending down to tie her shoelace, all the time being careful not to look at me.

And then I knew.

I had to sing to her.

Because singing is what I do.

Only there was no way I'd be doing another bedroom concert. Singing at parties, Savannah's or otherwise, was also out of the question.

What I needed, I realized, was somewhere intimate. The kind of place where people would respect the music. Where they would actually hear me.

Somewhere a little romantic. A little special.

Somewhere like that little wooden platform in Vox Vinyl, all strung with fairy lights.

Only it was closing at the end of the week.

And the end of the week was now.

Today.

"Jaz, I have to do a gig."

She laughed. "You really don't know when to stop, do you?"

Maybe not. "Listen, I know it's crazy, and I'll look like a jerk. I just think that maybe this is my last chance to, well, not make everything okay, but slightly less awful."

"When?"

"Tonight."

"What?!"

"I know! There's no time, but the shop's going to be closed tomorrow. Adrian will go away. It's my last chance."

I thought through what I'd have to do. Get Mom and Adrian and Amanda and Lacey into the room together and keep them there long enough to get through just a few songs, songs like "Sorry" and "Autocorrect" and "Song for a Broken Phone." And "Cake Boyfriend," which, while not completely relevant, had turned out to be really catchy.

"You want to arrange a gig for tonight?" said Jaz. "In the shop of a guy who has decided he doesn't want anything to do with you anymore? And you're going to invite your mom, who's split up with him and doesn't want to see him, and your sister, who doesn't want to see you?"

"And Lacey," I said, watching her swing her bat and miss. "Who hates me."

"You'll never manage it," said Jaz.

"Oh. Great. Thanks for the pep talk."

"Without me."

After all the surprising things that had happened, this was the most surprising. A million people watching my song, I could get my head around. But Jaz wanting to help?

It just goes to show that life is a journey which takes you to some very unexpected places.

"You're really saying that you can get Mom and Adrian and Amanda and Lacey into the shop to hear me sing?"

"If you give me their numbers."

Which, under any normal circumstances, would have been complete insanity.

Only I was starting to think that maybe something had changed. I'd gone so far down there wasn't really anywhere left to sink to, but there was Jaz, still at my side.

I handed her my phone. "Here."

"Am I allowed to lie?" said Jaz.

"No! Well, maybe. Only a little bit." I paused for a moment. "Just don't say anyone's dead."

"You are no fun," said Jaz.

♪♫♩♫

After that, I couldn't eat. I couldn't drink either for a while, only then my throat got really dry, and I found I could.

Mainly, though, I couldn't practice.

Knowing I was about to play to all the people I loved most in the entire world froze my fingers and made my voice go froggy. After three attempts at "Sorry," I gave up, opened my laptop, and put in my name.

And the video was gone. It really was over. One minute, a million hits. The next, nothing.

I tested out the feeling, like you do with your tongue after you lose a tooth. And…it was all right. Honestly, it was. A little painful, yes. But livable. Unlike some other stuff.

Then I noticed the clock in the corner of the screen. I'd told Jaz to have everyone there for seven o'clock. That was in less than an hour.

No time to brush my hair or put some makeup on or any of the things I'd been planning to do. Well, the people who'd be watching had all seen me without my eyeliner. They'd seen me wearing a cake. They wouldn't care.

If they even came.

I slung my guitar onto my back.

Six twenty-five. If I was going to leave, it would have to be now.

"You can do this, Katie," I said to myself.

Even though I really wasn't sure I could.

Chapter Thirty-Three

T HE FIRST PERSON I SAW was Adrian, unlocking the shop
door with this look of complete terror on his face. His
hands were shaking, and he dropped his keys. Twice.

Then Amanda came racing around the corner like she
was in the ocean and someone had shouted "Shark!"

"Are you okay?" she panted. "Adrian, *are you okay?*"

"I don't know. I'm not in yet." Adrian rattled at the
door. "Come *on!*" Then he was inside and turning frantic
circles. "Where is it?"

"What?"

"The fire. There's a fire in the shop. The shop is on fire."

"No it isn't," said Amanda. "But look, I need to get you
to a hospital, all right?"

"Not even any smoke," said Adrian.

"Just come with me, and everything will be all right,"
said Amanda.

"What…Why?"

"I had a text from Katie saying you'd tried to throw yourself into the river."

"I haven't tried to throw myself into the river."

Amanda stood back and looked at him. "Are you sure? Not even a little?"

"I'm sure. Really. I'm not the happiest guy in the world right now, but I'm not that bad."

"That is the last time I give my phone to Jaz," I said.

"*Amanda!*" Mom's car screeched onto the pavement, and she was out of it before the engine even stopped running. "Don't you even *think* about it."

"About what?"

"It's been a difficult few days," said Mom, "and we're all very tense, but I promise, getting a tattoo will not help. Especially not of a dragon. Especially not *on your face*."

"I'm not getting a tattoo," said Amanda. "Er, Katie, would you mind telling us what's going on?"

We went into the shop, everyone still a little shaken, to be honest, and then they looked at me.

"I'm sorry about…all…that," I said. "I just needed to get you here, and I knew you wouldn't want to come."

Mom and Adrian exchanged a glance—a glance that could have been the complete definition of the word "awkward."

"Why?" said Amanda.

This was so embarrassing. "Because," I said, my cheeks

hotter than the sun, "I sort of have some stuff I'd like to play for you."

"Really?" said Mom. "You really think that—"

"I know," I said. "But look. You're here now. It'll only take a few minutes. Promise me you'll stay and listen, just for a little while? And then we can all go home and pretend this never happened, if that's what you want."

Mom looked like she was ready to start pretending now, but Adrian pulled back the record racks and unfolded a few chairs while Manda switched on the fairy lights and made everyone some coffee. And said again and again and again that there really was no way she'd ever get a tattoo. Which wasn't entirely true. I knew she actually had a teensy little dolphin on her back that she'd gotten when she went to Ibiza after university entrance exams.

So while that was happening, I tuned my guitar, probably taking a little longer than was really necessary, then shuffled my chair into every possible position you can have a chair on a small wooden platform.

Mom and Adrian and Amanda were sitting, waiting.

"Okay," I said. "I'm ready now."

Was I ready? Was it about to be Savannah's party all over again? At least there weren't any cakes for me to destroy.

I cleared my throat.

"Okay," I said. "I've been doing a lot of thinking lately.

And a lot of writing. And I figure that the best way to show you what I've come up with is to sing. This first one's called 'Sorry.' And I really, really mean it."

I let the first chord trickle out from beneath my fingertips.

"I was wrong. So wrong.

Wrong about my life,

Wrong about my song."

As I sang, Jaz slipped through the door of the shop and gave me a big thumbs-up.

"Wrong about you,

Wrong about me.

All I can say

Is sorry"

That first song went by in a complete blur. I don't know where I looked or whether anyone was even listening. All I know is that I'd never meant anything more. I didn't even notice that I'd finished until they started to clap.

"Um, so that's the first one. The next one is…oh. Hey, Sofie."

Sofie, Paige, and Savannah had come in and were sitting down on the floor. And Dominic Preston, who was managing to be more good-looking than ever.

Aaaaaargh!

I glanced over at Jaz, who just grinned.

"The next one is…?" said Mom. I was pretty sure that

meant she wasn't about to leave. At least not for another song, anyway.

I swallowed. "The next one's called 'Autocorrect,'" I said.

And maybe I wasn't going to crash and burn, even when the door opened again, and Devi Lester came in and then Finlay, both of them holding up their phones and swaying the screens in time with the beat.

So I sang. I sang to them all. I sang all the stuff that I'd only ever admitted to my lyric book, stuff that I'd have thought would make them laugh and hate me. And perhaps it would later, or tomorrow.

But while I kept singing, they kept listening and clapping, and more people came: some sixth-graders from the bus, my guitar teacher Jill, Cindy from Cindy's, the weird boy Jaz had brought to the party. Even—oh Lord—even McAllister was there, and the principal, crowding in at the back, both wearing jeans. I don't know what was more surprising—that they'd turned up or that they knew how to dress casual.

Finally, when the shop was full to bursting, I said, "Why did you come?"

A silence. Then someone shouted, "Jaz!" and there was a lot of giggling.

"Oh no. What terrible, awful, hideous thing did she say to get you here?"

"She said that you'd be spilling your guts live in concert," said Sofie. "And that we had to tell everyone we knew."

Ah. Yes, that would do it.

Then, from Jaz, right at the front, "Why are *you* here, Katie?"

All those faces, open and waiting, lit in smudges from the fairy lights and phones.

"To say…to say that I was an idiot. This guy from Top Music, Tony, he told me he would release 'Just Me' as a single. He said I'd be going on tour. That I'd have everything I wanted—everything I thought I wanted. And I believed him…which was stupid. Because I've got everything I want here." I cleared my throat. "There isn't going to be a single. He lied. But that's a good thing. I think I just want to keep writing music. That's all." My voice went sort of funny. "Do you mind if I take a quick break? Is that okay?"

Everyone said that it was, and so I stopped and staggered into the stockroom on legs of jelly.

Mom and Adrian followed, as Amanda called, "Is it all right if I open up the register? People seem to want to buy things."

And as she said it, I heard someone out front saying, "I never knew this place existed!"

I sank down onto a box as Mom said, "Katie, that song, 'Autocorrect.'"

"Er." My eyes slid away. "Sorry. I…"

"Is that really how you've been feeling?"

"No!" Then I remembered why I was here. "I mean, yes."

Mom's face did something quite complicated, and then, completely unexpectedly, she pulled me into a hug.

"It's okay," I told her shoulder.

"It isn't," said Mom. "But we'll work on it."

We pulled apart, and I saw her eyes focus in on something behind me.

"Adrian, have you been sleeping in here?"

"Just a few nights," said Adrian.

"On this?" She pointed at the sleeping bag.

"Yeah," said Adrian.

"I thought you'd be in a hotel." As she said it, Mom leaned on the stack that was Adrian's drum set. Which fell down, made exactly as much noise as you'd expect.

"Kind of expensive," said Adrian quietly.

"So why didn't you go stay with Neil? Or your mom? Someone in the pub must have a spare room."

He rubbed at his cheek. "Wasn't really thinking straight."

We might have gone on like this for a while, since Mom hadn't even gotten as far as finding out where Adrian was brushing his teeth, only Jaz came shoving in.

"It's gone crazy out there."

"I know. McAllister? At my private gig? What were you thinking? And how did you even know her number?"

"You haven't noticed?" said Jaz, then, to the world at large, "She hasn't noticed!"

"Noticed what?! Jaz, you are making me crazy!"

In answer, Jaz took my hand and dragged me back into the shop, where Amanda appeared to be selling every record she had.

"Look," she said.

"What? What am I supposed to be seeing?"

"Outside," said Jaz.

I focused on what was behind the glass. Then I saw.

People. People pressed up against the window with their phones held high—not just a few, but rows and rows and rows so that every inch of the glass was filled, like we were in a zombie movie, only scarier. They saw me and began to wave and shout.

"Who are they?" I whispered.

"There's more of them," said Jaz. "I just looked down the street. They're everywhere."

I darted back into the stockroom and sat down on the floor until the world stopped spinning, only it wouldn't stop but just went faster and faster.

"How do they know you're here?" said Adrian. "I don't know how news can travel so quickly."

I knew.

Oh yes, I knew all too well. I don't know why I hadn't thought of it sooner.

"Um, Jaz. The people holding up their phones. Were they…putting this online?"

She nodded.

"And…" I said, slightly not wanting to know the answer, "are there people…out there…on the Internet…watching?"

Jaz nodded again. And as she did so, I heard a chant begin. "KA-TIE. KA-TIE. KA-TIE."

"Better go do the second half," said Adrian.

"But…I can't," I said. "This was supposed to be just us. Now it's everyone. Everyone except…"

"Except who?" said Mom.

"Except Lacey," I whispered.

"I did try to get her here," said Jaz, looking surprisingly defensive. "Even though she's an annoying drip with stupid hair. I did try."

Which gave me an idea. "I've got one more chance," I said. "Give me my phone." And then I texted:

Hey Lace.
We're not friends anymore and I get it. I don't deserve u.

But look, can u get to Vox Vinyl ASAP?

This is the last thing Ill eva ask, I promise.

I need u 2 cut me bangs

"That'll do it?" said Jaz, looking over my shoulder.

"KA-TIE. KA-TIE. KA-TIE."

"I don't know," I said. "Come on. I'd better finish this."

She didn't come. I sang "Cake Boyfriend" and "Respect Your Waist" and "London Yeah" and "Mobility Scooting On the Pavement." Then there was just one song left.

"'Just Me'!" shouted Devi. And then they were all at it. "'JUST ME'! 'JUST ME'!"

And I raised my eyes and looked into the audience to see that—

Adrian and Amanda had gone from the front row.

Walked out.

Abandoned me.

Mom was looking at her feet.

And Lacey still wasn't there.

It *was* just me.

And I thought, some things you just can't forgive.

And they shouldn't forgive me. Because I'd been stupid to show off like this. Stupid to think that getting up in front of everyone would help.

My guitar began to slip from my arms.

"'Scuse me."

It was Adrian, emerging from the stockroom with an armful of the drum set.

Amanda was clambering onto the teeny piece of stage that was left, slinging on one of Adrian's bass guitars. Jaz was coming up past me, drumsticks in her hands, and now—now it was just like my bedroom, only without…without…

It was at that moment that we all heard this rumble, like a wave, far away at first, then gathering into a roar. Outside, the people jumped apart, as something, some*one* came hurtling through the crowd, scattering phones this way and that like glowing Lego tiles.

And then I saw what it was…and it was like…it was like…It *wasn't* like anything I have ever seen or heard or imagined.

It was Lacey, being carried along above the mass of bodies, half surfing, half flying, while something—someone— charged through, ramming a path to the door.

Finally, as they broke through the front, I saw.

Bleeding from a scratch above the eye, hair crazy, eyes basically feral…

Lacey was riding Nicole, the sophomore.

And it was *magnificent.*

Adrian was holding a tambourine.

And as Lacey reached out her hand, I knew it was going to be all right.

IKES," SAID LACEY, STARING DOWN at her phone.
"Have you seen this? You have to see this."

COX IN CONCERT

She shot to fame with her homemade
video of the gloriously cheeky "Just Me,"
then vanished from view. But last night,
Katie Cox made a return to our computer
screens with an intimate, live-streamed,
one-off concert.

Cox seemed nervous at first, her hands
visibly shaking. But after a few stumbles,
she got into her stride with a set so electri-
fying, so well-crafted, and so heartfelt that
the early jitters were quickly forgotten.
Family matters came up again and again,
perhaps most memorably in plaintively

lovely "Autocorrect." And then there was a somewhat strange song titled "Cake Boyfriend," much appreciated by the audience but somewhat lost on this critic.

Explaining the recent disappearance of the video that made her name, Cox said that she'd recorded "Just Me" as a single with the über label Top Music (home to the likes of Karamel and Crystal Skye) but that her track had inexplicably been held from release.

Indeed, it was the teen anthem "Just Me" that finished the set, with the backing of the same ragtag group that had featured on that bedroom recording. Was it as good as the video watched by two million people?

No. If they'd rehearsed even once since making the original, then it didn't show. Endearingly, this did not seem to matter to Cox, whose smile lit up the room even as her song was abandoned before the second verse.

And perhaps it's that smile that so appeals to her fans. A number of different

recordings of the concert exist, of vary-
ing quality, but a rough tally of their
views thus far shows that from an initial
audience of a few hundred, the show
has already been downloaded more than
nine hundred thousand times.

Amid a frenzy of press interest, CEO
of Top Music Tony Topper vehemently
denied that the single "Just Me" had been
shelved, saying, "There must have been
some kind of miscommunication. I adore
Katie. We had a terrific time in the studio,
and she's back in soon to talk about her
album. We couldn't be more excited."

So basically, it was the next day and we were at school,
sitting around the back of the classroom, sharing a bar
of chocolate that Jaz said she'd swiped from Aldi. Only I
found a receipt in the bottom of the bag, so, you know.
Jaz says she's an anarchist who doesn't live by the rules, but
someone paid for that candy with exact change.

"The best part was when that girl got arrested for trying
to kick the door down," said Jaz.

"The best part was when you said nice stuff about me,"
said Lacey.

They were both good, although I have to say the girl trying to whack through the back door with steel-toed boots while screaming my name was a little worrying until the police got it straightened out.

Anyway, though, they were wrong. The best part was when I was putting my guitar away and I saw Adrian slip his arm around Mom's waist, and she didn't shrug him off or anything.

There were lots of great parts that night, and I hope it doesn't sound like showing off or anything, but I do want to say them because they are important.

The first was that I barely saw Amanda for the rest of the evening because they kept the shop open after I'd finished, and everyone was asking her where they could get my songs, but obviously they couldn't. Only Amanda didn't let that worry her at all and was getting people to sign up for her mailing list and promising another concert at the same time next week and recommending albums here, there, and everywhere, and best of all, people were actually buying them. I even heard one guy saying that he was happy that Harltree had finally opened up a music store because he'd been waiting long enough.

All while Amanda was rushing around in this happy blur, Mom and Adrian were off talking in the stockroom, and when I put my head around the door to see about maybe going to McDonald's or something, I found them kissing. I screamed, obviously, and said it was the most disgusting thing I'd ever seen, to which Mom made a rude gesture. While still mid-lip-lock.

Mom rocks.

After all that, the rest of the night was kind of anticlimactic, to be honest, as we waited around for the street to empty out and Lacey remembered about the bangs cutting and ended up with the stockroom scissors.

Eventually, it rained and everyone went off and we got in the car and drove home, where we found that a big new leak had appeared in the roof and part of the hall ceiling was now on the hall floor.

Weirdly, though, after all that craziness, and the fact that the house really did seem to be doing its best to fall down around our ears, I slept incredibly well that night. And even though I was woken up early by Adrian banging on my bedroom door, meaning he must have stayed over to finish what he and Mom had started in the stockroom, which is revolting, I felt this amazing sense of peace.

"Katie, can you get up? We need to have a chat about something. Everything. Up you get, Katie. I've put the kettle on."

He had also put on Mom's flowery dressing gown, which was such a crime against humanity that I said I would only come out if he got dressed. I did say it in a nice way though.

Well, fairly nice.

Half an hour later, and we were a reasonably okay-looking pair sitting at the kitchen table eating leftover Chinese takeout, although not the rice, because as I told Adrian, you shouldn't eat leftover rice. Nicole once had some half-heated, fried egg special rice and puked so hard that parts of her stomach came out, and she had to go on an IV.

"Right. I—" He saw my hair. "Oh dear."

"I know," I said, feeling around on my forehead. "It'll probably be okay once I've styled it. I hope."

"You think?" Adrian asked.

"No," I admitted. "But it was worth it to have Lacey back. Anyway, what's the drama?"

"I've gotten a message from Tony," said Adrian. "Quite a few, actually."

Bear in mind that it was still eight thirty in the morning.

He held out his phone. "Want to listen?"

"Not really," I said.

"Sure?" said Adrian. When he saw that I wasn't going to take it, he carried on talking. "He was calling to say that he was sorry if you and he had a bit of a misunderstanding in his office the other day…"

Which made me sit right up, I can tell you. "There was nothing to misunderstand! He was *very* clear."

"Well," said Adrian, sticking his fork into a sweet-and-sour chicken ball that I'd had my eye on, "Tony was very clear to me too. Your single is out."

My mouth went slack, so it's probably just as well I hadn't eaten it.

"*Out* out? As in, for people to buy?"

"Yup."

"But…why?"

"Doesn't look good, big music man bullying a teenager. I don't think he had any choice. Especially not once Karamel came out in your support."

"Karamel?" Savannah would *freak*.

"There's been some interest in your concert too. In fact, there's been some interest altogether. Online petitions, people calling from the papers… You should probably take a look."

"I'm going to have a break from the Internet for a few days," I told him, at which he nodded and said that was probably a good idea and he could see why I would want to but maybe not *these* few days.

Then the doorbell rang and it was a delivery guy with an enormous bunch of flowers. Not to sound ungrateful, because no one had ever sent me flowers before so it was really pretty excellent, but they looked a little too big and exotic for our house. As if we'd stolen them from a funeral. There were handmade chocolate truffles too (and I'm never going to be down on truffles), plus a card that said,

To Katie
With love from all at Top Music

It was signed by a load of people I didn't know, and there, in the bottom corner, *Tony*. The nerve!

I almost admired him.

Almost.

"So what are you going to do?" said Lacey, who was attempting to make a daisy chain and, I have to say, failing.

"Well, I've got detention every night for the next week for skipping school. Even though McAllister said she liked the concert. Can't have liked it that much, can she?"

"I meant about the music stuff," said Lacey.

"Oh. That," I said. Somehow, I was finding it all a little difficult to say. "They want me to go back and talk about doing an album."

"Cool."

"Do you want to be on it, Lace?"

"Seriously?" said Lacey.

"Seriously," I said, and I meant it too.

"Then, no, not really. Those music people sound horrible. But"—she gave my knee a squeeze—"thanks for asking."

"We're having this big fight with them because they are saying it has to be while school's in session and we're not going to take any days off."

"You have the option to miss school, and you're not even taking it? You are crazy," said Mad Jaz.

"Adrian's probably right," I admitted. "He was right about all the other stuff."

"So he's your manager again? I thought you hated him."

"He's fine," I said.

An then I got a little embarrassed and ducked my head, because I really don't like going back on myself like that. Luckily, I don't think anyone noticed.

We all sat there for a while, and I heard the people talking in the dining hall and the seagulls that hang out on the playing field and some sixth-graders having a fight, and I felt sort of happy. Like I was in the right place for a change. That the people I was with were the right people, and more than that, I was the right person. Which I hadn't experienced since the divorce. In fact, not for months and months.

"Give me some money, babes," said Savannah.

"No. Why?"

"I'm downloading your single, but I'm not paying for it."

It would have been nice for her to have made this clear

before she'd hit "buy," which I was about to tell her, when she gasped.

"What? Actually, don't tell me. I'm thinking I need a few days screen free—"

"Number two."

"Number two what?"

"'Just Me' is at number two."

"You are literally making no sense right now."

"You're at number two. In the iTunes chart. Between Karamel and Taylor Swift."

"Show me."

She did.

There was "Just Me," with my name underneath in those neat, gray letters, looking so incredibly proper. And there was a little picture of my face, a still from the video, with my mouth open.

Huh.

Was I ready? No. Not even slightly.

Was it what I wanted?

Not any more than I had to start with.

Probably, in some ways, quite a lot less.

There was only one way to deal with this.

"Lacey," I said, "can I come over to your place tonight? I really want to watch *Mean Girls*."

"*Mean Girls*! I'll be there," said Jaz.

To which Lacey folded her arms and said, "Er, I don't think so."

"Please?" said Jaz.

"Why?" said Lacey.

Jaz looked away and said, "You two seem like you have fun together."

I thought, *It must be pretty lonely being Jaz. Having to be mad all the time, when occasionally you just want to hang out and eat chips.*

And then I thought how lucky I was to have Lacey back as my BFF, and I gave her a look that said *let's open up the arms of friendship to someone less fortunate than we are, even though she is a bit crazy sometimes.*

"All right, you can come," said Lacey.

Which must be the first time one of my faces has ever worked. Ever.

"But don't steal anything," said Lacey. "And don't record us on your phone and stick it online, and don't mess with my mom because I've already had no allowance for the last two weeks in a row and there are things I need to buy."

Jaz said she wouldn't.

Savannah flicked her hair.

Nicole was attempting to remove her cuticles with a vegetable peeler.

And I tried to imagine all those people listening to

my song and watching the concert, all those pairs of eyes in bedrooms and on buses and maybe sitting behind the computers at their schools too, the millions of invisible connections between me and them, between my words and their ears, and for a second, just a second, I thought maybe I could.

And then the whole thing dissolved, and it was just me and Lacey—and Jaz and Nicole and Sofie and Savannah and Paige. And Amanda, over at the store, sending out the first message to her new mailing list, and Mom and Adrian calling the construction guys and probably doing something disgusting too.

I guess I knew that things were about to change, but in my head, just for that second, I pressed *pause* on the moment, so I could enjoy it. Come back and live in it sometimes, when things got difficult, which I knew they would. But having one moment when everything was in balance, maybe that would make it okay.

And then I thought, *Wow.*

That's a great idea for a song.

Can't wait for Katie Cox's next adventure?

Here's a sneak peek!

So THERE I WAS, STANDING in the wings, ready to do my first major concert. I mean, seriously major, with masses of people watching and who knows how many more online.

Even though I'd practiced and practiced, I was shaking so badly I could barely hold my guitar. My hands were dripping sweat, and there was a good chance that when I opened my mouth I'd barf all over the stage.

It was no use telling myself that everyone gets nervous. Because this was no ordinary concert.

I was about to sing live to twelve and a half thousand people.

And each and every one of them wanted to kill me.

ABOUT THE AUTHOR

Marianne Levy spent her twenties as an actor. She was in various TV shows and made a brief appearance in the film *Ali G Indahouse*, where she managed to forget both her lines. She's been the voice of a leading brand of makeup, a shopping center, and a yogurt company. Marianne is a regular contributor to the *Independent on Sunday*. She lives in London with her husband, daughter, and a bad-tempered cat. *Katie Cox Goes Viral* is her first novel for older readers, and she is working on the sequel. Learn more at mariannelevy.com.